WHEN THE
Time is Right

M. MABIE
USA TODAY BESTSELLING AUTHOR
ALY MARTINEZ

When the Time Is Right
Copyright © 2020 Aly Martinez and M. Mabie

All rights reserved. No part of this novel may be reproduced, distributed, or transmitted without written permission from the author except for the use of brief quotations in a book review. This eBook is licensed for your personal enjoyment only. If you would like to share this book with others please purchase a copy for each person. This eBook may not be re-sold or given away to other people.

WHEN THE TIME IS RIGHT is a work of fiction. All names, characters, places, and occurrences are the product of the author's imagination. Any resemblance to any persons, living or dead, events, or locations is purely coincidental.

WHEN THE
Time is Right

Prologue

Hudson

I blew every red light on the way to her parents' house.

    White knuckles.

    Heart pounding.

    Dread souring in my gut.

I'd been driving around town, searching for her for over an hour, and was now making the loop a second time. My phone was blowing up with texts and calls from her family, but with nothing new to report, I ignored them.

I was running out of time.

He was running out of time, and she didn't even know it yet.

He couldn't die. For fuck's sake, I'd talked to Brenden just that morning. We'd made plans to meet up with the rest of our crew and grab a burger for dinner. It was rare when Lauren and I were able to get out at the same time now that we had Jack, but damn if Brenden wasn't relentless.

Lex loved it when we were all together.

He just liked when she was happy.

It didn't seem fair. Not for him. Not for her. He was twenty-two, already at the top of his career, and had a woman who adored him. The same woman I was about to destroy with the news of his accident.

I dialed her number for what felt like the thousandth time and lifted my phone to my ear. Straight to voicemail. Even if she had picked up, I had no idea what I would have said. This wasn't news you shared over the phone, and I sure as hell didn't want her behind the wheel of a car while clinging to the edge of panic.

I'd known Alexis Lawson for over a decade, but I was nowhere near qualified to deliver this kind of devastation. But if not me, then who?

His friend who had found his lifeless body still trapped beneath the four-wheeler?

The cop who had been the first on the scene and requested every medical resource available when he couldn't find a pulse?

The EMT who had tirelessly performed CPR until the helicopter finally arrived to transport him to the hospital?

Her parents were at their beach house, and her brother Cal was a six-hour flight away at a medical conference. All of them would no doubt race home after hearing the news.

I was the only one there out of our makeshift family. It was my duty to break her heart even though the very thought of it felt like I was burning at the stake.

The world flew past me in a blur as I sped down the busy road, weaving through traffic and laying on the horn, but my mind barely registered any of it.

How was I going to do this to her?

"*It doesn't look good. You need to find her and prepare her to say goodbye.*" Those were the words Brenden's father had barely been able to utter, his voice cracking with grief as he'd explained to me when he couldn't get Lex on the phone.

What were the syllables required to prepare someone to say goodbye? I could have read straight from every dictionary in existence and never strung together the right thing to say.

He was my friend too, and I couldn't fathom losing him.

WHEN THE *Time* is *Right*

But he was the love of her life—there was no recovering from that kind of loss.

Maybe he'd pull through. Maybe by this time next week, we'd be having that burger, swapping stories about the day he'd almost died.

Or maybe I'd still be trapped inside this fucking truck on an endless road, unable to save him or protect her.

A wave of relief punched me in the gut as I turned into her parents' driveway and finally saw her car. Adrenaline exploded in my veins, but it was quickly iced by the reality of what was to come.

I needed to get my shit together and be there for her during one of the hardest moments she would ever face. God forbid, if the tables were turned, Lex would have been the first person standing at my door, ready to rage against the universe, if for no other reason than to make sure I wasn't alone. We shared no blood, but we were a family just the same.

As I threw my truck into park and then bolted up their massive front steps, my throat was so thick it felt like I was drowning. Though I had to push that aside to be her life raft.

None of this made sense.

Brenden had spent the majority of his life on two wheels. I'd never forget the first time Lex had dragged us to one of his races. I wasn't the one on the track, but the thrill still hit me as we watched him speed around, navigating steep jumps and obstacles with pinpoint precision. Dirt bikes had never been my thing, but it was easy to see why he got off on Motocross.

He lived on the edge, but it was fucking fishing at his own pond and a four-wheeler that had shoved him over it.

My heart sank as I opened the front door, the sounds of her off-pitch singing filled the entryway.

"Lex!" I yelled, marching toward her voice.

With a watering can in one hand, she stood in the kitchen, barefoot with her wild red hair piled on the top of her head, surrounded by her mother's menagerie of prized succulents.

"Hey, Hud. What are you doing here?" She smiled so innocently that it felt like razor blades to my heart.

I took a second to memorize it before being forced to wipe it away, maybe forever. "Where the hell have you been?" I snapped too roughly given the situation, but my nerves were shot. "I've spent the last hour searching the entire city for you."

Oblivious, she grinned. "I broke Mom's cactus, so I had to hit the nursery and find an exact cacti-match so she didn't cut me out of the will. What's up? Why were you looking for me?" She propped a hand on her hip and teased, "Can't find anyone else to insult you properly?"

"Why weren't you answering your phone?"

Her eyes narrowed. "Uh, it's dead."

My chest ached as I stared at her. She had no idea what was coming. That was literally the last moment before I was forced to ruin her life. "We gotta go, Kid."

Her smile melted as she placed the watering can on the table and took a slow step toward me. "What's wrong?"

Shit, this was going to hurt.

"There's been an accident. And we need to get to the hospital as quickly as we can. So I need you to grab your shoes and purse and get in my truck."

She stood there blinking at me, her lashes fluttering as if they could bat away the words that hung in the air. Then, all at once, she burst into action, rushing past me to the sink to dump the watering can. With an edge of panic lacing her voice, she asked, "Is Jack okay?"

Life wasn't fucking fair.

I was about to drop the weight of the world on her and she was worried about *my* son.

"Jack's fine." I rumbled, and my throat filled with shards of broken glass. "It's…Brenden."

Her face paled, and her lips tipped into a paper-thin smile. "Shut up. What are you talking about?"

If I had any chance of getting her to that hospital in time to see Brenden while he was still alive, I needed her to get in the damn truck. "He flipped the four-wheeler, Kid. I got a call from his dad when they couldn't reach you."

She shook her head, her green eyes filling with tears even as she fell into a pit of denial. "Is this a joke? Did he put you up to this? He's such a shit. This is probably payback for me telling him to release anything he caught. We just don't have the freezer space anymore."

I closed the distance between us, hooking my arm through hers. "I'm not fucking around. Please just get in the truck."

She peered up at me for a long beat, her chin quivering as she tried to make sense of the unfathomable.

Then I lost her.

Lex snatched her arm away and spun all at once. She was a tornado touching down with deafening lulls and violent whirls.

"Where's my phone?!" she shrieked at a soul-crushing octave. "Where's my fucking phone! I'll call him. I'll prove he's fine." With wild eyes, she darted around her parents' kitchen, looking for a phone that she'd told me only minutes ago was dead.

I followed after her, my heart in my throat, the seconds on the clock ticking away at an agonizing speed. "We gotta go, Lex."

With trembling hands, she found her purse on the island and dumped it out, the contents rolling off the counter, crashing to the floor right along with her heart. "This is bullshit. He knows how to ride a four-wheeler, Hudson. He wouldn't fucking flip it."

She pushed past me, but I caught her by the arm. It would be years before I forgave myself for the way I jerked her against me and shouted, "I wouldn't lie about this! Please, fuck, we need to go." It was louder than I'd intended, but it momentarily snapped her out of it.

Her head tipped up, her life-altering green eyes pleading with me long before her words did. "How bad?" When I didn't immediately respond, she yelled, "How fucking bad, Hudson?"

I could have lived a thousand years and I'd never forget the complete and utter devastation on her face. I fought the urge to squeeze my eyes shut to block out the searing pain of reality. But if I did, she'd be forced to live this hell alone.

Holding her gaze, I whispered, "Bad."

With that one single syllable, she flew away from me as though I were her mortal enemy. In that second, I guess in a lot of ways, I was.

When her back hit the wall, she managed to rasp, "Is…is he alive?"

"Yes!" I exclaimed, jumping on the only good news I had to offer her. It was one tiny morsel of hope, and I prayed it was enough. "The four-wheeler flipped on his way back from the pond. They life-flighted him out, but…" Fuck. *Fuck!* I moved into her, stopping only inches away. Careful not to touch her again, but close enough to catch her if her knees buckled. "It's bad, Lex. Like really fucking bad. But Brenden's a fighter, and the sooner we get there, the sooner we can get answers."

She was frozen in place, her hands in midair as though she were about to reach for my biceps, tears dripping from the corners of her eyes as she searched my face. "So he's okay?"

He wasn't. Not even close.

But the spark of hope that lit her eyes turned that rock in my stomach into a boulder, and I knew there was no way I would get her out of the house in one piece if I told her the absolute truth.

So, even though I prided myself in being honest to a fault, I swallowed my pride and told the biggest lie of my entire life. Staring into the terrified face of a woman I would burn down the world to protect, I forced a nod. "Yeah, Kid. He's gonna be fine."

She sprang back into action, her emotions spinning so fast her legs couldn't keep up and she nearly tripped. After a few eternally long seconds of searching for her shoes, I told her to forget them.

I carried her from the house that day, barefoot, sobbing, and tearing apart at the seams.

Held her hand on the way to the hospital.

Stood behind her as she sat at his bedside—a million tubes and wires making him unrecognizable—begging the only man she had ever loved not to leave her.

I slept in a chair in the waiting room for a week when she refused to go home.

And I held her, wrapped in my arms, her tears soaking my chest, agony ravaging her, the day Brenden's body finally gave out.

Cal, Lauren, and I did everything we could to ease Lex's pain. But it was an impossible job.

I couldn't fix it for her, but I never stopped trying.

Not when she fell into the depths of depression.

Not when the darkness closed in.

Especially not when the simple task of breathing became too much.

Looking back, I was so damn thankful I'd taken the second to memorize her face before I shattered her dreams, because it took years before I saw another genuine smile grace her face again.

CHAPTER
One

Lex

Six years later…

I stared down the aisle and could barely believe it was really happening. I had on the dress, the shoes, the jewelry, and my hair was exactly as I'd been instructed. *Big.*

There were a lot of people, and as at any wedding, their eyes were trained on the door I was about to walk through—that was if he would just get over here and take my damn arm.

Did he have to pick today to become social?

The music began, and it took everything in me not to scream to get his attention. My only option was the Jedi death stare. If you could hear a glare, mine would have been deafening, but it worked.

He leisurely strutted over and linked his arm with mine as if it were no big deal that we were up and everyone was waiting. It wasn't like we hadn't been forced into practicing this very thing the evening before.

"You look like a clown with all that makeup on," Hudson whispered as he leaned into my side.

"Yeah, well, I didn't think they made tuxedos in size Sasquatch, either. Yet here we are."

Leave it to him to say something totally blunt and slightly rude, but he wasn't wrong. I normally wore *some* makeup, but never to this level. It had taken forever for the hundred-dollar-an-hour makeup artist to smear it all on. But again, I was just going along with what had been forced upon me.

I wasn't the kind of woman who fawned over the idea of holy matrimony or happily-ever-afters—at least not anymore. Because, although I loved the company of men, I was a single mom to two cats. Beep and Boop's half-assed brand of tough love was all I needed in my life. Not that my meddling parents understood that.

A wave from the uppity wedding coordinator, whose hair was higher than the steeple on the church, put our feet in motion.

"We can always object," he said and then cleared his throat. "Rock, paper, scissors for which one of us does it."

I grinned at my aunt and uncle as we slowly marched closer to the altar. With a bright smile on my face, I replied, "He'd kill us."

"The lesser of two evils." He pretended to shiver. "At least we'd get out of this stupid wedding pageant quicker."

He had a point.

Still, there was no way I was going to ruin my brother Calvin's wedding day—crazy debutant bride or not. And deep down, Hudson would never do that to his best friend, either. It was bad enough that Lauren wasn't there. We'd all done our fair share of shit to each other over the course of our lifetimes, but objecting would be a step too far—even for us.

At the pulpit, before we split, he leaned over again and muttered, "I can't wait to hear all about how it's going with you and that mouth-breather you brought, Lex." He hung his jaw open, panted, turned on his heel, and clapped Calvin on the shoulder, taking his place beside him as best man.

Holding my bouquet, I flipped him off where no one else could see, and he gave me a smug wink.

At least I have a date, cocksucker.

He'd brought a seven-year-old.

Yes. That's right. I was the maid of honor in this circus. Not because Vanessa and I were close—or even friends for that matter. Truth be told, if she hadn't had a collar around my brother's neck for the past two years, I wouldn't have given a shit about knowing her at all. But for whatever reason, they were getting married. *Hooray.*

As far as I was concerned, I was only looking forward to all of the planning and fittings and rehearsals and showers, ad nauseam, being almost over. I'd spent a small fortune on this fucking dog and pony show and had literally nothing to show for it. The bright, intoxicating light at the end of this long, dark, annoying tunnel was me getting shit-hammered later at their reception.

I deserved an open bar and wasn't afraid to use it.

I meant that from the bottom of my cold, dead heart.

Okay, so my heart wasn't really all that cold or dead, but as I stood up front and looked into the congregation, my hooker-painted eyes landing on my date—if you could call him that—I was again reminded of how dumb all of this was.

My feet had started hurting before the ceremony had even begun, but by the time it ended and Hudson and I were paired again to leave the altar, I was preparing for a new life as a double amputee. Only a troll would force her wedding party to wear four-inch stilettos to a Catholic wedding. A fucking troll, I tell you.

"Are you crying?" Hudson asked as I hung my wrist on his tree trunk of a forearm for support.

"No."

"Yes, you are. You bawl bag."

I did my best to again offer smiles as we passed row after row of family and attendees. "I think I lost a toe about an hour ago. I'm mourning."

He stretched his thick neck to the side and tugged at the

collar. "I know what you mean. I can't wait to get out of this fucking thing. It's choking the shit out of me."

I laughed, a full belly laugh. What a sucker.

"What?" He glared down at me, his stern brow proof of how serious he was about getting out of the formal wear.

"It's funny that you think you get to change anytime soon."

"Oh, I am," he stated as if he'd gotten permission in writing, which I was certain he had not.

"Dude, we still have pictures and dances and God only knows what else before we're set free. You're looking at another few hours."

"You've got to be out of your ever-loving, fu—" Hudson cut himself off as his son ran up to us. Releasing my arm, he picked Jack up in one swift motion. But don't be mistaken: He silently finished the sentence while staring me down.

"Lex, you look funny." Jack was seven and spoke nothing but the facts.

"You're right. I do." I poked him in the side. "You gonna save me a dance later anyway?"

His eyes lit up, but he argued, "You don't know my dances."

Just to prove a point and see the little fart's reaction, with my bouquet in hand, I gave him a sample of my best Floss moves.

"Dad, she can do it!"

"Alexis," someone called from near the chapel doors. "We need you, Sugar."

Sugar. If that wedding planner called me Sugar one more time, I was going to trip her ass the next chance I got. That just goes to show you how well she didn't know me.

In my best, thick Southern drawl, I called back, "All right, Snickerdoodle. I'll be there in two shakes of a dog's tail."

"Go on, Sugar," Hudson quipped.

"Yeah, Sugar," Jack added. *Like father, like son.*

Dutifully, I did what had been asked of me. Pictures. Train fluffing. Flower holding. *Smiling.* All the while losing, my best estimate, a pint of blood a minute from the holes worn into my feet.

My older brother owed me big time, and I had no issue at all with sending him links to a few high-end thank-you gifts I'd had my eye on.

Besides, he had plenty of money. Hence the Stepford wife he now belonged to. Dr. Calvin Lawson could afford to splurge on the Kate Spade purse I had in my online Nordstrom cart—and the matching wallet. The Lord knew I wasn't going to be dropping that kind of money for a while.

I'd only recently regained employment when one of my old waitressing friends moved back to town, and I was about a month into my new job at Warren and Warren Consulting. Sure, it was an entry-level position, mostly doing administrative work. Assistant stuff. Running errands. Still, it was good experience and any marketing knowledge I gained wouldn't hurt. But with both Warrens expecting their first child and opening a new office in Atlanta, my need for employment couldn't have come at a better time for all of us.

So, as the afternoon went on, I kept my mouth shut and fulfilled my sisterly obligations. The second I got to the reception venue, I limped my saintly ass up to the bar with my stupid date trailing behind me.

Normally, I wouldn't have brought Craig—or even dated him for that matter. We'd only been out a handful of times, but his family knew my mom and she'd basically invited him after our second date.

Don't get me wrong. Craig was an okay guy. Nothing special, but I supposed, with also still being single as fuck at twenty-eight, I was no prize peach, either.

"Two Captain and Cokes, please," I ordered at the first port-a-bar I came to.

"Oh, no, thanks, Alexis," Craig said after catching up to me, waving off the first cocktail that was set in front of us.

"These are both mine," I explained.

He didn't look impressed, but that would only cushion the blow when I let him down gently, probably the next day on the phone. It didn't bother me one iota if he thought I was being a bad date.

I *was* a bad date, but that wasn't anything new.

I was simply one of those people who knew what they liked and what they didn't. If and when the right guy came along again, I'd know right away. Although I wasn't holding my breath. Mostly because I didn't really care about many people, except the ones I chose to keep around me.

They were irreplaceable.

Besides, I had more important things to worry about. A new job that was going to run me ragged over the coming weeks, two fur balls that demanded my unwavering devotion, and a small starter house I'd bought just before I'd been laid off a few months ago. Without much income, my savings—which I'd planned on spending on renovations and some other now sidelined plans—had dwindled. So I would have to be creative with my budget.

Like, pronto.

Because the leaks in my guest bathroom weren't getting fixed by a plumber. The low-hanging tree branch and overgrown bushes out front wouldn't be touched by a professional landscaper, and the drywall and paint the walls needed were probably going to be poorly repaired and only slightly improved by yours truly.

I wasn't afraid of the challenge though, and I wasn't scared to get my hands dirty. Hell, I'd grown up in the Georgian dirt with my brother, playing with bugs and chasing snakes with the neighborhood kids. Granted, our neighborhood was pretty tame, and we weren't trudging through any wild forests, but rather a creek bed that ran through the adjacent golf course.

Regardless, I could take care of myself.

Plus, you could learn how to do just about anything on YouTube. So that left me no time or interest in a love life. Then again, everyone gets a scratch they can't itch themselves from time to time.

I'd let Craig give me a scratching the weekend before and it had left a lot to be desired. *A whole lot.*

From then on, with regard to me, Craig wasn't going to be itching anything other than the flaky, mysterious skin thing he had going on. Maybe I'd mention it when I called him the next day. I didn't want to date him, but sometimes a guy needed a friend to nudge him in the right direction. And the only helpful direction I could point him was to a good dermatologist.

"I'll have a Sprite," he told the bartender as I pulled tip money from my wristlet and slugged back about half of my first rum and Coke.

When we both had our drinks, it was time to find our table. So I headed up front, knowing as part of the wedding party I'd be seated near the lucky couple. I spotted Hudson and snaked my way through the others filing in.

"Double-fisting it tonight?" Hudson made the gesture for shame-shame with his hands.

I sat and hooked my finger around the back strap of the torture devices melded to my blood-encrusted feet. "I only have two hands. Otherwise, I'd have more."

"Craig, good to see you again." Hudson's voice was full of phony enthusiasm. "Lex's mom told me you two were coming together, but I could hardly believe it until I saw you with my own eyes."

If I could have pulled the straw from my mouth, I would have sassed back, but I couldn't. My priority was to get the alcohol inside my body as soon and efficiently as possible. However, without my strongest line of defense—my smart-ass mouth—at my disposal, I was left feeling Craig's arm wrap around the back of my chair. *Ew.*

Hudson grinned. "Just think, in a year or two, that might be you two up there."

My nostrils burned as the drink reversed course and sprayed out of my face. I hacked and coughed, gasping for air. Crusty Craig patted my back as I choked.

"Dad, did you and Mom have a wedding?" Jack asked, effectively saving his father's life. He'd been standing beside his dad, and as Hudson refocused his attention on his child, he perched Jack up on his knee.

"No, Mom and I never got married," he answered simply.

For all of his many faults, being a good father wasn't one of them. And since I'd always wondered what Hudson and Lauren had told Jack, I quelled the urge to kick the chair out from under him in order to find out.

"Why?" the golden-headed boy asked, his head tipping to one side.

"Because we were better at being friends. And when you came along, we decided we wanted to be the best mom and dad we could be instead of being just an okay husband and wife."

It was a good, honest answer, which seemed to satisfy the kid, and then the rascal turned to me.

"Okay, so, why aren't you married yet?"

I took a break from my deadly drink to answer, "I don't know, Jack. But as soon as I find out, you and my mom will be the first to know."

Disappointed that the dip-your-nose-into-Alexis's-relationship-status had spread to Jack, I went back to my cocktail.

Shit. He'd been one of the few people in the room I didn't have to explain my life to.

Now, it was just me and Captain Morgan.

CHAPTER
Two

Hudson

In high school, I had been an all-state wide receiver. Before that, I'd played catcher for the county's World Series winning Little League team. Before that, I had been the undisputed best lightning bug trapper in my entire neighborhood. Hell, I'd once caught my son in midair when he'd launched himself off a swing as a toddler.

But when Calvin shot that garter belt in my direction, I didn't bother pulling my hands from my pockets as I let that fucker bounce right off my chest.

No way was I catching it. I mean, seriously, how was the tradition of tossing something that had been rubbing between your new wife's thighs for the better part of the day to a group of single men still a thing at modern-day weddings? Yet there I was. Middle of a country club dance floor, surrounded by pimple-faced teens and balding divorcées, all of whom were ready to fight to the death over the superstition that whoever caught it would be the next to get married.

What a shit time to be sober.

"Dad!" Jack scolded from the corner of the stage. Clearly, he was unimpressed with how his old man hadn't made the coveted catch. He'd have to find a way to get over it though, because I wasn't even willing to bend over to pick up the garter.

WHEN THE *Time is Right*

Vanessa's sixty-year-old uncle, who was on his fifth divorce and still looking for "the one," slid across the dance floor, quite possibly breaking a hip while snagging the equivalent of his niece's dirty panties from my feet. Not creepy at all. The room erupted in cheers, and for once, I joined along with them because that fucked-up tradition marked the end of my best man duties.

Don't get me wrong. I loved Calvin. We'd been best friends since our first day in high school, when I'd snagged a rare athletic scholarship to Willowing Creek Preparatory School. Yes, it was exactly as uppity, snobby, and pretentious as it sounded. Especially for a foster kid who had been in and out of the system for as long as I could remember. By the time high school had rolled around, I was living with my mom again and quickly coming to the realization that if I didn't get my shit together, I'd be living with her until I ultimately became her.

Cal and I had become close almost immediately, and it wasn't long until I was spending more time at the Lawsons' house than my own. In a lot of ways, Cal, Alexis, and their parents, Judy and David Lawson, had saved my life. So, needless to say, I would walk through fire for that man, and that was exactly what the last six months of wedding planning had felt like. Today had felt more like I was being offered as the human sacrifice to a volcano.

The blushing bride's family was absolutely insane, and I had somehow gotten tasked with running interference. Her mom hated her dad, who had brought his once mistress, now wife, with him to the ceremony. Her sister hated her mom, so she refused to so much as use the same public restroom with the woman. Her dad hated her mother's brother Saul, though there were five of her brothers at the wedding, and so far, I was zero for three in guessing which balding New Yorker was Saul. And that's not even to mention Grandma Marie, who had spent the entire day mad-dogging Cal.

It was a nightmare trying to keep all the family feuds straight. My strategy had been to bulldoze any conversation in which two of Vanessa's family members were involved. I'd been positive I was going to be the wedding's most hated guest before it was all said and done. However, now that it was the end of the night, I had not one single fuck to give.

"You ready to go, bud?" I asked Jack when I made my way off the dance floor.

He leveled me with a hard glare and crossed his arms over his chest. "What is wrong with you? You didn't even try to catch it!"

Chuckling, I ruffled the top of his thick, blond hair. "That's because I didn't *want* to catch it."

He let out a low growl and stomped his foot. "Why not?"

"Because." I jerked my chin. "Come on. Go grab your jacket so we can get out of here."

"Because isn't an answer."

He wasn't wrong. But I was dying to get out of there, out of that suffocating suit, and possibly grab something that didn't end in "tartare" to eat on the way home. I suspected explaining to my son why I had zero plans of ever getting married was going to take longer than the thirty seconds I had to spare.

"Jack, seriously, go get your jacket. And the bubble lawn mower Vanessa gave you for being the ring bearer, and—"

Thoroughly affronted, he balled his fists at his sides. "I'm not taking that thing home. All the guys will laugh at me."

"I'm not sure we can count Nolan as *all the guys*, but sure. Of course. How silly of me."

Lauren and I had taught our son to read when he was four. Usually, I was proud of this, watching people's jaws slack open as he perused the adult menu at restaurants, pronouncing words like *linguine*, *parmesan*, and *Bolognese* with ease. However, the minute he'd opened that bubble mower and read the recommended ages were twelve to thirty-six months, I'd never regretted anything more.

Cal had always been shit at buying gifts for Jack. He tried. He really did, but after the four-hundred-dollar ninja throwing stars he'd given my son for his third birthday, Lauren had forbidden Calvin from giving him anything other than cash or a donation to Jack's college savings account.

Vanessa had not gotten the memo.

Still, I believed wholeheartedly in being grateful for the things you were given, and I worked hard to instill that in my son. But seriously, my boy was quite possibly the easiest kid in the world to shop for. He loved every sport imaginable. The last time Cal had been over to the house, Jack had wiped the floor with him at an extremely competitive game of lacrosse. Vanessa could have bought him any ball in existence and it would have been the highlight of his life. Actually, I believed those were the exact words I'd used when she'd texted me to ask what he might like. Yet Vanessa had gotten him a bubble-blowing lawn mower for toddlers.

I loved Cal, but the only thing worse than his taste in gifts was his taste in women.

"You don't have to play with it, bud. How about first thing tomorrow morning, I give you a screwdriver and you can use my workbench in the garage to take it apart."

His eyes lit. "Can I use the circular saw?"

Oh, yeah. He was totally my kid.

"Nope. If I send you back to your mom missing a finger, I'll be missing my head. Now, come on and hurry up. I'm starving, and this tie is cutting off the blood to my brain." I made a show of staggering from side to side, tugging at my collar. "Must. Get. This. Off."

He giggled, and just as it had since the day I'd heard his first cry, the sound of his voice filled my heart in unimaginable ways.

Truth be told, I'd never wanted kids. After the way I'd grown up, bouncing around from relatives and foster care, I knew firsthand that not everyone was cracked up for parenthood. Though, at twenty-two, without so much as a serious girlfriend, I hadn't given it a ton of thought, either.

However, that was all before I'd fallen in love with my best friend.

No. Not Cal. Though that would have been an interesting plot twist in my fucked-up life.

Lauren Rafferty. The girl next door.

Well, the girl next door to Cal. Her family had a boatload of money. No way had she lived in the slums with me. While she was a year younger than Cal and me, Lauren slipped right into our crew, making our duo a trio. Then, a year later, when Lex joined the ranks of Willowing Creek High, our trio became a quartet. The four of us did everything together. Lauren and I naturally gravitated to each other though. She had this laid-back, easygoing way about her that I so desperately needed in my life.

She didn't judge when I unloaded a mountain of baggage about my mom or my desire to finally meet my dad so I could punch him in the fucking face. Lauren just smiled, told me to consider wearing my state championship ring when I punched him, and then passed me a can of Coke.

On the flip side, I didn't judge her, either. I listened to her vent about her overbearing mother and her workaholic father. I just smiled and offered to let her borrow my ring, should she ever decide to punch him in the face.

It was never romantic between the two of us. That wasn't how we worked. We were just two friends who understood each other in a way no one else could.

WHEN THE *Time* is *Right*

After Cal and I went off to The University of Georgia—me on a football scholarship, him on a path for medical school—things became strained for our little clique. Lex and Lauren had never been particularly close on their own, and without Cal and me there as buffers, they went their separate directions. However, when we came home for the holidays, everything fell back into place like nothing had changed.

Until my mom died. Then every-fucking-thing changed.

I'd just graduated college with a bachelor's in communications—a.k.a.: the easiest, most useless degree UGA had to offer. Cal was heading to Emory, but the Lawsons had been kind enough to let me crash at their place while they, Lex, and her boyfriend spent the summer at their Hilton Head Island beach house.

I'd never forget that phone call. I hadn't spoken to my mom in years, with the exception of when she called to borrow money, but the finality of finding out she was dead rocked me to the core.

I raged.

I collapsed.

And I was bitter as fuck that I even cared at all.

I don't remember when she'd shown up. Or how she had known to come over to begin with. But when Lauren Rafferty appeared, the weight of the universe somehow seemed lighter. While everyone else was supportive and there for me, she never left my side that summer.

As my mother's closest surviving relative, I was stuck with handling all the details. The funeral, the legalities, cleaning out her piece-of-shit apartment. God bless the Lawsons, they'd loaned me the money to pay for everything—a debt I repaid the second I was able.

But through it all, Lauren was there.

That was when I knew I loved her. It was the kind of love

that burrowed deep into the marrow of my bones. She was beautiful, and funny, and sweet. What was there not to love?

One night in late August, days before she was supposed to start her last year at Georgia Tech, we got drunk and my dumb ass confessed my feelings. She was shocked. A little weirded out. But see the aforementioned drunk part.

Under the stars that night, Lauren and I had the most awkward, uncomfortable, horrible sex of my entire life.

Seriously, almost eight years later, I still cringed when I thought about it.

We decided the very next day that the love I was feeling *deep in the marrow of my bones* was the thank-you-for being-there-when-I-needed-you kind and *not* of the let-me-strip-you-naked variety. Four weeks later though, when she came to me crying and holding a pregnancy test, I was grateful there was at least some love between us, no matter the variety.

I'd been terrified about having a baby. Scared I was going to fail my kid the same way my parents had failed me. Scared that I was twenty-two, unemployed, living with my best friend's family, and had no fucking idea what the hell I wanted to do with my life.

But once again, Lauren was there to quell the storm, and nine months later, our little man, Jackson David Bradley was born.

Let me be honest, there was nothing and I mean *nothing* that could test the bonds of a friendship more than co-parenting with someone. Through the years, there had been times when Lauren and I were at each other's throats. There were also days when she'd call me to see if I needed anything from the grocery store, or I'd run over to her place to fix her leaky pipes. It was a process we took day by day, but all in all, I thought we were doing a pretty remarkable job at giving our son the life he deserved.

So, no. Long story long, I had zero interest in getting married.

Besides, while I was no expert, I assumed dating was required before the whole tying-the-knot thing anyway. I was far from celibate, but the idea of bringing another woman into Jack's life and flipping our entire comfortable world upside down was a hard no. There was no amount of shit Cal, Lex, or even Lauren could give me that would change that.

"You owe Aunt Lex twenty bucks," Jack said, falling into step beside me.

"What? Why?"

"Because she bet me you wouldn't catch that rubber band thing Uncle Cal threw at you. I told her you used to play football, so there was no way you were going to miss. You should have warned me your nickname was actually Butter Fingers."

I shot him a glare. "First, you're seven. You aren't allowed to gamble yet. Second, for the last time, my nickname was Sticky Hands. Get it right."

He let out a surly scoff, which I chose to ignore in the name of picking my battles while trying to parent a twenty-five-year-old first grader.

"And third, it sounds like *you* owe her twenty bucks, not me."

"Oh, no way! You missed it on purpose. That bet was rigged from the start. You two are lucky I don't get a lawyer."

I stared at my son, a grin trying to work its way out. It was official. I was raising a monster. A brilliant, stubborn, and hilarious monster, but a monster nonetheless.

"All right, in thirty seconds, if you don't have all your stuff, I'm going to invite 'all the guys' over tomorrow to watch you suds up the grass with the bubble mower. Yeah?"

His eyes flared wide, but his feet got moving.

He stomped straight to our table and snagged his jacket off the back of his chair.

"Pay up, sucker," Lex taunted with her feet propped up on a chair, a pyramid of empty glasses stacked in front of her.

"You're a cheater," Jack accused.

She snapped her fingers and held her palm out. "No. I just know your dad better than you do. I'd like to say you'll get on my level one day, but the truth is, if you weren't there to witness the travesty of him wearing leather pants and puka shells in high school, you'll never truly understand the inner workings of his psyche." She snapped again. "Grease the palm, Jackie Boy." A wicked glimmer suddenly hit her drunken eyes and she tapped her cheek. "Orrrrrrr you could pay me with a smooch-a-roo right here. Your call. But a deal's a deal."

Jack loved his Aunt Lex. She'd been a fixture in his life since the day he was born. She'd attended every school play, field day, and birthday party. But recently, he'd come to the conclusion that he was too cool for her hugs and kisses.

This explained the disgust and panic on his face as he turned to me and begged, "Dad, you gotta let me borrow twenty bucks. Please. Please. *Please.*"

I shook my head. "Sorry. I'm fresh out of cash. Go hit up your grampa. But make it quick. I need a burger stat."

He took off in a dead sprint, barreling through a crowd of people to get to Lex and Cal's dad.

I had no family to speak of, but I'd always felt gratitude that the Lawsons had accepted Jack as one of their own. It shouldn't have been surprising though. They'd always been like parents to me. But they took the doting-grandparent thing to a whole new level. I'd never forget the tears in Mr. Lawson's eyes when I'd told him we were using David for Jack's middle name. He'd wrapped me in a bear hug, slapping my back almost painfully as he'd mumbled around the emotion, "It's a good name, son. A real good name."

It wasn't the first time he'd called me son. It was, however, the first time I'd allowed myself to believe it.

They were good people, the Lawsons. Even the drunk one sitting in front of me, hustling my kid for cash. But if there was ever a day she deserved to utilize an open bar, this was it. She liked to put on a good show, but deep down, we all knew that weddings were never easy on her.

"You ready to go?" I asked.

Lex swung her adoring gaze from Jack to me. "Depends. How much longer till the bar closes?"

"For you? It should have closed two hours ago. But for everyone else, I think they are shutting down shop now." I shoved my hands into my pockets and dug my keys out. "Come on. I'll buy you a burger on the way home."

"Mmmm," she hummed, her head falling back and her long, auburn hair cascading over the chair. "That sounds amazing. I nearly gagged on that last cucumber creme de la frufru, but I should probably find Craig."

"No need. I sent him home an hour ago after you and Jack requested the Chicken Dance for the third time." Only part of that was because I didn't trust that idiot to take her anywhere in her current state, and Lex could do a hell of a lot better.

"And he just left me here? What kind of date does that?"

"Clearly, you have not seen yourself do the Chicken Dance…thrice."

Laughing, she stumbled to her feet and drained the last inch of her Captain and Coke. "Hey, my main man Jack seemed to like it just fine." She bent over to pick her shoes up and lost her balance, nearly taking a header into the floor.

I caught her arm at the last second. "Whoa. Easy there, Kid."

She clung to me, swaying ever so slightly. "I knew those

damn shoes were going to kill me. They've been plotting my demise all day."

Careful not to release her, I hooked her arm through mine, dipped low to grab her heels, and passed them her way. "Right. Let's make that a burger *and* some coffee, then."

As if on cue, Jack reappeared beside us. "Dang it, all Grampa had was a hundred-dollar bill, and Mimi tried to give me her credit card."

"I'll take it!" Lex declared, thrusting her hand in his direction.

Jack rolled his eyes. "Can I give you an IOU for now? My mom still owes me, like, seven years of allowance. I'm sure I can get it to you by next week."

Her green eyes lifted to mine. "I don't know. What do you think, Hud? Is he good for it?"

"Considering I have no idea what he thinks he did to earn an allowance for the first three years of his life besides drool and poop in his pants, I'd advise against it."

"Oh, come on, Dad!"

Lex shot him a wink. "It's okay. I'm holding out for that kiss anyway."

With Lex on one arm, her heels dangling from her fingers, and Jack on my other, a bubble lawn mower dragging behind him, the three of us said our goodbyes and then meandered to the valet.

It was no 1970 Chevelle like hers, but when my black Hud Construction pickup came into view, Lex called "Shotgun!" knowing good and damn well my son rode in a booster seat in the back.

Still, Jack mumbled, "Dang it."

We got burgers, coffee, and then milkshakes even after I'd said no, but Lex snuck up to the counter with Jack while I threw the trash away. Such was my life wrangling two kids.

I didn't complain though; some of the best nights of my life had been spent like that. Lex had this way about her that made the most mundane activities feel like special occasions. Plus, she'd bought a chocolate shake for me too.

By the time we pulled into Lex's driveway, the eleven-p.m. sugar rush was in full force. They were laughing and discussing the finer things in life. Specifically, SpongeBob memes. I almost hated to ruin the moment.

"What in the holy hell is that?" I rumbled, slanting my head as if it would give me a better view through the windshield.

"What?" she asked, mirroring my position.

"That," I said roughly, pointing at the giant tree branch I'd never noticed before hanging over her small, three-bedroom ranch. Additionally, I'd not noticed how ominous her front door was in the dark, hiding behind her overgrown bushes.

"Oh, yeah. I've been meaning to trim it back a little. I just have to get my ladder back from Cal first."

It was my ladder. She had borrowed it. Then Cal had borrowed it from her. Now, she was borrowing it back from Cal. It was safe to say I was never getting that one back.

It was also safe to say Lex wielding a saw—on said ladder—was literally the very last thing I needed in my life. I wasn't about to volunteer to put on another suit for her funeral when I was so damn close to taking this one off.

Over the years, I'd learned there were three different versions of Alexis Lawson.

Sweet and caring.

Sarcastic and mouthy.

Drunk and argumentative as fuck.

If I said anything about cutting those branches down on her own, she was going to plant both feet in the drunk-and-argumentative territory and I'd spend the rest of my night sitting in her driveway, listening to her go on and on.

Therefore, my response was, "Okay."

It wasn't okay. It would make me absolutely crazy until I knew that damn limb was gone and it wasn't going to break free and fall through her roof at the slightest breeze.

I'd take care of it.

When I put the truck into park, she shot me a tight smile. "Thanks for the ride."

"No problem."

She extended the remnants of her milkshake. "Can you hold that for a second?"

I arched my brow but took it. No sooner than the cup had left her hand did she dive over the center console, leaving her legs in the front and her upper torso in the back, and pepper kisses all over Jack's face.

"Dad, help!" He laughed, trying to fight her off.

I smiled, watching them in the rearview mirror. "You're on your own, bud."

"Mwah, mwah, mwah," she chanted, kiss after kiss after kiss.

"Ew, ew, ew," he complained, all the while laughing hysterically.

When she was finally done torturing him, she righted herself in her seat again, taking her milkshake as if nothing had happened. "You have until next week to pay up, Jackie Boy. After that? There's more where that came from."

"Jeez," Jack groaned, wiping his face, but he did it smiling from ear to ear.

I couldn't help but chuckle.

At the sound, Lex's gaze bounced to mine, a gorgeous white smile stretching her mouth. "Be careful on the way home. Love you."

I jerked my chin. "You too, Kid."

She swung her door open and did a strange combination of a roll and a tumble that I was absolutely certain could never be replicated. But she landed on her feet without dropping a shoe or spilling her shake, so I chalked it up as a win.

"Love you, Jackie Boy," she chirped.

My son had finally gotten his smile under control and was almost convincing as he grumbled back, "Yeah, yeah, yeah. Love you too."

We watched as she zigzagged up the sidewalk and then punched her code into the smart lock I'd installed after the second time she'd locked herself out. She pushed the door open and stepped inside, stopping only to give us one last wave before shutting the door.

"Man, Aunt Lex is—"

Oh, there were so many adjectives he could have used to finish that sentence. And at one point in time, she had probably resembled each and every one of them.

Though, on that night in particular…

"A mess," I finished for him. "She's a total mess."

CHAPTER
Three

Lex

There was this recurring dream I had sometimes. It was nothing wild or scandalous, but it was odd. Basically, I was naked and jumping on a trampoline. All night long. That's it.

And that's exactly what I was doing when a loud noise coming from outside my bedroom window startled me awake. Noticing the mess my full face of glamour had left on my pillowcase, I craned my neck to look outside.

My head pounded.

Like a baby fawn on new legs, I wobbled to the window with only a tank top and my underwear on. Scratching my hairspray-encrusted rat's nest, I squinted to see what was going on, but it took a few seconds for it to make sense.

Parked in front of my little fixer-upper were two Hud Construction trucks. I always thought it was cool how he hadn't given his company his family's name, but part of his first name instead. Hudson had built the company with his bare hands and he deserved all the glory.

Blinking away the sleep that was still making my vision blurry, I scanned the yard for him. I recognized a few of the guys and the one woman he'd sent over, but I didn't catch sight of his mug anywhere. Hobbling to my closet, I nearly stumbled over Beep, the most fabulous orange tabby cat to have ever been found under a dumpster. I bent to give her a scratch on the head and she purred against my hand and then stood up on her hind legs to ask for more lovin'. Beep was the sweet one. Boop, on the other hand, was somewhere in my house, hiding under the sofa or a bed, waging a war plan that would no doubt scare the absolute shit out of me. Mostly black with white socks and a thumb shape on her face and forehead, she was a nighttime snuggler and a daytime ankle beast.

After finally breaking free of Beep's impromptu morning lovefest, I threw on a bra and a pair of shorts, all the while keeping an eye out for Boop's first attack of the day. Then I went to the bathroom for a little damage control. If there were going to be people helping at my place, I didn't want to scare them away by looking like a creature from the depths of hooker hell.

And, yeah, it was that bad.

But after a good hot water scrub, pulling a brush through my tangles, and returning my forbidden-from-the-wedding nose ring—thankfully, the tiny stud went in without trouble—I was good enough to do some work outside.

I found my wristlet on the small kitchen table and fished my phone out. As the line rang, I shook out two Tylenol and carried them to the sink for a glass of water. It was going to be a loud day for a hangover.

"Yo," Hudson barked through the line.

I tossed the painkillers back and swallowed. "You're a dick boss."

"What are you talking about?"

"It's Sunday, Hudson. You have a crew at my house."

"I know. You're welcome. But how am I a dick though?"

"Shouldn't they be off? I can't believe you'd call people in to clean up my yard on a Sunday morning."

He chuckled, almost sounding evil. Or maybe powerful. Sometimes those sounded the same.

"Lex, those people volunteered to go to your shack. I mean, they're getting paid, but I have crews working damn near twenty-four-seven. When I offered to let a few of them run over to your place for a few hours to cut back those gnarly limbs and some bushes, they jumped at the chance. It sure as hell beats pouring concrete, which was what they would be doing."

Oh.

"And another thing," he added. "It's almost one. It was about time your drunk ass got up and got around anyway. By the looks of that old heap, you've got a lot of work to do yourself."

I yanked the phone from my ear and checked the time.

Shit. He was right.

I hated that.

"I've been up."

"Liar. You still sound like you have gravel stuck in your gullet."

I coughed and cleared my throat. "Allergies."

"Whatever. You wouldn't have been able to do all that yourself anyway. That's why I sent the bucket truck. Your yard was dangerous at night, but you'd straight up murder yourself trying to get that big limb down alone." He grumbled something under his breath, but I didn't hear it. Then he added, "You with a chainsaw is my worst nightmare."

With nothing left to argue, in true Lawson family fashion, I changed the subject. "Well, what are you doing?" I asked and then chugged the rest of the water in my glass.

"Lauren's trip got extended a few days, so Jack and I are getting some pizza and then hitting a ball game. He's still laughing at your *unique* dance moves from last night."

I smiled, remembering how much fun it had been, even if my feet were still in critical condition. They would be touch and go for a while.

"My moves are good."

"Your moves look like upright seizures."

"Shut up." I rolled my eyes, listening to the pair of them

chuckle at my expense. "Anyway, have fun at the game, and thank you."

"We still on for Huey's Thursday?"

Drinks didn't sound good, even days away. "Cal will be on his honeymoon. If you want to cancel, that's fine."

"No way. You're not ditching me. I've had to miss the last two." Hudson could only make it to our weekly night out when Lauren was in town. Life of a single dad and all. "Come on. I can't play darts by myself. That's too pathetic," he complained and then sweetened the pot. "*I'll buy.*"

"Deal. See you Thursday."

The beer was usually a little too warm and the wings were on the dry side, but free beer and wings would always hit the spot. Surely, I'd recover before then.

I helped Hudson's crew with cleaning up and thanked them all. He'd of course been right. They were tickled pink to have what they considered a "puss day." But if it hadn't been for them—and him—I would have likely never gotten around to it, and I had to admit that it looked ten times better than before.

My porch was now visible from the street and I didn't have to worry about someone scary jumping out from the bushes to get me. I could check "major yard overhaul and cleanup" off my list thanks to Hudson and company.

Then there was the other thing I had to do that day, but Craig took the breakup—if you could really call it that—pretty well. That was until I learned right after our call that he'd called his mom, who called my mom, who I then had to talk to for thirty minutes about why I'd broken her friend's son's heart.

Truthfully, if a man's heart was that weak, he shouldn't be wearing it on his sleeve to begin with. I'd been dumb enough to do that once, and I wouldn't be making that mistake again anytime soon.

The beginning of the week flew by. The closer my bosses, Maggie and Shane, got to the arrival of their baby, the more they were delegating tasks and projects to us in the office, but I didn't mind. They paid me well; plus, I got along with everyone else they'd hired.

That's kind of what made it nice at Warren and Warren Consulting. We'd all been brought on around the same time, so there wasn't any real hierarchy to speak of. We were all new and doing our best. Not to mention, I was getting some real hands-on marketing experience, which would hopefully come in handy soon.

"Are you sure you don't mind waiting?" Maggie asked from the front doors Thursday evening as she was heading out. Shane was already in their truck, honking for her. FedEx was running late, and part of the last major campaign she'd been working on was supposed to show up that day.

"I'm fine. They'll probably only be a few more minutes." It was only five thirty, but everyone else had already left. "It's no trouble. I'll lock up."

"Thank you. You're the best, Lex. I'll bring you a good coffee and breakfast in the morning." She waved as she waddled out the door.

I sat at my desk and sent off a few more emails. Then it hit me: I should message Hudson since I was running late, because without Cal there, he'd be waiting by himself.

Me: Shit for brains, I gotta wait on a delivery. I'll be a few minutes behind you.

Hudson: We're already here. Don't stand us up…or I'll tell your dad where you really went on spring break your junior year.

That motherfucker wouldn't dare.

Wait. *We're?* The hell? Had he brought someone to Huey's? A date? Ugh, I didn't want to be a third wheel.

Me: I'm coming. Who is we?

Hudson: Me and Craig. Your boyfriend. I invited him for you. You can be so rude sometimes.

My mouth hung open and I stared at the screen. No. No. No. *No!*

Adrenaline started to sing in my veins. I was going to kill him. My tongue swept back and forth inside my bottom lip, a true tell that I was pissed if I ever had one. Wrestling with my anger, I was blank about what to reply.

Thank God I didn't have to, because just then, another message came through.

Hudson: I'm teasing you, Kid. I heard he hit the road. I was just giving you shit.

He was lucky, because I didn't just get mad—I got even. And usually then some. Controlling my temper could be tricky at times. Especially when I had grown up with one older brother who liked to test my sanity and a second honorary-ish brother who thrived on pissing me off.

Breaking me out of my thoughts was the bell above the door when the FedEx guy popped his head in and set the poster tube on the chair. "Sorry I'm so late today. It's been a long one." The man who was about my age—and not half bad to look at—smiled at me and winked. "I'm glad I caught someone still here. Seeing you is literally the best way to end my day."

"No problem," I replied as I stood and turned my monitor off, smiling back at him. Maybe if I ever got desperate, I'd ask him out. FedEx guy, if not punctual, was tall and tan and handsome. He filled out the uniform if you know what I mean. "Glad I was here too."

I was still smiling about the foxy FedEx guy flirting with me when I walked into Huey's.

"What's that grin for?" Hudson asked and poured me a glass from the pitcher.

"Oh, nothing. Just thinking, and it's almost the weekend." I tossed my bag into the booth and slid in across from him.

"I'll drink to that." He lifted his glass in my direction and waited, his T-shirt stretching around his bicep.

Hudson had always had a nice body, but lately, he was totally shredded. It was probably all the hard work, and also, God thought it was funny to give certain people a perfect metabolism while the rest of us could literally feel every calorie they consumed stick to their bones.

Oh well. I'd been a good girl and hadn't had a drop of alcohol since my bender at Cal's reception. It hadn't even sounded good until now. But my liver's vacation was over, and I clinked my glass with Hudson's.

"Your little joke text wasn't that funny," I said.

He pressed his hand against his chest, feigning innocence. "I'm so sorry. I had no idea you were so upset about things with you and Craig the Stud ending." He smirked. "Did he let you down gently?"

I glared, hoping it had enough intensity to melt his smug face off. It didn't; he just sat there completely immune and proud as ever.

"I broke up with him, Bradley, and you know it."

He chuckled and relaxed into the booth, stretching his thick arm across the back of his seat. "Another man who couldn't satisfy the insatiable Alexis Lawson."

I chuffed. "Well, he tried. *Once.*"

His blue eyes bugged out of his face. "No fucking way. You slept with him?"

"I was dating him. Why not?" I took another sip, surprised with how refreshing and cold our pitcher was this time. I chalked it up to the fact that it was on his tab and not my own.

"I didn't even think you liked him." He squinted and his square jaw rocked to one side.

"I didn't."

"Then why sleep with him? You were only dating him because your mother—who I love as my own—doesn't know how to take no for an answer."

I took a deep breath and gave him the ugly truth. "I was hoping he had secret big dick energy."

He leaned in and lowered his voice. "I'm sorry, come again? Big *dick* what?"

"You know. Some guys"—I gestured to him—"just exude this big dick energy. I was hoping he had *hidden* big dick energy."

"And?" He blinked at me, waiting.

I shrugged. "Not so much." Then I took another long drink and stared down into the glass, totally convinced that the beer was colder than it had ever been. I wasn't complaining though. It was getting me through this conversation.

"Wait." One of his eyebrows lifted, and I could have sworn he blushed. "You think I have big dick energy?"

I didn't have anything to hide. "Hell yeah. You're all buff and manly and stacked. All that swagger you toss around. Plus, I *know* your dick is big." Facts were facts. Big dicks were big dicks. And I didn't make the rules or hand out the dicks.

I refilled my glass and poured a little more in his.

"You've never seen my dick."

"Oh, yes I have. I saw that monster your senior year of high school when we went skinny dipping at the Foresters' pond."

He scratched the back of his neck and grimaced. "Don't look at my dick."

"Well, I haven't since then." I laughed. "But I bet the damn thing is even bigger now."

He readjusted in his seat, seemingly uncomfortable about talking about the size of his genitals. Though he had nothing to worry about. I had seen it for sure. Forgive the pun, but I had a really good, *hard* look at it—and it was impressive. If he weren't close enough to be family, I would have chased him and his big ol' hog around that whole summer until I'd gotten him. Well, that and our neighbor Lauren and him had something going on—or at least that was the feeling I got when she'd been around back then. Turned out they kind of did, then really did, and then didn't at all.

It's a shame she let that beautiful wiener go.

He waved his hands in front of his face. "Mercy. Uncle. *Shut up.* I don't want to talk about my cock with you."

"You don't talk to *anyone* about your cock, let alone show it. Craig wasn't a winner, but at least I got laid this year." For the record, it had not been good, and in hindsight, no sex would have been better. I wasn't going to let Hudson know that though.

"I'll have you know I get laid. *Plenty.* Thank you very much."

I nodded, pursing my lips sarcastically. "Sure you do."

"I'm serious." He stood and nodded at the dart board near our table, and I slid out too. "At least I don't have to have my mommy get me any dates."

Now I'm not advocating for violence, and believe me, I'd never really hurt the big oaf, but I might have gut-checked him.

"Uff," he groaned when my fist connected with his rock-hard stomach.

WHEN THE *Time is Right*

I shook my hand, wondering who'd been injured more. Watching me flex my grip open and closed, he chuckled. "Serves you right. Didn't Cal or I ever teach you how to throw a punch?"

"Guess not." I bent over the booth to retrieve my darts. Yes, I had my own. The ones at Huey's were shit, and we all had our own for that reason. I had kickass black ones with neon-pink-and-green tails, and Hudson's were a boring matte gunmetal gray. "I think you just said that because you can't win unless my hand is as jacked as your dick."

I straightened, wishing for the millionth time I was a few inches taller so I could measure up to Hudson or my brother. But there I was, just under his shoulder, glaring up at him and pursing my lips like the smartass I was.

He grinned down at me, not commenting on my theory. "You know what, Lex. You're smart. You're pretty. You're loyal. If it weren't for your smart mouth and your no-fucks-given attitude, you'd be a good catch."

My second punch must have shown improvement, because he was still buckled over after I shot a one-seventeen and my hand felt fine.

CHAPTER
Four

Hudson

"Hudson?" my secretary, Libby, called over the intercom that Saturday morning. It was Lauren's weekend with Jack, so Libby had met me at the office to work on the mile-high stack of filing that had gotten backed up over the last few weeks.

We'd been slammed with new jobs and all the warranty work on the subdivision we'd completed last year. Working six days a week was the only way to catch up. Most everyone, including Libby, liked the overtime, so it was something of a win-win.

"Yeah?" With sweat beading on my forehead, I kept doing sit-ups. I'd gone for a run that morning, but with no way to break away for a trip to the gym at lunch, the floor of my office would have to do.

"Dr. Calvin Targaryen Lawson, MD is here to see you."

I barked a laugh, which gave me a stitch in my side. That motherfucker.

"Let his royal highness in," I called back, but Cal was already strutting through my door at least three shades darker than he'd been when I'd seen him last. A honeymoon in Bermuda would do that to a man.

I pushed up off the floor, wiping my hands on my shorts before shoving one in his direction. "You do realize it's not necessary for her to announce your arrival like a damn sultan every time you get here, right?"

Normally, he would have brought it in for a back pat, but after eyeing my sweaty T-shirt, he kept it to a brisk handshake. "It's been three years, Hudson. I've gone through the entire cast of The Office, Parks and Rec, Harry Potter, and now, next week's Dr. Calvin Khal Drogo Lawson, MD will round out Game of Thrones. Why does she *still* ask my name every time I get here?"

"Probably the same reason you told her your name was Dr. Calvin Dumbledore Lawson, MD the first time you met."

"Yeah, but that was funny. This is...odd. She's, like, eighty. What if she has dementia?" He scratched his head. "Oh shit, you aren't letting her do your payroll, are you?"

No. I wasn't letting her do my payroll. And only part of that was because she was in fact eighty-four and not as sharp as she'd once been, according to her. Libby Patterson was something of the Hud Construction grandmother. She knitted booties and a blanket each time one of the crew had a baby, and she kept a spiral-bound planner with every single employee's birthday handwritten inside. Not a day passed when she wasn't shuffling out into the equipment bay to give one of her "loves" a special celebratory hard candy. To be honest, filing, keeping up with birthdays, answering the phones, and announcing Cal over the intercom were the brunt of her duties, but she was part of the Hud family, so she wasn't going anywhere.

"Nah, she just does my taxes. Good news, I got a refund last year."

His mouth fell open. "You've got to be shitting me."

For one of the smartest men I'd ever met, Cal was also the most gullible. Being an orthopedic surgeon, his brain worked in logic and reason. He was funny as hell, but his humor was so damn literal that sarcasm sometimes floated right over his head.

I was sure that growing up with Lex's smart mouth had to have been an absolute hell for him, but somehow, they got along.

I walked around my desk and sank into my chair. "Yes, of course I'm shitting you. Now, tell me all about losing your virginity in Bermuda."

Grinning, he settled into one of the chairs on the other side of the desk and stretched his legs out, crossing them at the ankle. "Says the workaholic at the office on a Saturday who hasn't been laid in so long I'm relatively sure his hymen has grown back at this point."

"Spoken like a true medical professional."

Intertwining his fingers, he rested them on his stomach. "They don't call me Dr. Targaryen for nothing. So, listen, I *distinctly* remember telling you Vanessa registered us at Pottery Barn, yet somehow, when we opened wedding presents last night, I found a card that contained a design for a hundred-thousand-dollar swimming pool. Care to explain?"

I mirrored his posture, resting my joined hands on my abs. "Well, first, my guys dig a hole in the ground in your backyard. Then they lay a steel rebar frame, rough-in the plumbing, spray in a concrete shell, and then..." I shrugged. "You know what, it's all very technical. All you need to know is it will be done in about a month, and I took the liberty of adding a diving board to the plans. It's going to cost you a fortune in homeowners insurance, but Jack will love it." I smiled. "You're welcome by the way."

He blinked at me for several seconds. I'd known Cal long enough to be able to see the gears turning in his head. Vanessa was probably at home, already scheduling pool parties with her girlfriends, and he was sitting in my office, debating if he could live with himself for accepting such an exorbitant gift from his best friend in the name of *happy wife, happy life*. Deep down, he wanted it though because Cal would do damn near anything to make Vanessa happy.

He'd come around. Eventually.

I was prepared for him and had played out our argument in my head long before I'd pulled the trigger on the pool.

Lurching to his feet, he started to pace. "There is no damn way I'm letting you buy us a pool as a wedding gift. Or any kind of gift, for that matter. And what the hell is wrong with you for trying? I know business is going well right now, but you have a kid, Hudson."

"Yeah. A kid who will be swimming in your pool all the damn time. Honestly, this isn't a hardship."

My computer chimed with an incoming email notification, but I did my best to ignore it.

He stopped pacing and planted his hands on his hips. "So put the pool at your house."

"What? Are you crazy? I've got a kid. He'll drown."

He ran a hand through the top of his hair. "He'll drown at my place too!"

"Don't be ridiculous. He doesn't sleepwalk at *your* house." I leaned forward and propped my elbows on my desk. "Wait? Has Jack been hitchhiking to your house in the middle of the night again? That little punk."

Cal shot me an unimpressed glare.

I had at least another week of this back-and-forth before he'd finally accept the pool, but if I didn't want to make it a month, I needed to set the framework now. "Would you sit down and relax? Christ, I figured a week of getting laid would mellow you out. Though, judging by that tan, you spent more time on the beach than you did between the sheets. Trouble in paradise already?"

"Fuck off," he shot back, but he finally relaxed into his chair.

"Look, it's not a big deal. I own all the equipment, I've got a couple of guys who could really use the extra hours, and I called in a few favors on the shit I can't do. It'll cost me ten grand max."

He barked a loud, humorless laugh. "Ten grand is still a lot of fucking money."

He didn't have to tell me that.

My financial situation had changed drastically over the six years since I had started Hud Construction. When Jack was first born, I was working for a different construction company across town and sleeping on Lauren's couch. It wasn't the best arrangement, but I'd wanted to be there those first few months to help out and bond with my son. Though, from watching Lauren struggle to finish school while my paycheck barely covered the power bill and formula, I'd been hungry for more.

So. Fucking. Hungry.

Taking handouts from her family wasn't my style. So I worked every waking hour, trying to build Hud Construction from the ground up, all the while framing houses and pouring concrete at my nine-to-five to keep my boy in diapers. It was the most grueling year of my life.

But so incredibly worth it.

Repaying all the people who had stood by my side in the years when I'd had absolutely nothing to offer anyone—including myself—was priority number one.

If that meant buying a pool for my best friend, a kid who had paid for my football cleats senior year so I hadn't looked like a slouch in front of the college recruiters and then stayed up all damn night to help me study to take the SATs a third time when it didn't look like I was going to get picked up at all—the very same man who had sat beside me at my mother's funeral, never once mentioning the tears I'd cried for a woman who didn't deserve them—then so fucking be it.

As far as I was concerned, ten grand was almost an insult after everything Dr. Calvin whatever-the-hell-he-wanted-his-middle-name-to-be-that-day Lawson, MD had done for me.

I'd let him argue. I'd even let him think he was winning at times. But he was getting a pool if I had to dig that thing in the middle of the night, one shovel of dirt at a time.

"Just think about it, Cal."

He shook his head. "No. No pool. Final answer."

I lifted my hands in what he probably assumed was surrender. "Okay. Okay. But you have to break the news to Vanessa."

He dropped his head back and stared up at the ceiling. Oh, yeah. He was going to need divine intervention for that conversation. While he let that sink in, he rubbed his forehead with the tips of his fingers.

Meanwhile, I glanced at my inbox.

Saved by the hellion.

I clicked on Lex's latest email with the subject line reading: *I'm still waiting on my quote, asshole.*

"Your sister is a lunatic."

He huffed at my understatement. "What did she do now?"

"She drew up this crazy blueprint of a stupid cat condo she wants to put in her guest bedroom."

"Like a cat tree?"

"No. Although it does have three stories, two balconies, three bedrooms, two baths, and a cat den. She also wants these tandem bubble window porthole things that go through her exterior wall so they can—and I quote—*work on their tans*. And it also has a pair of porch swings."

It did make me laugh though, because her design was meticulously professional and included all the measurements I'd need. I supposed she had learned a thing or two in design school, because barring how absurd it was, her prints were impressive.

Cal chuckled. "You think that's bad? She sent me a photo while I was gone of her and the cats with a text message that read: *I'm up to my eyeballs in pussy. Hope you are too.*" He shook his head. "It wasn't what I intended to use my international data plan for, but it was my fault for telling her I got one. Over the course of the week, she sent me sixty messages and at least a dozen pictures and videos." He shrugged and grinned. "She's nuts, but I guess that's why we love her."

He wasn't wrong there. Being best friends with Cal meant dealing with Lex's personal style of insanity for well over a decade. I was a trained professional.

While Cal rattled off random stories from his honeymoon, all talks of the pool temporarily forgotten, I half listened and half put together an estimate for Alexis's cat condo. Sure, I quoted all top-grade materials including quartz countertops and bamboo flooring, I even added gold leafing to the ceilings, bringing the grand total to over seventy thousand dollars.

Don't worry. Before I hit send, I made sure to deduct her Friends and Family discount of fifty dollars. I was a real giver like that.

Her text reply was so fast that I wasn't sure how she'd had time to even download my proposal.

Lex: Seventy Gs?! Have you lost your board-cutting, lumber-yard-loitering, power-tool-crazed ever-loving mind?

Me: Sticker shock? Cat mansions aren't cheap, Kid.

Lex: Being a CEO has gone to your head. You egocentric, price-gouging whoremonger. What exactly is the point of having a contractor for a best friend?

Me: Well, obviously my stunning good looks and flawless wit. Why else?

Lex: Stunning? Flawless? So humble. No wonder my cats hate you.

I chuckled and clicked the reply button when Cal's voice broke through my thoughts.

"And then a gang of iguanas swarmed our room, grabbed Vanessa, and dragged her into the woods to be their new queen."

I leaned back in my chair and stared at Cal. "Wait, what? Whose queen?"

He shot me a glower. "Oh, good. I have your attention again."

"Sorry, Lex was just—"

"Lex is always just fill-in-the-blank-with-something-ridiculous-and-crazy with you these days. I swear, you two are like an old married couple at this point."

"What the hell are you talking about? Of course we're closer now. You abandoned us and spent the last six months planning a three-ring circus with Vanessa. For real, man. I was shocked she allowed you to attend your own bachelor party."

He arched an eyebrow incredulously. "You mean the bachelor party you invited my sister to? Let me tell you, there wasn't enough eye bleach in the world to end my suffering after watching my Lex tuck dollar bills into a stripper's thong with her teeth."

I barked a loud laugh. "Okay, first off. She wasn't a stripper, nor was she wearing a thong. She was a bartender who danced on the bar for one song. You were just too damn busy standing outside, talking to your fiancée on the phone, to see the part where Lex took a shot from her cleavage. She had to pay for the drink somehow."

His mouth fell open, and I paused for a brief second.

"You know what? On second thought, it's probably good you missed that."

He nodded emphatically. "Ya think?"

"Relax. It was a fun night."

"It was, but only because watching Lex hustle you out of a hundred dollars on the pool table really took the sting out of the dancing bartender."

"How the hell is she so good at pool? Did you have a table growing up?"

"Nope." He stood from his chair. "How is she so good at *everything* competitive? It's Lex. I've learned not to question or challenge the secrets of the universe." Heading for the door, he shoved his hand into the pocket of his slacks. Yes, he was wearing khakis on a Saturday. How we were friends, I'd never understand.

"Where are you going? You didn't finish telling me about Bermuda."

"I'm going to find my wife while you sit and giggle on the computer with my sister all day. Tell her I said hi. I'm sure you'll see her before I do."

"Not if you actually showed up to Huey's on Thursday!" I called after him. "Last I checked, you're allowed to have a life even after you get married."

He stopped at the door and turned to face me. "One day, Hudson, you'll meet a woman who will actually want to put her mouth on your cock, and I promise you hanging out at Huey's, playing Laverne and Shirley with Lex, will no longer be a priority for you, either."

"You're a dick." I laughed and rocked back in my chair. Though he...had a point. A blow job did sound pretty fucking nice. "We can talk about the plans for the pool if you show on Thursday."

"No pool. Just be a normal person for once and go buy a damn set of crystal salt and pepper shakers like everyone else."

My brow shot up my forehead. "Shit. Who buys crystal salt and pepper shakers?"

He let out a long-suffering sigh. "Judging by the box of them in my car on the way back to Pottery Barn, about thirty percent of our wedding guests." He patted the door frame. "I'll try to make it on Thursday, but if Vanessa surprises me with more lingerie, just know that I love you like a brother, but I'll never choose you over that."

I gave him a curt nod. "I would expect nothing less, Dr. Targaryen."

With that, he was gone, and I spent the next hour going back and forth with Lex over a damn cat condo.

Shit...did that make me Laverne or Shirley?

CHAPTER
Five

Lex

It was that time again. Sunday lunch with my mom and dad. Only, this week, I was solo. No Cal and Vanessa because they'd just returned from their honeymoon on the Island of Misfit Toys. Not even their wedding plans were left to dominate the conversation. Hudson hadn't been able to make it because of work, so I couldn't even fall back on them fawning over Jack.

In a nutshell, I was preparing to get railroaded by both of them and considered giving my worrywart parents a rain check. The problem with that was they'd still ask questions. They'd still worry. They'd still meddle. They'd still be Judy and David Lawson—just over the phone.

Make no mistake. My parents were basically *the* best. They'd loved us. Provided for us. Given us a dreamlike childhood. Practically cheered all of us through high school and college. And they were an excellent example of what a marriage could—and should—be.

As I drove down their boulevard, I wondered if I'd already missed my shot at even a fraction of what they'd built together. But before I got all up in my own head—Lord knew my parents would do it for me—I distracted myself with thoughts of the flirtatious FedEx guy.

By the time I pulled into their drive, I was fantasizing about

WHEN THE *Time is Right*

two or thirty-six naughty things I'd like to do to him and at least ninety lewd things I'd let him do to me. I stepped out of my Kelly Blue Book Top-Safety-Rated Thank You Very Much GMC Acadia to find my favorite seven-year-old ambling down the driveway next door. With a game in his hands, he didn't even notice when he'd passed the back door to his mom's car, but he paused when he hit the trunk and looked up.

"Hey, Jack, you pay attention about as well as you do your debts," I called over to him from about ten feet away, and then I made a smoochie face to remind him of the penalty for nonpayment.

He squinted at me, the same as his dad did when I was being a shit, and asked, "What?"

Oh, he was going to play dumb, but I was boss at dumb and not letting him off that easily.

Lauren was now at her door, and we exchanged smiles. She put a hand on the roof of her luxury sedan and glanced at her son to watch our exchange play out.

"You owe me money, man. Where's my twenty bucks?"

"Um…" He grinned, but he had adorable guilt written all over his face. "Mom?"

Lauren had known me all my life, and although we were polar opposites, we'd always gotten along—especially when it came to our guys, including Jack. I mean, we weren't calling each other up to gossip about celebrities, who we'd hooked up with, or to share smoothie recipes, but we were cool. She was good people, just not my crowd. Except for the handful of random times she'd shown up at Huey's for darts and beer when Hudson had forced her to leave the house when Jack was younger and a few other novel occasions when we were all together. Other than that, we were friendly acquaintances these days.

"Do you owe Alexis money?" she pointedly teased her son.

Swinging from side to side and perching his game on top of his head, he explained, "Kinda. I lost a bet."

In his defense, most people who made bets with me lost. He just hadn't learned that yet.

These were the kinds of life lessons I had to offer, and I proudly took the responsibility of making this dude someone no one would be able to fool in the future. It first began with teaching him how to ask for cash when someone asked what he wanted for Christmas, although that was mostly due to my brother's shitty gift-giving issues. Then my wisdom manifested in bedtime negotiations when I'd babysat him. Can you believe the kid just went to bed when I'd asked him to? I had to let him in on how powerful bedtime was and how he could occasionally get something out of his no-nonsense compliance. And now we were onto the petty gambling and hustling portion of my contribution to this young man's education.

"What was the bet?" Lauren asked, tightening her nearly perfect strawberry-blond ponytail.

"Dad was supposed to catch Vanessa's leg scrunchy thing. Uncle Cal shot it right at him."

Lauren's face lit up, knowing what I did. Sure, Hudson would look the part and diligently fill all his roles as best man, but there wasn't an ice cube's chance in Hell that he'd ever catch the garter.

"Sounds like she won, buddy." His mom shrugged with mock sympathy. "Bet's a bet."

Lauren might have been as prim and proper as they came, but there'd been a time when she'd had mud under her fingernails just like me. She'd been the only child next door, and our house had been the hub when it came to stray kids. Not that she was neglected in the slightest, but her parents were a shit-ton more intense than mine. I could only imagine how they'd reacted to her getting pregnant her senior year at Georgia Tech.

WHEN THE Time is Right

"If you don't have the cash on you now, that's fine. But next time I see you, it's gonna be twenty-one." Life was hard, but the sooner he learned how the games were played, the sooner he'd quit losing. But to let his mom know I wasn't being a total asshole because I'd never actually keep it, I winked at her and added, "Late fees."

"Late fees? Aw, man. What?" he whined.

"It's a cruel world, my man."

"So that's why your dad warned me you might hit me up for back pay on an allowance I know nothing about," Lauren teased.

"All the guys get allowances," he contended with gusto, even tilting his head to the side. He was going to be a handful in his teens.

With that thought, I chuckled because I couldn't wait to see how Lauren and Hud would deal with him. With his father's blue eyes and stubbornness and his mother's brains, Jack was going to be a force.

"Who are these guys? It's just you and Nolan," she said, shaking her head.

I poked the bear. "Yeah, don't you still sleep with a nightlight?"

He rolled his eyes and groaned, heaving the door open and then slamming it when he got inside.

"I hated missing the wedding," Lauren said.

I could see she was sincere, but she was focused on her career and I respected that. "How does it feel to be God's favorite? You missed a circus."

She covered her mouth as she laughed. "I heard."

"Oh, well. Mrs. and Mr. Vanessa Lawson are happy. I guess that's all that matters."

From inside their car, I heard her son chide, "Are we going? I'm hungry."

"Always hungry," she replied under her breath. "Tell Judy and David hi for me." Then she got in her car. Off to feed the poor, starving child.

"Craig left me at the reception," I contended—as if I could blame him. Although it wasn't a bad excuse. After all, he could have said goodbye.

"Well, honey, some people don't want to party all night," my mother explained as she took a bite of her homemade chicken salad sandwich.

"Exactly. That's not the kind of energy I'm looking for. Besides, it literally was a party and it lasted until *midnight*. It's not like I was doing body shots at four in the morning." *Anymore.* College had been fun, and so were many of the nights I'd spent traveling the country with Brenden. But that was neither here nor there.

"Okay. Okay," my dad interjected in his even-keeled *I've had enough* voice. "She didn't like him, Judy. She'll find somebody else."

I picked up a chip and replied, "Or not." Then popped it into my mouth.

Yes, I sometimes made things harder for myself. Still, I was twenty-eight and had a lot of experience being on my own, and I didn't need a man. Sure, it sucked sometimes. That's life.

"Anyway, are you guys going to Hilton Head?" A perfectly timed change of topics if ever there was one. They wouldn't be able to resist talking about their favorite place on Earth. The pristine vacation home they had right on the ocean—and predictably right next door to Lauren's family there too.

Dad bobbed his salt-and-pepper-covered head as he chewed

and swallowed. "Next week. Wanna go? Come up for a long weekend?"

Oh, how I missed the sand and the early mornings, watching the sun come up. "I'd love to, but I'm not sure I'll be able to take off. Maggie is due soon. So work is kinda hectic."

"How do you like your new job, sweetie? I bet it's fun working with Maggie again. A bit different from the waitressing you two did back in the day, huh?"

"Yeah. My attitude wasn't really conducive to tips."

"It's a wonder you made any money at all," my father teased.

"Watch it, Davie," I warned and shoved my index finger into his shoulder. "I believe I come by it honest, Mr. I-Almost-Didn't-Walk-In-My-Own-Graduation-Because-Of-A-Senior-Prank."

"Yeah. Yeah. Yeah." He tipped his sweet tea to his lips and shrugged at my mom, who was glaring at him as if it had happened only yesterday.

"Your father almost killed you, David," my mom reminded him.

"He would have had to catch me first." Mischief sparked in his green eyes as he winked at me.

"Anyway," my mother said, shifting the conversation back. "You said Maggie was having a boy. He's going to have them wrapped around his little finger from day one."

"Just like Prince Calvin," I quipped. *Mama's boy.*

A sweet smile spread across her face, and she tossed her napkin onto her plate. "Do I need to remind you that your *daddy* slept beside your crib for the first three weeks after you came home from the hospital?"

She didn't need to remind anyone of that story. It was her favorite—and one of mine too. Regardless, we knew the next words that were about to come out of her mouth.

In unison, my dad and I squawked, "Only four pounds. One ounce."

I'd been born a few weeks early and had stayed in the hospital for a week or so before coming home. That's probably why I couldn't even reach the top of my refrigerator. Being a preemie had stunted my growth. Or maybe not. But it was a pain in the ass being five foot three *and three quarters*.

"Oh, shut up. Both of you."

"Mother, we don't say shut up in this house."

She laughed. "Yeah, well, maybe we should have. You smartasses always have some bullshit to say."

"Judith Millicent Draper Lawson, *your language*." I wiped an invisible tear from my eye. "It's amazing."

Dad sat back in his chair, rubbing his full pot belly, with a smile that could light the Olympic torch. "I miss this."

"Don't you go soft on me now, old man," I said. One would think my mother was the biggest advocate for my reproductive journey, but one would be wrong. My daddio was champing at the bit for grandbabies. "And don't even start in. We just got Mom to swear. Do not ruin this for me." It was a rare occasion when her potty mouth came out to play, but I was rather good at coaxing it out. Actually, the best.

"Hear me out a minute, Alexis." Full first name. He was serious. "We want to see you happy. You and your brother are the lights of our lives. You can't blame us for wanting that for you."

I couldn't blame them for loving me, so I kept my typical argument that Beep and Boop were their grandkittens—who they neglected—out of the dialogue.

But some choices we didn't get to make for ourselves. My life certainly wasn't exactly how I'd once planned. *A single mother, raising two cats on her own.* But there were times when you could either let life run you over or hide, and hiding was sometimes easier.

Those days, I mostly hid from myself.

WHEN THE *Time* is *Right*

It was getting too deep though, and in self-defense, I forced myself to daydream about the hot FedEx guy as they both blathered on. It was easier to just let them get it out every now and then anyway. As if telling me about everything I was missing out on was ever going to help me get any of it.

So there I sat, in the sun, nodding and eating the last of my chips, fantasizing about the deliveryman as my parents got it all off their chests.

Who knew? Maybe one day, I'd be sitting there with someone and not pretending like there wasn't a massive hole in my chest.

CHAPTER
Six

Hudson

"The wave was so big it nearly ripped us both out to sea," Cal said with wild storytelling hands slicing through the air.

Smiling, Vanessa hooked her arm through her husband's and cuddled into his side. "But then my hubby saved the day. Did you know he used to be a lifeguard?"

Of course we knew. Back when Vanessa was still debating which sorority to pledge, Lex and I had been creating a fake email account and forging a dress code policy to inform Cal that the uniform for the lifeguards at the country club pool had switched to speedos. We were also there—front and center—to witness the horror in his eyes when he reported for his first day on the job in the aforementioned speedo while everyone else was in trunks. It was a personal highlight in my life.

But reminiscing on it now, I let out a silent groan.

Vanessa always did that crap. When they'd first started dating, I hadn't thought much of it. She was proud of her man. Good on her. Most of all, good for Cal for finding a woman who wanted to dote on his adolescent achievements. As time passed though, it became more and more apparent that Vanessa's pride was nothing but a pop quiz to prove who knew him best. A competition she couldn't possibly win when going toe-to-toe with his sister and his best friend of over fifteen years, but that never dissuaded her from trying.

I did a lot of pretending when Vanessa was around.

Pretending I didn't know things about Cal to allow her a victory.

Pretending she didn't grate on my nerves.

Pretending I wouldn't rather throw myself in front of a bus than listen to her talk.

But she made Cal happy. So I bit my tongue.

Lex on the other hand...

"A lifeguard? No way!" she gasped, sarcasm dripping so thick in her tone that it was a wonder it didn't puddle in her lap.

I swept a leg out to the side to kick her under the table, but Cal beat me to it, catching her right in the shin.

"Ow!" she exclaimed.

"Shit. Sorry about that," he lied, shooting her a quit-being-a-dick smile. It was his very own signature mixture of his what-the-hell-is-wrong-with-you glare and his how-am-I-related-to-you grin.

Never one to be outdone, Lex leveled him with a I-will-murder-you-in-your-sleep scowl.

Ahhhhh, the joys of family.

No, really. I fucking loved this shit. Finally having Cal and, yes, even Vanessa back for our weekly ritual of beer and darts was a welcome return to normalcy. Outside of work, I didn't have much of a life, but when I didn't have Jack, I could always count on something going down at Huey's.

Okay, maybe "something going down" was an exaggeration. The up-all-night, wake-up-for-work-still-half-drunk days were long gone. But they were typically good for a couple of hours of bullshitting in our favorite booth, a shared pitcher of beer, a basket of wings. You know, real wild shit.

Lex and Cal were still locked in a glare-off when another chair suddenly appeared at the end of the table.

"Hey, guys," Lauren chirped, giving my shoulder a squeeze before sitting down.

"Hey, what are you doing here?" I glanced around her. "Where's Jack?"

"Ah, he couldn't get in, so I ditched him with the bouncer. We really need to get him a better fake ID."

"What?" Cal exclaimed, knee-deep in his lifelong struggle with sarcasm.

"I'm kidding," Lauren said. "He's actually with Judy and David. They called and asked if they could take him to see a movie."

Like a good uncle, Cal visibly relaxed.

Vanessa clutched her heart. "Awww. That's so sweet. Those two are desperate for more grandkids." Tilting her head back, she silently asked Cal for a kiss. "We better get working on that, *hubby*. We might be their only hope left."

I didn't even have to look at Lex to see the verbal slap hit her. I also didn't need to wait to see how she was going to react.

Tossing an arm around her shoulders, I cupped a hand over her mouth and kept talking to Lauren. "Ah, so you're free tonight and decided to finally grace us with your presence? How generous of you."

"Something like that," she mumbled.

Cal slid her the empty cup Carmen, our favorite waitress, had brought out for Vanessa before she'd ordered a cosmo and asked, "Did they finally find a cure for your allergy to social gatherings, or was that specific to my wedding?"

She wrinkled her nose, flipping him off as she scratched it. "Good to see you too, asshole." Her blond hair brushed her shoulders as she looked at Vanessa. "Sorry I missed the wedding.

WHEN THE *Time* is *Right*

I would have done anything to be there, but with the way things are at work right now and all these automation upgrades, they've got me flying out at the drop of a hat. I couldn't get out of it. Just know I went in halfsies on whatever Hudson bought for a present."

Vanessa's pink-painted lips formed a tight line. "Oh, you mean the pool Cal won't let us have?"

"And here we go." Cal rolled his eyes and grabbed the pitcher, spreading the last few sips around to everyone's glasses.

Lauren swung an incredulous gaze my way, mouthing, "You bought them a pool?"

I took a page from her playbook and mumbled, "Something like that."

Just as quickly, Lex tore my hand off her mouth and turned to face me in the booth. "I'm sorry. You gave me a fifty-dollar discount on a seventy-thousand-dollar cat condo, but you bought them *a pool?* I thought we were friends."

And just like that, it was old times again.

Shrugging, I relaxed deeper into my seat. "We are. Hence the discount."

She scoffed. "You can keep your crappy discount. Besides, after reviewing all the bids, I've decided to go with Delaney Construction for the cat condo. Your loss."

"No, you aren't."

"Yes, I am. His bid was a tenth of yours. You need to work on those prices or you're going to be out of business soon."

"No. I mean, you *really* aren't. I emailed every contractor within a hundred-mile radius yesterday and told them you stiffed me on a job. You'll be lucky if you can find a neighborhood handyman to hang a picture for you with that kind of track record."

The rest of the table broke into laughter as Lex's eyes stretched wide. "You didn't!"

"I did. But I'll keep my prices in mind. Though, if I suddenly go out of business, it will free up my schedule to install Cal's pool." The side of my mouth hiked as I chanced a glance at my best friend.

"No pool!" he declared. "Jesus, Hudson, let it go. It's too much."

"I agree," Lauren stated with a nod and lifted her palm my way. "I'm going to need my half of that purchase back."

My brows shot up my forehead. "Oh, you mean the money you never paid me for the gift you had no part in? Yeah. I'll get right on that."

"You know what's not too much?" Vanessa asked, her eyes filled with a sparkle that did not bode well for Cal. "A sunset party around *our pool* for our first anniversary."

Lex's head snapped in my direction, the antithesis of Vanessa's sparkle showing in her dread-filled face. "Please tell me we don't have to attend anniversary parties too?"

"No parties," Cal declared, curling his arm around his wife's shoulder. "And no pools." He leveled me with a pointed glare before turning it on his sister. "And for the love of God, who will hopefully one day find a man crazy enough to date you, *no* cat condos."

"What about fiancés?" Lauren asked. "Are we allowed to have those?"

Four sets of eyes jumped her way.

"Fiancé?" Cal said.

Followed by Lex's, "What the fresh hell?"

Followed by Vanessa's, "You're getting married!"

Followed by my, "I'm sorry, come again?"

She flashed them all a bright smile, which dimmed when it landed on me. Damn if that didn't sting, but fuck, I hadn't even known she was dating anyone. Not that I cared. It had been almost eight years since our one night of stomach-churning passion that had given us a son. In that time, she'd had several boyfriends, a few I'd even liked.

A fiancé was a completely different story though. A fiancé meant moving in and getting married and becoming a permanent figure in my son's life, and I hadn't even known that the guy existed.

"He asked, but I didn't say yes…yet," she whispered, a pair of baby-blue eyes that matched my son's staring back at me.

"Oh-kay," I drawled suspiciously. "Want to tell me who he is?"

Her cheeks flushed as she nervously tucked her hair behind her ears. "Um, well, his name is Mark Garrett, and he's an investment banker who I met after my parents kinda-sorta set us up on a blind date."

Lex leaned forward, propping both arms on the table. "Dear God, do not let your parents give my mother the idea that that actually works. I just got rid of my last 'perfect match.'"

Lauren giggled softly but kept her gaze on mine. "We've been dating for about a month now. And I was going to talk to you about him, but I've been so busy at work and you with Cal's wedding. Things have moved really fast. And I know if I was in your shoes, I'd be freaking out about you bringing a stranger into Jack's life so quickly. But, Hudson, I swear to you. He's such a good guy. Just give him a chance. Maybe we can all have dinner one night. Then, if you're cool with it, you can be there when we introduce him to Jack. Whatever you feel comfortable with."

It had been bound to happen one day. Lauren was a catch. Smart. Funny. Beautiful inside and out. There were a lot of times when she had started pulling away from our little gang of misfits to concentrate on her career and being the best mom imaginable that I'd wished she'd had someone. But despite the fact that

I'd met several of her boyfriends, most of which she'd casually brought to Huey's for darts and wings, Jack had never met a single one.

This was a huge deal and not just for me.

There were a few perks to having a child with one of your best friends. Absolute trust was at the very top of that list. We didn't always agree how much screen time Jack should have or if tackle football was safe for a kid his age, but I knew with absolute certainty Lauren would never bring a man she didn't trust implicitly into our son's life.

Sure, I could have put my foot down and lectured her about how we'd discussed in great detail while she was still pregnant how we were going to handle relationships in the future. We were never going to be together, but we'd both wanted with our whole hearts to do what was best for our son. She'd made me pinky swear a dozen times that if I ever got serious about a woman, I would let her know immediately. Say, before I got to the point of proposals and marriage. But bitching and arguing wasn't going to change her relationship—at least not with her soon-to-be fiancé anyway.

Besides, I was sure investment banker Mark would be a good guy. Though, before dragging my son into the middle, I had every intention of finding out for myself.

"Okay," I replied.

She eyed me skeptically. "Okay?"

I shrugged. "Yeah. Okay. I'll meet him. I've got to be at Cal's all day on Saturday to get the pool measured off. But after that, I should be free if you want to set something up."

"I said no pool," he rumbled, but it was drowned out by a very uncharacteristic squeal from the usually cool, calm, and collected mother of my child.

Diving from her chair, she threw her arms around my neck.

WHEN THE *Time is Right*

"Oh my God. Thank you so much. You are so amazing. Seriously, Hudson. This completely makes up for how bad you were in bed and accidentally knocking me up."

"Hey!" I complained, peeling her arms off my neck and shifting her back into her chair. "I don't exactly remember you being any better. I should probably warn Mark."

"Trust me. He already knows better." She shot me a wink and then stood up. "I need to get going."

"What?" Lex complained. "You can't leave. You're almost engaged. This calls for champagne on Cal's bill." She lifted the empty pitcher. "Or at the very least another round."

"I can't," Lauren said without the faintest hint of regret coloring her voice. "Judy and David have Jack for a few more hours, so I promised Mark if all went well here, I'd meet him for drinks some place"—her cheeks pinked all over again—"*private*."

Jesus. She'd caught it bad. As far as I knew, the only time her face had turned that red was when Jack was three and packed his sword—a.k.a. a pink dildo—in his overnight bag he took to her parents'. It was a lot of fun when she'd lied and told them it was mine. I was told her parents still prayed for me every Sunday at church.

We all slid out of the booth, and one by one, we took turns hugging her, exchanging greetings, congratulations, and goodbyes in one simple gesture.

And then she was gone again. Unfortunately, that was how the majority of our interactions went with Lauren.

"I, uh, think we're going to head out too," Cal announced.

Vanessa peered up at him, a huge smile on her face. For all of her annoying qualities, she did love Cal something fierce.

"What?" Lex exclaimed. "You can't leave. You just got here. We haven't even ordered food yet."

"Yeah, well, you two are on your own for dinner tonight." His lips split into a wolfish grin, and if I wasn't mistaken, his hand slipped down to his wife's ass. "Vanessa and I have more *pressing* things to do at the moment."

Lex curled her lip and balled up a napkin before throwing it at her brother. "Gross. Get out of here with that shit."

He waggled his dark brows and then knocked his knuckles on the table. "Have a good night. I know we will."

"See you on Saturday!" I called after him.

He spun to face me and pointed. "No pool, Hudson. I'm serious."

I had no doubt he was. He was also getting a fucking pool.

"Okay," I lied, lifting my hands in surrender.

He gave me a quick chin jerk and then ushered his wife out of the bar.

"He's getting a pool, isn't he?" Lex slid into the booth across from me.

I lifted my beer to my lips and mumbled, "Abso-fucking-lutely."

"You in for another pitcher?" she asked, searching the bar for Carmen.

"Depends. You think we can drink away the fact that Cal *and* Lauren are both getting laid tonight and we're two sad sacks alone at a bar, debating if we can split a second pitcher?"

She stared at me in all seriousness, her long lashes blinking over her deep-green eyes. "I mean, I'm willing to give it a shot if you are."

I was, and only part of that had to do with the fact that I'd just found out I had to meet my son's future *stepfather* on Saturday night.

I pinched the bridge of my nose. "Yeah. I could do another drink."

We spent so much time at Huey's that it didn't require ordering anymore. Lex made eye contact with Carmen and, a few minutes later, a fresh pitcher of beer landed on the table between us.

Lex gave us each a cold pour, asking, "So, how do you really feel about the whole Lauren thing?"

I slanted my head to the side and eyed her curiously. "About the same as I felt when Cal told us he was going to propose."

Her face lit. "Oh, so we're doing shots tonight?"

Chuckling, I shook my head. "No, smartass. I'm fine with *Lauren* getting married. She's my friend. You know it was never like that with us."

"What kind of friend? The kind that gets a fifty-dollar discount or a whole damn swimming pool?"

I loved fucking with her, so I pretended to think about it for a minute. "Good point. You think I can get a two-for-one deal with my plumbers if I do her pool at the same time as Cal's?"

Her eyes narrowed into slits. "That's it. As soon as I get home, I'm forbidding Beep and Boop from ever speaking to you again."

I feigned agony and clutched my chest. "How will I ever recover?"

She rolled her eyes and lifted her cup into the air, and I followed suit, ready for whatever ridiculous toast she'd no doubt been preparing all night. "To never getting married." Her glass tipped forward.

Mine sloshed all over the table as I snatched it out of the way before they had the chance to clink. "Whoa, what the hell was that?"

"What the hell was what?" she parroted, tossing a handful of napkins onto my spill.

"Who says I'm *never* getting married?"

She laughed loud and rich. "Uhhh, the universe at this point. When's the last time you went on a date?"

Truth? A long fucking time ago, and I suspected being on

the very welcomed receiving end of a booty call from Rebecca Florence, my tenth-grade girlfriend, last summer was not what she was talking about.

I scoffed. "When was the last time *you* went on a date?"

"Cal's wedding, thank you very much."

I quickly amended. "With a guy who didn't make you dry-heave?"

Her shoulders fell. "A...while."

Try at least six years.

I had no life due to the circumstances of being a part-time workaholic, part-time single dad. Lex, however, was a master at distracting herself. Dating meant giving a guy a chance. And giving a guy a chance meant opening herself up. And opening herself up meant facing the facts that no one would ever be Brenden.

It had been six years since she'd lost him—since we'd *all* lost him. Lex had moved on, but it wasn't on the same trajectory. The once serial-dating fiery redhead was now the crazy cat lady about three decades too soon. Judy Lawson loved nothing more than to pry in her daughter's life, and I think Lex allowed it because her mom had absolute shit taste in men.

Lex didn't need Craig Lewis, a whiny shit stain of a man. She needed someone she couldn't plow over with her larger than life personality. A man confident enough to sit in her shadow while she forged her own path. She was a handful. There was no denying that. But somewhere out there was a man aching for a challenge because he knew, at the end of the day, the sweet she gave would always be worth the chaos.

Brenden had been one of the few men who had ever been able to withstand the natural disaster that was Alexis Lawson.

And then he was gone.

And then Cal got married.

Next, Lauren was getting married.

WHEN THE *Time* *is* *Right*

And, now, it was just the two of us, alone at Huey's with a pitcher of beer.

One day, I wasn't going to be there anymore, either. Like, for example, next week when I had Jack.

Lex was a twenty-eight-year-old knockout. Men couldn't pass her on the street without stopping to stare. I'd love to say that she didn't know it, but that wasn't Lex's style. She knew she was gorgeous and could have the pick of any guy she wanted.

She just hadn't found anyone she wanted yet.

Yet.

Yet.

"Hey." I leaned forward when an idea struck me. "Why don't you let me set you up with someone?"

"Because if your taste in women is anything to go off, your taste in men will be awful too?"

It was my turn to be offended. "What the hell is wrong with my taste in women?"

"You don't have any. Like none. The last date you went on was a woman who had been divorced but still cried about her socks-with-sandals-wearing ex-husband. And I'm not talking about three-a.m. calls from Rebecca Flojob, who has an ancient Egyptian scroll of her own problems."

Holy. Shit. Atlanta was a huge city, but in a lot of ways, it could be a really small town.

I glanced around the bar before lowering my voice. "How the hell do you know about Rebecca?"

"Because shortly after that night, she had a hair appointment and gave the entire salon a play-by-play. Don't worry. You were a lot better in bed in her story than you were in Lauren's. So good they were still talking about it a week later when I went in for a trim."

I thrust a hand into the top of my hair. "Jesus, don't you and your mom go to the same salon?"

She shot a mischievous grin. "Judy was simply happy to hear you were getting some. That pink dildo of yours had her worried for a while."

Rolling my shoulders, I faked a gag and then tipped my beer up for a long sip. "Anyway... Let's get back to me setting you up."

She propped her elbow on the table and then her chin on her fist. "Okay. What do I get out of it?"

"Uhhh... A date?"

"Not good enough."

I arched an eyebrow. "Okaaay, a date who will buy you dinner and drinks?"

She lifted her chin, a smile pulling at her full lips. "I want the Purrrr-fect Pretty Pink Palace."

"I don't know any men who will pony up five figures before they even meet you."

"Not from them. I want it from *you*. I'll pay for all the supplies, though we are going to have to seriously cut down on all your additional quartz and gold leafing."

I brought my hand up to cover my mouth in a worthless attempt to hide my smile as she continued.

"*And* I want to set you up too. I'm not the only loser at this table. If you think it's so easy to find me Mr. Right, then it's only fair you have to suffer through Mrs. Right along with me."

"So let me get this straight. First, I have to find a man willing to go out with you. Then convert your guest room into an apartment for your cats *and* pay for dinner and drinks for a woman I have zero interest in going out with?"

She nodded like a genie. "That's correct."

I mimicked her nod. "Hard no."

Remember that part about how much I loved to fuck with her? Well, it could be said that she loved to fuck with me more. So. Much. More. I could only imagine who Lex would set me up with if she thought it was out of some kind of revenge for me forcing her to go out with a completely decent guy. I wasn't sure if she had a connection with the trolls who lived under the bridge, but I'd have been willing to bet she'd sell her soul to make them in order to give me hell. No fucking way I was signing up for that cruel and unusual punishment.

Unless...

"You let me buy the Chevelle."

Her mouth fell open. "No fucking way."

I wasn't much of a car guy. I had my work truck and had been toying with the idea of buying an SUV for the weekends, though her grandfather's fully restored cherry-red-with-white-racing-stripes 1970 Chevelle SS was enough to make my cock hard. That car was the pinup model of vehicles. She'd inherited it when he'd passed away four years earlier, and in that time, it had sat in a storage unit across town. A beauty like that deserved the open road where she could let all four hundred and fifty of her horses run. But no, Lex kept that fine piece of American craftsmanship locked away like her private automotive captive.

I slid forward in my seat, resting both arms on the table. "Hear me out. What's to say you aren't going to set me up with someone awful just to have a little fun? We gotta have stakes in this *bet*."

Bet. Three simple letters, but it might as well have been a flute-playing snake charmer for her.

She straightened her back and brushed her long, red hair off her shoulder. "You have my attention."

Of course I did. The only thing more lethal than a bet would have been the reemergence of the triple-dog dare from our childhood, but I wasn't about to pull out all the guns just yet.

"Three dates," I said. "Three *good* dates. No funny business. No games. I'm talking real people we think the other might like.

If you find someone for me and we hit it off in a way that ultimately ends in a relationship, I'll build you the cat-astrophe in your guest room."

Her eyes lit.

And I lifted a finger in the air. "But! If I find someone for you, you have to sell me the Chevelle."

She stared at me for a long beat, but I'd already won. I had no idea if I could find the perfect guy for her. But suffering through three dates was a small price to pay for her finally letting me try.

The Chevelle was just a bonus.

Maybe she could find me someone that would slip into my life the way Mark had slipped into Lauren's. Or Vanessa into Cal's. Though I wouldn't be ordering the braided trim for Boop and Beep's custom balcony anytime soon.

"Deal," she said, extending her hand across the table.

I gave her hand a firm shake. "Just make sure the tank is full when you deliver my new baby."

CHAPTER Seven

Lex

I'd been pretty confident, initially, that I could beat Hudson. That was until I actually had to put my money where my mouth was and find him a date. Trouble with that was he was only looking for someone who was right or at least tolerable for *me*, and I was shopping for two.

Hudson and Jack.

And let me tell you: Finding a date for an overbearing, bossy stick in the mud and a seven-year-old who was more mature than I was was a challenge.

I'd gone through my phone, but all the women in it were married, in a relationship, or way too into themselves to have enough to give two of my guys. I needed a woman who was sweet and nurturing. Someone I could trust to take care of them.

Nearly a week after our bet, I lay on my fur-covered bed, wiggling to get my date-night jeans zipped, mentally patting myself on the back. Hudson had a date I could feel good about.

I really wasn't worried about who he'd set me up with. He wasn't going to win. However, I was getting tacos out of the deal, so I cleaned myself up, and for the most part, I was optimistic about the whole thing.

Was Hudson going to make me a love connection? Hell fucking no.

Was Hudson going to win my Chevelle? Again, not a chance.

Were my cats going to live a life in the lap of luxury? You're damn right. I would inadvertently get to see how some of my extra, *extra* bells and whistles looked in my design.

So I had plenty to be positive about. Plus, as bratty as I was, I knew how to be a good sport.

Knowing I'd need at least one strong margarita, I called a Lyft to take me to Mejor Mexicano, where Hud had arranged for my date to take place. My mouth watered the whole ride. To be honest, my palms were a little sweaty too. I wasn't nervous per se, but what if Hudson had found someone quasi-decent for me?

I'd have to cross that bridge when I got to it—and then set the bitch on fire. How had I found myself—yet again—pacifying another person by going out with someone I knew I'd never end up with?

"Thanks," I called to the driver while walking to the restaurant's door, straightening my tank top and wiping the corners of my mouth. There was no way I was getting into a relationship, but being the optimist I was, I reminded myself that maybe I'd get lucky and still have fun. Hopefully, Chase, my blind date, would be pleasant to talk to, easy on the eyes, and—if all went well—a good kisser too.

Maybe I was more of an opportunist than an optimist. Fuck if I knew.

At the very least, I was getting a great dinner, so the smile on my face as I walked in was genuine. The familiar scents of Mexican food hitting my nose made my stomach growl, and then I saw who I assumed was my date at the bar, where Hudson had told me he'd be. Plus, he was the only guy at the bar, so I didn't feel too weird approaching him. The odds were in my favor.

"Chase?"

He glanced over his shoulder, smiled, and then stood. "Alexis?"

I held my hand out to shake his in greeting. His was soft and smooth, and his grip was a tad weak. But I pushed that out of my mind as I stared at his face. He looked so familiar. Brown hair. Blue eyes. Tall, probably over six-three, his head an easy foot higher than mine.

"Nice to meet you," I told him.

"You too. I just ordered a drink while I was waiting. I thought I was early."

Chase's style was clean cut and strait laced, but there was something about him that was throwing me off a bit—purely on first impression. I couldn't put my red-tipped finger on it yet. Maggie and I had gone for manis and pedis that week in the name of first dates and due dates. So I peeked around him to see what he was having: Stella Artois in a gold-rimmed chalice.

"Can I get you a drink? Or if you're hungry, we can get a table and order."

"A table would be great," I answered as my tummy rumbled again.

"Sure. I'll be right back."

Quickly, while he went to the front to get a server, I pulled my phone out and sent Hudson a quick text. It was unlikely that he'd answer since he was on a date too, but my mind was racing, trying to place Chase.

Me: Where do I know this guy from?

Seconds later, while Chase was still waiting to be assisted, Hudson replied.

Hudson: I don't think you do. He's not from Atlanta. He moved here a few years ago. He's a good guy though. Why? Are you okay?

Me: I'm fine. Just thought I recognized him from somewhere.

Hudson: Nah, I doubt it. I don't think he gets out that much.

"They have a table ready for us," Chase said when he returned for me and his goblet of fancy beer.

I offered him a smile and let him usher me in the direction where we'd be seated.

After ordering a margarita on the rocks roughly the size of my head, I couldn't help but subtly watch him over my menu. There was no real reason for me to be looking at it anyway. I knew what I was getting, but he was intently reading his, so I pretended to do the same.

When the waiter returned, I ordered my steak tacos with extra meat and extra queso to pour on top, and then I listened to Chase place his.

"Is the rice cooked with chicken or vegetable stock?" He was either vegan or allergic to chicken, which I'd never heard of, so my money was on the former.

"Chicken stock, sir," the server answered.

"And the beans?"

"Yes, a little in there too, I believe."

Chase closed his menu. "Okay. Thank you. I think I'll have veggie fajitas. Please add mushrooms if they don't come with. No beans. No cheese. No rice. And a side of pico."

He wasn't a dick about it, but I prayed—after ordering what I had—that I wasn't in for a lecture. In my opinion, everyone was entitled to believe and eat what they wanted, but I wasn't there to learn about the atrocities of animal cruelty. I was there to have dinner and possibly find a man to curl my toes later.

But I was already losing hope about the hooking-up-afterward part though because something was off.

"So you know Hudson well, then?" I asked while he took a sip of his drink.

"Not all that well. Actually, I was kind of taken aback by his phone call to set this up."

"Oh, well, how do you know each other?" Maybe I'd get a hint about why I felt like I was having some twisted version of déjà vu.

"We played eighteen holes together at a charity fundraiser for the hospital. I'm his son's pediatrician."

Listening, I sucked my golden cocktail through the straw until the pieces began to click into place.

A doctor.

Short, dark hair.

Blue eyes.

Tall.

Picky eater.

Kind of geeky.

Hudson, the motherfucker, had essentially set me up with Calvin. I was on a date with my damn brother.

The ick factor that hit me was strong. Yet not powerful enough to quell my appetite. So, from then on, I didn't worry if shoveling beef into my gaping maw bothered him. There was no chance this was going any further than the check at the end of dinner.

Strike one for Hudson, and if Hudson's date was even a fraction better than the one I was on, Beep and Boop were one sad date closer to their kitty palace. So all wasn't lost.

After a pretty dull conversation, Chase went up front to pay for our meals, which was nice, and I retrieved my phone from my purse again to get another Lyft when another message came through.

Hudson: Well, my date is over. You should just give me the keys now and forfeit.

Me: No way, my dude. Mine's over too. And I have a major bone to pick with you.

Hudson: Do I need to kick someone's ass? I'm at Huey's now, but I can be at Mejor Mexicano in ten minutes.

I pecked at my phone and ordered a ride to the bar from the restaurant.

Me: Don't move, killer. I'll be right there.

I met Chase up front and together we walked out the door.

"It was nice meeting you, Chase. Thanks for dinner."

He smiled, and if he hadn't looked and reminded me so much of my Goddamned lame-ass brother, whom I loved dearly, he might have been handsome and charming. But the mere thought of leading him on or giving him any kind of encouragement about us ever being a thing was wrong and frankly disgusting.

"You're welcome. Can I give you a ride somewhere? Wanna go have another drink? We could go for a walk?" It was sweet and absolutely something I could hear my sibling saying. So much so that, now, his voice was even giving me yucky Cal vibes.

Inwardly, I cringed.

Outwardly, I returned the smile and said, "No, thanks though. I called for a ride already."

"Well, can I get your number?"

I straightened and put it out there. "I hate to be rude and this may sound sort of blunt, but you and I aren't going to happen. *Ever.*"

His brows bunched. "Oh. I just thought… I mean…I had a good time."

"Don't get me wrong, I did too." It was time for a truth bomb, so I lit the fuse. "And I think you're great. It's that you're way, way, *way* too much like my brother. I just—"

"Calvin?"

"You know him?"

"Sure. We work at the same hospital. He played in the tournament with Hudson and me."

I put my hand over my heart and exhaled. "So you get it? You see it?"

He shrugged. "Not really. But I have two sisters, and if I were ever on a date with someone who I thought resembled either of them, I'd probably feel the same."

"Yeah. It's really weird." The uncomfortableness of the moment was causing my neck to itch. "You look alike. Act a lot like each other. Talk the same. You're both doctors. It's just too much. Again, thank you for dinner, but I just can't see this going anywhere beyond this evening."

Scratching the back of his neck, he chuckled. "I guess, thanks for being honest." He looked toward the parking lot and then started to say something else, but I interrupted.

"My Lyft will be here any minute. You can go."

Awkwardly, he snickered again. "Okay, then. I'll…"

I waited as he searched for the words, but evidently, he couldn't find any, and left me with, "Bye. I guess?"

As soon as he was out of sight, I shivered and shook off the heebie-jeebies as my ride pulled up.

―

"What the fuck is wrong with you?" I accused as I threw myself into our booth.

"Currently, I'm pissed at you. But what are you talking about?"

I rested my face in my palms and sweetly answered, "Chase. I'm talking about Chase, Hudson."

He sat back and flagged Carmen down to get another glass for me. "What was wrong with him? He has a good job. A clean criminal history. His credit score is over eight hundred and—"

I slapped the table, causing the beer to slosh in the half empty pitcher. "How do you know about his credit?"

"What? We're putting a rental unit over his garage. *And* he is the slowest, most cautious golf cart driver I've ever had the unfortunate pleasure of riding with for eighteen holes. He's perfect for you. He even has a damn cat. Did he tell you about his cat?"

Yeah, on paper, I could see why Hudson, a.k.a. Mr. Practical, would like him. Therefore, I couldn't be too mad. That didn't change the fact that even the idea of Chase touching me in any sort of sexual way made my skin crawl.

"All of that is fine and good, but—you blind Neanderthal—he's Calvin!"

His face bunched up, and he leveled me with that classic deep-in-thought squint of his. "No."

"Tall? Dark hair? Blue eyes? Puny? Vegan? Ringing any bells?"

"Calvin was only vegan for a few months," he interjected with an ornery grin.

"He's a Goddamned doctor."

"Okay, you have me on that one."

My head shook at the thought of Calvin-slash-Chase leaning in to kiss me. "You're sick. In the head. You can't be trusted. I need new friends. Maybe a lobotomy."

He finished a long drink and set his glass down. "You should be one to talk. You think I wanna fuck Mary Poppins?"

I couldn't help the laugh that ripped up my throat at his twisted face and his tongue hanging out in disgust.

"Seriously, Lex. Why? Just why?"

"Mrs. Hort—I mean, Susan is nice."

"She smelled like oatmeal raisin cookies."

I giggled again. "Well, she's a baker, Hudson. What did you expect her to smell like? Leather and strawberry lube?"

His lip curled and he rolled his eyes as he filled the glass Carmen had brought for me. Then he topped his off while she waited. "We're gonna need another one of these," he told her. When she was out of earshot, he leaned in and discreetly answered my question, "I would have been more interested in the leather. She wore sneakers, Kid."

Inside, I was rolling, but I remained calm and pretended to be offended. I'd thought she would have dolled herself up for a date. Guess not. "So? Women can't wear athletic footwear now?"

"I took her to a nice Italian restaurant."

I licked my lips to hide the smile threatening to spread across my face. "So no kiss on the first date?"

"I don't mean to be disrespectful, but I suspect her teeth were false. She had to be around thirty years older than me? You're cheating on this bet."

"Hey, she's sweet and I thought Jack would like her. At least I'd know you two were eating more than delivered pizzas and Hot Pockets when you had him. You probably eat even less when he's not around."

"Bullshit. You sabotaged me."

After a few sips and a long pause, I said, "You sabotaged me too. And I was in a rush to find someone for you. But I will say this: I already have your second date in mind. And you—you giant asshole—will be happy to know she's more your age."

He opened the pouch he kept his darts in, which prompted me to dig mine out of my purse. "Good."

Before it slipped my mind, I had to know how last weekend

had gone. "Hey, how'd it go with Lauren and her beau? Was he cool?"

"Got rescheduled." His brows lifted. "They're supposed to get back to me with another night." He shrugged and I could see the disappointment.

I changed the subject, not wanting to make his night any worse. "Oh, and for my second date, could you *please*, for the love of my shriveled twat, keep in mind that I'm looking for big dick energy and not some incestuous dinner company. Please and thank you."

"Jesus," he muttered, pointing to the board with the tip of his dart, a smug grin lifting one side of his mouth. "You're up first, but don't expect me to go easy on you. I'm playing to win, Kid."

CHAPTER
Eight

Hudson

What a fucking day.

No, strike that. What a fucking *week*.

I'd spent the majority of it in Cal's backyard. For seven days, I gave the great pool debate a rest, long enough to give him the illusion that I'd dropped it. Then on Monday, when I was sure he'd be at work, I'd broken into their backyard with a team of my guys. As I'd suspected, Vanessa didn't say a word. It had taken us two full days to get the utility lines marked and the area prepped. So imagine my surprise on Wednesday morning when I'd shown up with a trailer full of equipment including a backhoe and a mini excavator to find all of our hard work gone. Cal had been standing in the bay windows of his kitchen, a cup of coffee in his hands and a shit-eating grin on his face. But that little stunt was far from the victory he'd hoped for.

We'd had to work our asses off to get things back on schedule, but when he came home from work that afternoon, there was a concrete hole in his backyard, ready and waiting for plumbing to be hooked up. I didn't give a fuck if he filled it with water and let his wife float in it or turned it into the neighborhood skatepark. There was no turning back.

That should have felt like a victory. And in some ways, it did, but I was exhausted, and despite that, I hadn't been to the gym all week, so my whole fucking body hurt. I wasn't a stranger to hard work, but with Hud Construction's rapid growth over the last few years, I'd basically worked myself into a desk job. It felt nice to be back at it—at least in my mind. My traps were a different story though.

On top of all that, I missed Jack. He'd spent the week with Lauren's parents at their beach house on Hilton Head Island. Judy and David owned the house next door, so I was positive my boy was having a blast and being spoiled in ways only grandparents knew how to do, but damn, a week was a long time. Technically, I only had him every other week as it was, but Lauren and I made sure he never went a whole week without seeing both of us. Sunday couldn't come soon enough.

Oh, and speaking of Lauren, she'd had to reschedule my little meeting with investment banker Mark for the *fourth* time in two weeks. Apparently, he was just as busy at work as she was. How the hell they had spent more than an hour-long lunch together in the month they'd been dating, I'd never know. But it sure as hell kept me up at night, reeling through worst-case scenarios. The longer she put this off, the less I felt like "the best baby daddy ever," but more accurately, "the most understanding and flexible baby daddy ever."

And then there was this fucking bet with Lex. It was finally Friday, and Jesus, I'd have given my left nut to sit on my couch with a beer before calling it an early night.

But no. I had a cherry-red Chevelle to win first.

After the Chase/Cal fiasco from the week before, I'd spent a lot of time trying to pick Lex's next date. I didn't know him well, but I had faith Hank Davis was going to win me that pink slip.

He was a solid six-foot, so shorter than Cal, but at least a head taller than Lex. He also had short, blond hair that told me he liked to take care of himself and a good build that made me feel like in a pinch he could take care of her. Lastly, he was successful with a laid-back personality, so I knew he had drive and, most of all, *patience*.

According to Libby, all the girls went wild for him at the accounting firm he worked at. Okay, fine. Yes. Eighty-four-year-old Libby had found this date. He was her friend's grandson. But I'd seen pictures and asked around about him. I didn't know his credit score, but it was entirely (read: definitely) possible I'd had a buddy pull a background check on him. Short of his middle name being Elenor, he didn't appear to have any deep, dark secrets.

So, while Lex was off at The Lobster Claw with Hank for some of the city's most prized seafood, I was walking into The Porterhouse, home of Atlanta's best steak, to meet my date, Sandra.

Things I knew about Sandra:
Her name was Sandra. The end.

As I walked to the bar, I prayed like hell Lex had given her a tad more information about me, because there had to have been at least a dozen women at the bar. I stood there like an idiot waiting for someone to notice me, all the while scanning the women for my date. A brunette at the end of the bar caught my attention. She was beautiful. Long, brown hair, tan skin, and wearing a pair of jeans and a fitted black top. Simple, but nice.

"Um, hi. Any chance your name is Sandra?" I asked.

Her head snapped in my direction, a pair of startled big, brown eyes staring back at me. "Nope. As far as I know, I'm still Charlotte."

"Oh, I'm sorry. I'm supposed to be meeting my date here." I swayed my head from side to side. "And it's a blind date thing. So you know."

She lifted her hand, revealing a large diamond stacked on top of a wedding band. "Definitely not me."

A big guy in a Porterhouse polo shirt came strolling behind the bar. When he stopped in front of her, he didn't say anything. He just smiled and stood there. The husband no doubt. Not awkward at all.

Right. Okay. I gave them both a curt nod and turned around ready to continue my search when a woman a few stools down called, "Hudson?"

Oh, thank fuck.

And then I saw her. Blond hair. Bright smile. Gorgeous blue eyes.

Oh, double thank fuck.

I walked over and extended my hand. "Sandra?"

"That's me," she chirped, taking my hand. "You can call me Sandy though. All my friends do."

Okay. So, Lex did good this time.

I smiled, and she shifted her giant purse in her lap and motioned for me to sit down next to her.

"Actually," I said. "We're going to be late for our reservation. Are you okay if we grab a drink at the table?"

"Sure," she said, rising to her feet. Resting her hand on her very round stomach, she finished with, "Though *we* aren't drinking tonight."

I blinked. Once, twice, seven thousand times. But the fact that this woman had to have been at least six months pregnant did. Not. Change.

This had to have been a joke. This was what I'd assumed was going to happen if I allowed Lex to set me up. But there was a bet involved and the stakes were a three-bedroom, two-litter-filled-bathroom monstrosity. There was no way she'd risk losing that for a good laugh.

I forced an expression that I feared only loosely resembled a smile and turned to make my way to the hostess. Sandy and her fetus followed hot on my heels.

Swapping uncomfortable smiles—or at least mine were uncomfortable—we were quickly guided to our table. The place was nice, and I made a mental note to bring Lex here for her birthday if I hadn't killed her by then.

When the waitress dropped off two waters, I ordered a much-needed double Jameson neat and then slyly retrieved my phone from my back pocket, keeping it tucked under the table as Sandy listened to the night's special.

Me: What the fucking fuck did you do?

It wasn't a good sign for my Chevelle that her reply was immediate.

Lex: What do you mean, what did I do? What did YOU do? I've been here five minutes and so far Handsy Hank has traced a finger down my neck, twirled my hair, and I swear to God, Hudson, I think he kissed the top of my head when he slid my chair out for me.

A surge of adrenaline hit me, all frustration with Sandy's reproductive system momentarily forgotten.

Me: Kick him in the dick if he touches you again. I'm on my way.

The waitress was still talking about Wagyu when I looked up. I was going to wait for her to finish before breaking the news to my dates—*plural*. But my phone vibrated again first.

Lex: Relax. I just ordered two appetizers and the lobster. I'll make his wallet hurt far more than you could make his face. And I won't have to explain to my mother why her precious golden boy was arrested for assaulting an accountant. Win. Win.

Lex: P.S. Seriously? An accountant? It's like you don't know me at all.

She could take care of herself. Anyone who had ever met Lex knew that, but it didn't make my blood boil any less that this prick thought he could put his hands on her.

Me: Ask for a to-go box and I'll come pick you up.

Lex: Are you crazy? Lobster is terrible cold.

Me: I'll buy you another damn lobster. It will be cheaper than me paying his medical bills when I amputate his arms.

Lex: Chill, Tarzan. I'm not drinking, he's safely across the table, and I'll tuck my legs beneath me in case he gets any ideas about a round of footsy. Now, put your loincloth away and tell me what's wrong with Sandra.

I blew out a ragged breath. Damn it, I really should have set her up with Cal again.

"So," Sandy said, pulling up my attention. "Alexis told me you have kids."

Typing, I replied absently. "A son. Jack. He's seven."

Me: Well, for starters, she's pregnant.

Lex: Holy shit, you work fast.

Sandy kept talking. "That's great. You may have noticed that I have a little one on the way. A girl, actually. But don't worry.

No daddy drama from me. Sperm donor three-oh-five and I get along really well." She laughed at her joke.

I smiled. *Where was that drink?*

Lex: Wait? Are you serious?

I kept my eyes on Sandy, hoping I wasn't coming off as a total asshole for texting at the table, all the while texting at the table.

Me: Completely.

Lex: How pregnant are we talking?

Me: Does it matter? But let's just say pregnant enough that our second date would have to be at Lamaze class.

I looked up and she was staring at me expectantly. Shit. I was being a dick. I should say something.
Though my mind was still distracted with all things Lex and Handsy Hank. "So, when are you due?"
Add that to the list of questions I never expected to ask on a first date.
Her eyes sparkled with excitement. "August twelfth. My little Petunia is going to be a Leo."
Okay, so she was pregnant with a sperm donor. So what? Honestly, that was a brave choice and I respected the shit out of her for making it. But I drew a hard line at dating a woman who would name her daughter *Petunia*.
The waitress set my drink in front of me, and I decided right then and there that I'd be calling one of the guys to pick up my work truck because I'd be catching an Uber home. Whiskey

was meant to be sipped. And I sipped this one all in one swallow, motioning for the waitress to bring me another.

My phone vibrated again, and knowing it was sure to be Lex, I excused myself from the table before reading it.

Lex: Shit. I'm sorry. I haven't seen Sandra in a while. I had no idea.

I stood in the hallway outside the men's restroom as I typed out my reply.

Me: Well, apparently, all her friends call her Sandy. So I'm not sure you really know Sandra at all.

Lex: We've met! Like…twice. Let's be real here. You've always wanted more kids, right?

Me: Yes. But preferably with a woman my cock has met at least once.

Lex: Minor formality. The meeting part, I mean. We've already covered that there is nothing minor about your cock.

I glared at my screen, and like most of our interactions, I ended up shaking my head.

Me: Right. Anyway. Has Hank touched you again?

Lex: No. Though I'm fairly sure he's given up on me. He's flirting with the waitress now. I'm not particularly devastated about it.

Me: Good. That changes though and I expect a call.

Lex: 10-4, good buddy. Since tonight seems to be a bust for both of us, you want to meet at Huey's for a drink later?

Me: Yeah. I'm going to be a few drinks ahead of you though. Text me when you leave.

Lex: OK. Be sure to find out where "Sandy" is registered for me. I should at least send the baby a gift.

Me: Ass.

After several seconds with no reply, I headed back to the table. Sandy was still sitting there, perusing the menu, and she shot me a smile when I sat down.

"Sorry about that. Alexis is on a date too, and apparently, it's not going so well."

"So, pretty much just like this one?"

I sighed. "Shit. I'm sorry. I…didn't know you were pregnant. I'll be honest here. I haven't been in a relationship in years. I'm really going to need someone who can take it slow with me, and…well, August isn't that far away."

She grinned and removed the napkin from her lap, tossing it onto the table. "It's okay. I know this is kind of strange. It's been a while for me too. Hence my torrid affair with donor three-oh-five."

I chuckled, and she slowly stood up, her belly bumping the table.

"It was nice to meet you, Hudson."

Truthfully, I felt guilty, but I was starving, and I had at least an hour and a half before Lex would be at Huey's. It was Friday night, she was pregnant and alone, and despite how it looked, I wasn't a total prick.

"Sandy, wait. Don't go. Just because this isn't going to work out doesn't mean we can't share a meal. Let me buy you and Petunia dinner. Fair warning, I'm missing my son something crazy like, so I'll probably ramble your ear off with stories from when he was a baby. But I hear the food here is amazing, so it shouldn't be too torturous."

She twisted her lips. "Really?"

"Really."

Turned out, Sandy wasn't the worst dinner company I'd ever had. Baby aside, we never would have worked out though. She spent over an hour telling me all about her homemade herbal tinctures she'd been preparing for little Petunia's arrival. She didn't believe in TV. Electronics. Or really anything that required a power cord. She frowned a lot when I told her I was in construction, but to her credit, she only made one snide comment about trees and the environment.

We said goodbye with a handshake and then she and Petunia were on their way in her smart car which was the size of a shoebox.

Donor 305 had lucked out though. She'd be a good mom to his offspring.

Three doubles later, I was already tipsy when I arrived at Huey's, but without dick all to do the next day except sit in the office, I figured a few more couldn't hurt. Above and beyond a few beers, I wasn't much of a drinker. So by the time Lex got there about twenty minutes later, I was straddling the line of too much and oh-holy-shit too much.

"What's that?" I asked as she plopped down a plastic bag on the table. I reached for it and my hand hit my empty glass, nearly knocking it off the tabletop.

She plucked it out of the air before it crashed to the floor.

"Nice catch," I laughed.

She stood there for a second, her deep-red brow arched. "Are you drunk?"

"Short answer: yes. Long answer: Yesssssss."

She barked a loud laugh and lifted my glass to her nose for a sniff. "Whiskey? God, how bad was Sandy?"

"Not as terrible as you'd think. What about Hank? He get any better?"

She settled into the booth across from me and began unpacking two takeout boxes from the plastic bag. "No. He was exactly as terrible as you'd think. He stared at the waitress until we left and then tried to grab my ass on the way out."

I slapped my hand on the table, almost making my drink fall all over again. "What?!"

She chuckled. "I ordered extra *extra* dessert before we left. You feel like a brownie or cheesecake?"

"Um...whiskey."

"Too bad." She slid the cheesecake my way and then gave our bartender a nod while unwrapping two sets of plastic silverware.

Carmen suddenly appeared beside us. "Hey, did you bring me any?"

"You know it," Lex replied, pulling out another box from her magical bag.

"Sweet," Carmen replied. "Another whiskey, Hud?"

"Yes," I hissed.

"No," Lex stated definitively.

"What the hell!" I was a grown-ass man and I still had the agency to order whatever the hell I wanted.

Lex looked up at Carmen and gave her a pretty grin. "Mr. Jameson Gold Reserve has left the building. Mr. Whatever Light Draught Beer You Have On Tap would like a pitcher and I'll have a Coke."

I wanted to be angry, but the fact that she knew what

whiskey I was drinking had me leveling her over the table as Carmen left for our drinks. "You think you know so much about me, don't you?"

She relaxed into her seat and crossed her arms over her chest, making her cleavage look… Never mind.

With one brow quirked, she answered, "I know everything about you, down to the fact that you're one hundred percent, without a doubt wearing dark-gray boxer briefs."

"Oh, yeah. How do you know that?"

"Because your fly is down, Buster. It's a good thing you're sitting or the whole bar would know too."

I checked my lap and fuck all if she wasn't right. I hadn't even fastened my buckle. It was gonna be one of those nights, but at least Lex was there now. So the night wasn't a total bust.

CHAPTER
Nine

Lex

It had been a long, long time since I'd seen Hudson tie one on like he was. The typically calm, cool, annoyingly collected big brother of our group was now my tour guide down memory lane.

"Look how small he was, Lex." For the thirtieth time, he shoved his cell phone with a photo of baby Jack in my face. "How is he already seven?"

Thank God I'd already successfully steered him away from the hard liquor and back to beer. Otherwise, I'd probably have been watching videos of the all-natural birth too.

"I know. He'll be older than me before we know it." My joke fell on deaf ears. He was in his feelings.

The only reasons I was letting this one-man bender go on was that it wasn't too late yet, I had nothing better to do, and drunk Hudson was uncharacteristically charming—not to mention elusive. Plus, if anyone deserved to cut loose every now and then, it was him.

He grinned proudly, thinking about his boy. "He's already smarter than both of us." He closed the screen and put his cell down. "Do you think I'm a good dad?"

Without hesitation, I answered, "The best."

"Right? I'm doing the damn thing. Lord only knows how, but we're not messing him up too bad."

"Haven't had to bail him out of the clink once," I teased.

Jack couldn't have asked for better parents. Yeah, his dad and mom worked a lot, but they managed their time with him well. Especially considering how Hudson had only had my parents for positive role models and Lauren's had been so overprotective when she was younger. It was a wonder that either of them knew how to raise a well-adjusted, independent, brilliant kid like they had.

"I miss him," he confessed.

"You make it sound like he's in outer space. He's just across town."

He shook his head. "No, he's been in Hilton Head with all the grandparents. Lauren's folks took him with them to hang out with Judy and David earlier this week."

Lucky bastard. When Mom and Dad asked me to go up, I'd balked, but now that they were there, I was wishing I'd bit the bullet and driven out for a day. I could use some salty air and sunshine. Especially since Maggie's doctor had told her that she was no way near where she needed to be for delivery and they were pretty confident Baby Warren was going to keep them waiting.

"Hey, I've got an idea."

His glassy, blue eyes met mine. "What? Now you want Bleep and Blooper to have their own private residence?"

It wasn't a terrible suggestion. They'd both had shots that week and were still giving me the stink-eye every time I tried to pet one of their bitchy asses. "Not exactly, but we might circle back to that sometime." I adjusted in my seat and prepared to give him a very convincing argument for a taste of spontaneity, something he knew little about. "What if..."

He rolled his eyes, already expecting the worst.

"What if we get you home to dry out for the night, you play hooky from work for once on a Saturday, and we drive out early tomorrow and stay at the beach house with Mom and Dad too?"

He squinted but didn't fight me. Yet.

Sweetly, I continued, "You can get some quality Jack time, and I can get some sun and ocean."

Hudson drew in a deep breath.

But before he could contest my amazing plan, I added, "It'll be a quick trip. There tomorrow and back on Sunday evening. You won't miss a thing."

He moaned and groaned.

So, before I lost him, I dialed up the guilt. "Jack will be so happy, and my parents haven't seen you in weeks."

Looking like he was physically in pain, he tipped back the last of his beer, swallowed, and surrendered. "Fine. Drive me home."

He didn't have to tell me twice. Winning an argument with Hudson was about as likely as hitting the jackpot in the Georgia State Lottery. So as not to give him a chance to change his mind, I pulled some bills out of my wallet, tossed them onto the table, and tugged my bag's strap over my head.

As he rose, he kicked a chair at the empty table beside ours and he wobbled on unsteady feet.

"Whoa there, big fella."

He paused with his hands out to his sides to get his bearings. "I meant to do that."

With my ninja-like reflexes, I dipped under his arm and wrapped one of mine around his muscular waist. Then I gave Carmen a wink as we stumbled to the door. She covered her mouth to hide a laugh I could hear across the room. Apparently, I wasn't the only one getting a kick out of Hudson's drunken state.

It was a rare sight for sure, but he wasn't falling down or tripping over his own feet too badly, so we made it to the passenger side of my SUV with little trouble. The funniest part about the whole thing was how comfortable I was with Hudson's giant arm draped over my shoulder when, only a few hours earlier, Handsy Hank almost got a swift kick in the nuts for doing the same damn thing.

Then again, it was Hudson. I'd known him forever and that was probably why. He was like my other brother. Yet that didn't explain why he smelled so good beside me or why I kept tilting my head closer to get a bigger sniff of whatever he was wearing. The way it had my head spinning, I bet it'd cost a fortune.

"Hey, drunko," I said as I got him settled in my vehicle. "What cologne is that?"

He pulled the neck of his black T-shirt out and stuck his face into it, chuckling and sniffing himself. "It's not cologne, Kid. It's just SpeedStick." He laughed even harder, letting the stretched-out fabric fall against his chest. "You like it? It's musk."

I kicked his boot, which was still anchored to the asphalt parking lot. "What I'd really like is for you to put all your tree-trunk-ass appendages inside the car so I can shut the door."

He snickered again but complied, repeating, "Tree trunk ass."

After I passed him his safety belt to fasten, I closed him in.

Fucker thought he was really funny too, because as I rounded the hood, he honked my horn and yelled, "Get your tree trunk ass in the car!"

Okay. Drunk Hudson was obnoxious too. That was usually my job, but I'd let him have it for the night.

Inside, I turned the ignition and corrected, "I don't have a tree trunk ass. I happen to have a great ass. Not that you would notice, but it's one of my finer attributes." I pulled onto the road and headed toward his place.

"Oh, I know all about your nice ass."

I swallowed and reminded myself he was drunk. It was the whiskey talking, and historically speaking, Jameson always had a thing for my butt.

Hudson fumbled with the seat's adjustments, trying to make himself more comfortable in my small SUV, but he ended up reclining it all the way back. As if he'd intentionally done it, while he was on his back, he dug into his pocket, pulled out a pack of gum, and held a stick out to me. "You wanna piece of this?"

No. *No.* I didn't want anything from him. But as hard up for decent companionship as I was lately, everything was starting to sound like innuendo.

"No, thanks. And you don't know a thing about my ass. So check yourself."

He righted his seat beside me and argued, "Yes, I do. I know about all the asses. That's what I do. I'm an ass man."

"You're an ass period."

He fiddled with the radio but gave up when he couldn't turn it on. "And as a world-class connoisseur of backsides, I can tell you that you have a good one. Perfect to be honest. Some guy is gonna be lucky to have your cheeks—" He gestured as if he were sinking his fingers into a nice, big butt in front of himself. "Right in the palms of his hands."

I was watching the road, but seeing his massive paws squeeze an imaginary butt in the front seat of my vehicle was almost like I could feel him—*or someone*—touch me like that.

Probably because I hadn't been laid—or laid well—in a long damn time, but my heart raced as I turned down his road. "Shut up. We're almost there."

"I'm serious, Lex. When you finally let someone in one day, that guy is going to be one lucky sonofabitch. You're the total package. Fuck-hot body. Gorgeous face. Big, green eyes. A rack like blam. You're smart and independent."

As he listed things off, I was reminded of how this very same conversation had gone the last time when we were fighting at Huey's.

This time, I didn't wait for him to get to the punchline though. "Yeah, all except for this bad attitude and mouth, right?"

He turned to face me and a wicked smile bent both corners of his mouth, but he didn't answer. As I passed under a street light, his drunken eyes locked on mine, but I had to pay attention to the road and looked away. When he didn't say anything and nearly burned a whole in the side of my face with his laser-like stare, finally I asked, "What?"

"Yeah, your attitude is something, but your mouth isn't all that bad." Missing on the first swipe, he reached out again and touched my bottom lip with his index finger.

My breath caught and a cool sweat broke across my skin. What the fuck was happening?

"Your mouth might be nicer than your ass now that I'm looking at it."

I swatted his hand away and pulled into his drive. The ride was almost over, and I could go home and sleep away all these weird fe—well, whatever the fuck was happening.

"Yeah, you're definitely drunk."

And he was, but that didn't explain why my chest was seriously pounding.

Maybe I was sick.

Maybe I was chronically horny or something.

Maybe I was too sober to be around a handsome drunk guy.

Because surely, in the back of my mind, I wasn't thinking why I couldn't find someone more like him.

He was Hudson.

My brother's best friend.

My reluctant partner in crime—or at least the man there to bail me out when I was partnering in crime alone. He was...a really fucking good guy. *Not to mention stupid hot and all that masculine energy I craved.*

Shit, was I having a nervous breakdown? At the very least, it had to be a momentary lapse of judgment.

I should have skipped the beach and hauled myself to a doctor the next morning instead.

Afraid to look at him again for fear of the horrible, disgusting, but so, so very sexy thoughts my brain was going to fire off next, I kept my eyes on his two-story brick house and said, "Your chariot has arrived. Get out."

Pulling his hand back to his lap, he spoke in a low, gruff voice that did not at all travel down my spine and send chills over my skin. "I'm sorry. I just don't think I ever noticed so much of you before."

"Wow, you sure know how to give a compliment."

"You know what I mean."

And I did. Because as he sat there, his messy hair falling over his forehead while the veins on his forearms taunted me out of the corner of my eye, I suddenly realized there was a lot I hadn't noticed about Hudson before too.

"Well, stop," I snapped roughly because I was, without question, freaking the fuck out. "You don't mean it. You're just drunk and lonely."

What did that make me? Sober and pathetic for buying into it?

I knew better.

"It's all true. Some man is going to come along, and so help me fucking God, if he doesn't treat you right, I'm going to kill him." He shifted in his seat and pressed his back against the window, giving me his full attention. "Because, Lex, after all you've been through—"

And just like that, I was snapped back to reality. I held my hand up between us to make him stop right there. It wasn't the time or the place to go down that dark alley on memory lane.

And it never would be.

"Okay," he relented. "I'm just saying they'd be lucky is all. Even if you do have an attitude and a sharp tongue, you're easy to love too. I hope whoever he is can see the real you."

His hand stretched out and landed on my thigh, causing me to freeze, but it had been so long since a real man had touched me in a way that made me feel like I was melting inside. It was far different from the non-feelings I'd had when I'd been with Craig. It should have been gross, like being on a date with Chase, my brother's long-lost twin. Hell, it should have even made me want to slap him away like earlier with Hank.

But at the moment, it didn't.

His thumb rubbed across my jeans, and for a second, I let my eyes fall shut. In that instant, I didn't retreat, didn't run away, didn't want to hide or make it end. I just wanted to fucking be and have a brief glimpse, just a taste, of intimacy.

But the cold, hard truth was: Hudson had had way too much to drink. We weren't who the other wanted; we were simply the only ones left. And I didn't want a consolation prize any more than I wanted to be one. So after…probably too long, I cleared my throat and did what I had to do for both of us.

"It's time you go in, Hud."

Pulling away, he wiped his hand over his face and shook off the *almost* connection that never should have been.

"Yeah, you're right." He twisted in the seat and opened his door. "Um. Pick me up at six. That'll get us there before noon." He climbed out and looked as if he'd found his footing better than he had at the bar.

"Are you okay to make it inside by yourself?" I asked before he shut the door, all the while hoping he'd say yes. I wasn't prepared to spend any more time with him that night.

"I'll be fine. Drive safe." He paused and flashed me a

heart-stopping grin. Or at least, in that moment, it stopped mine.

"Love you, Kid."

Hudson had been calling me Kid dating back to when I had actually been a kid. I'd never so much as given it a second thought. Though, in my current state of *what-the-fuck*, I'd never in all my years hated that damn nickname more.

"Love you too, Hud." I watched as he slowly lumbered around the house to let himself in through the back door. And when I saw lights come on inside, I pulled away and drove home.

The night had started out shitty, but after ditching Hank, the stage-five clinger, it had turned out not that bad. Still, as I closed my eyes, I pretended I couldn't feel Hudson's touch. I pretended he hadn't said so many things I'd needed to hear. I pretended my body hadn't reacted to his and that my heart wasn't still racing.

But it was all for nothing, because no amount of pretending would change the fact that I'd liked it. And fuck if that wasn't *so* inconvenient.

CHAPTER
Ten

Hudson

Me: Wake up, Sleepyhead. You were supposed to be at my house ten minutes ago.

Lex: I'm out front. You were supposed to be outside ten minutes ago. Unlike some people who shall remain nameless, I wasn't drunk last night.

Me: Funny. I'm standing outside and you aren't here.

Lex: Okay fine. I snoozed a few extra times. I'm at the stoplight about to turn into your neighborhood. Any chance you can bring me some coffee?

With two travel mugs sitting on the step beside me, I was way ahead of her. I'd woken up early, and after consuming approximately two rivers' worth of water and a fist full of Advil, I'd gone for a run to clear my head and hopefully some of the lingering whiskey in my veins.

But there was nothing and I mean *nothing* that could clear my head of the memories of telling Lex all about her perfect ass and sexy mouth.

My personal favorite, a bile-inducing memory of that drive

WHEN THE *Time* *is* *Right*

home through the Twilight Zone, was when I air-palmed her invisible ass. Just the fucking gesture had been bad enough, but secretly her boobs had been in my face when I'd imagined her sitting on top of me. That was one fun fact I was taking to the grave though. I owed her a serious apology and possibly free gold leafing for her cat condo after that bullshit.

It was all true. Lex was gorgeous. She wasn't so much of a sister to me that I hadn't noticed that over the years. She was just...Lex.

It had been a while since my late-night call from Rebecca Florence. Salon gossip aside, maybe it was time I utilized her phone number and gave her a booty call for a change. For fuck's sake, something had to change in my sex-crazed brain if I was daydreaming about Lex straddling my cock, out loud, while talking to fucking Lex.

Oh, did I forget to mention my cock was involved in that little *Black Mirror* version of my drunken fantasy too?

Fuck. My. Life.

When I got home from my run, I quickly packed a bag and rehearsed six different versions of an apology all to the gist of, "Sorry for mentally perving on you last night. Please accept this travel mug of coffee as a token of my sincerest apology."

When she'd been late, something that was far from unusual for her, I'd worried she wasn't going to show at all. With my luck, she was still dry-heaving over the toilet—and rightly so—after the garbage I'd spewed at her. Thankfully, the worst of it had happened in the confines of my own mind, and as soon as she got there, I was going to apologize and then seal that shit in a mental compartment labeled Naked Pictures of Grandma to be sure it never got opened again.

A loud rumble echoed off the houses on my sleepy cul-de-sac and my head jerked up just in time to see the most incredible cherry-red muscle car turn onto my street. A huge smile split my face when she stopped in front of my house and revved the engine.

I was probably going to get no fewer than six letters from my homeowners association about the noise at six a.m. But this was nothing new when it came to her. For my thirtieth birthday, she'd paid to have three hundred (actual number) plastic pink flamingos decorate my lawn. Jack thought it was hilarious. My neighbors were slightly less enthusiastic.

Yes, it was ridiculous. This was what I had learned was something of a personal brand for Lex. And on that particular morning, sitting there in huge sunglasses, her arm hanging out of the open window, and a floral scarf tied around her head like Thelma—or maybe it was Louise—she looked every bit of the part.

Pushing her shades down to the end of her nose, she leaned over and shot me an evil grin through the window. "Need a ride?"

I gave her a smile and gathered my bag and our coffees. "I know Hank wasn't a match, but did you decide to go ahead and bring me my winnings early?"

"Oh, please. You aren't winning anything except the honor of carpeting Beep's new bedroom." She gave the engine another rev, more than likely doubling my HOA fine, before cutting it and swinging her door open. She marched directly over to me and plucked a to-go mug from my hands. "I decided to take pity on you and give you a little joyride as a consolation prize." She tipped the coffee back and chugged it like water, punctuating the scene with a loud, satisfying, "Ahhhhh."

"Starbucks closed?" I asked, popping the seat up and then shoving my overnight bag into the back through the open driver's side door.

"I hit snooze too many times to stop. How the hell are you up so bright and early? After last night, I figured you'd look like the crypt keeper when I got here."

"I don't get hungover. It's a gift." I turned to face her. "Listen, um, about that shit I said last night."

Her eyes flashed wide, but she immediately waved me off. "Oh, please. Don't worry about that. You were drunk."

"I still shouldn't have said any of that—"

"Hudson, it's not a big deal. Just forget about it."

I studied her closely for several seconds. "You sure? Cause if you want to talk about it—"

"Relax, Dr. Phil. I said it's fine. Now, come on. Let's get this show on the road."

I grinned, relief blazing through my veins. I'd at least expected her to give me shit before letting me off the hook, but this worked too. "Okay, then. I packed a few protein bars and some of those fruit snacks you steal from Jack all the time, but if you need to hit the bathroom, do it now. I'm not stopping for you to pee every fifteen minutes."

"That was one time and we both know it was Cal's fault. I am the Big Gulp champion. I won it fair and square when I was twelve. He had no business waiting over a decade to ask for a rematch." She clicked the seat back into place and started to slide behind the wheel with her coffee in hand.

This was going to be a fight. Quite possibly to the death or until one of us—cough, her—cried uncle, whichever came first. No one other than her grandfather or Lex had ever driven that Chevelle. And it wasn't for a lack of trying, either. Cal and I had been frothing at the mouth over that car long before Lex had a driver's license. Cal loved his grandfather, but that wasn't why he had cried when he saw a copy of the will. So, yeah. I knew this was going to be a battle, but it wasn't often that car even saw the light of day. There was no chance in hell I was missing my opportunity to get behind the wheel.

"I'm driving," I announced, hooking an arm around her

middle. Her small body became flush with mine, and in one fluid movement, I lifted her off her feet and spun her away from the door.

About halfway around, I realized something was wrong. She didn't kick or fight.

She didn't even scream or cuss at me.

From head to toe, her body flashed hard, turning her into a statue. And not even the statue of a pissed-off fireball. When I placed her on her feet, I couldn't see her eyes through her sunglasses, but her cheeks were bright red as though we were back at the Jonas Brothers concert Judy and David had made me and Cal take her to when she was sixteen.

Keeping a hand on her hip, I slanted my head to try to get a better read on her face. "What's wrong with you?"

She stared at me for several beats, with God only knew what was happening behind those shades, before finally finding two breathy syllables. "Nothing."

I eyed her skeptically. "You sure? Because you look like you're about to take your bra off and throw it on stage again."

Her lips thinned, and she took a giant step out of my reach. "We should go."

"Okay, but you're riding shotgun."

"No way," she snapped, suddenly coming unstuck. Lurching forward, she attempted to duck around me, but I extended an arm for another hook-and-move maneuver.

This was the exact moment I became a leper. I don't know when or how it'd happened, but she jumped away so fast there was no other explanation.

Her shoulders rose and fell with labored breathing as she stared at me from what had to have been six feet away. Jesus, I should have known dragging her out of bed before ten was a bad idea.

WHEN THE *Time* is *Right*

"All right. What the hell is going on with you? Are you having some kind of seizure from a lack of caffeine? Should I run in and grab you the coffee grounds so we can rub them directly onto your skin?"

She licked her lips and then blew out a ragged breath. "I have self-diagnosed myself with a stroke, but a seizure is not out of the question. I'll need to do more research before I can confirm."

"Riiiiight," I drawled with a slow nod. "Any chance you can do that in the car on the way to the beach? I'd really like to get there before lunch."

And then, just as quickly as I had become a leper, a miracle happened.

Alexis Lawson didn't argue. She didn't rage. No one said uncle. She didn't even make eye contact as she shuffled around the hood of the car and slid into the passenger seat.

For fear of sounding ungrateful for what could only be described as the Lord's handiwork, I kept my mouth closed as she wedged her coffee between her thighs and tugged her seat belt on.

The urge to text Cal and gloat that I was about to spend the next four hours behind the wheel of the Chevelle was strong. The damn near orgasmic vibrations when I started the engine were stronger.

Fuck, that car was a beast. I really needed to figure out who the hell I could set her up with next week to secure its place in my garage.

For the majority of the ride, Lex was on her phone. Her fingers frantically tapping the screen. She'd whisper the occasional, "You've got to be kidding me," followed by a loud groan. I think, once, there was an, "Oh, God, this isn't happening."

When I questioned her about what the hell she was doing, her only answer was a shrieked, "Shut up and drive!"

I went so far as to ply her with Slim Jims and a king-sized Snickers at our one and only bathroom stop, but nothing helped. She'd eventually tell me what was wrong, and if she didn't, I had no qualms about wading into the quicksand in her head to pull her out. With nothing but the open road, the hum of the engine, and the wind in my hair, I decided to first go for the tried-and-true method of letting her nap it off.

And sure enough, after another fifty miles or so, she took her scarf and sunglasses off and fell asleep with her head propped against the window.

"Dad!" Jack yelled, running down the front steps as I put the old Chevelle into park.

Damn, I had missed that kid. I hated to be "that dad," but I was going to have to have a talk with Lauren's parents before their next beach trip. A week was too damn long.

Lex's eyes flashed open and she bolted upright, already sporting a giant smile and furthering my belief that there wasn't much a nap couldn't fix. Judy and David were standing on the front porch, waving as though we'd just come back from war, and I climbed out in time to scoop Jack off his feet before he crashed into the side of the car.

"Hey, buddy!" I laughed, planting him on my hip. I would get about thirty seconds of holding him like a baby before he started to complain.

"Guess what! Guess what!" he said, already squirming to get down.

I pretended not to notice. "What?"

"Grampa bought a Jet Ski and I got to drive it."

"Rented!" David corrected from the porch, curling his wife into his side. "I only rented it."

Jack gave him a blink, which I knew all too well was supposed to be a wink, and then let out a soft giggle. "He totally bought it, but then Mimi said it was a death trap, so now we're pretending that he only rented it so she doesn't bury him in the sand and never come back for him."

Lex came walking around the hood, her bag already thrown over her shoulder. "He let you drive the Jet Ski? You're, like, four. He still won't even let me drive his car to the grocery store and back."

"I'm seven and three eighths, thank you very much. I guess that means he likes me more than you."

She faked a wounded gasp and dropped her bag. "Your words slay me, Jackie Boy." She dove in to tickle him, and Jack finally wriggled out of my grip.

I put him down and he took off at a dead sprint toward the beach, laughing at the top of his lungs, with Lex hot on his heels.

I shook my head, but that was basically business as usual when those two got together. I'd be lying if I didn't admit that I fucking loved it. Crazy as she was, she was good for Jack. And most of all, Jack was good for her.

I grabbed her bag off the ground and hooked it over my shoulder before making my way up the drive.

David extended his hand in my direction for a quick shake before taking his daughter's bag. "So, riddle me this, son. What kind of blackmail do you have on Alexis that landed you behind the wheel of the old Chevelle?"

I shot him a wink. "Now I can't tell you or she won't let me drive home. Though, if you happen to mention to Cal that you saw me driving it the next time you two talk, that would be much appreciated."

He chuckled.

Judy dragged me into a hug. "Well, I for one am happy you two came. You sure you can't stay for more than one night?"

"I wish, but we both have to work on Monday. I promise we'll be back for Fourth of July. Especially now that I know David has a Jet Ski." His eyes flashed wide, and I smiled as I finished with, "That we can *rent*."

"Oh, that reminds me," Judy chirped. "Hudson, you head down to the water and hang out with Jack and Alexis for a bit. David and I will be down shortly after he helps me with the chicken salad lettuce wraps and explains why it cost ten thousand dollars to *rent* a Jet Ski for the week."

I pulled the screen door open and waited for them to file inside. David paused long enough to give me a quick elbow to the side before following his wife.

After dropping my bag in the room Jack and I often shared, I changed into a set of trunks and made my way down to the beach. David had already set up Jack's bucket of balls, boogie board, and an elaborate array of pails and shovels beside the sun canopy, so I grabbed the sunscreen and headed down to the water.

"One, two, three, jump!" Lex yelled, tugging on Jack's arm and all but dragging him over the top of a breaking wave.

They both had their backs to me, so when I got close, I called, "How's the water?"

Jack giggled before replying, "Cold as tits."

"Tips!" Lex yelled. "I said cold as *tips*, remember?"

Jack tilted his head up to look at her. "But cold as tips doesn't make any sense."

Lex at least had the good taste to look sheepish when she turned around. "It slipped, okay? Sorr—" The words died on her tongue when her gaze landed on me. Or, more accurately, when her gaze landed on my...abs?

"Shit," she breathed, quickly turning back to the water.

"What?" I asked, looking down at my stomach, fully

expecting to find a rogue hair or at the very least some belly button lint. There was nothing though and this meant she was back to acting weird. Which unfortunately meant a nap couldn't cure everything.

"Jack, go play football or something with your dad. I'm going for a swim. I'll be back in a few," she announced.

"Hey, wait, I need you to sunscreen my back!"

"Oh God!" she shouted before diving into the water and swimming away as though the world had suddenly caught fire.

Jack moseyed over to stand beside me and shielded his eyes as we watched her go. "Jeez, what's her problem?"

I shook my head, a sense of unease settling in my stomach. "I honestly don't know."

But she couldn't stay in that water forever.

Something was definitely up with her, but if history had taught me anything, it was that she wasn't going to talk until she was ready. Whatever was on her mind, it stung that she couldn't talk to me about it, because for the rest of the night, she avoided me. Even when I asked her if she wanted to have a nightcap on the porch, she turned me down and went to bed.

I stood in the dark dining room, two beers in my hand by the sliding deck door. "Are you sure?"

She glanced down the hall toward the room she always stayed in and then back at me as if she were warring with herself over one lousy beer. "Not tonight, Hud. I'm tired. Good night."

Hell, without her joining me, I didn't even want the drink. I'd only used them as an excuse for her to maybe tell me what was up. Striking out, I put them back in the fridge and went to bed too.

CHAPTER
Eleven

Lex

At home, I wasn't a stranger to sleeping in on my days off, but at the beach, the sunrise called to me. *The real me.*

It was still dark out when I threw on a pair of shorts and a hoodie, grabbed a blanket off the back of the couch, and slipped my feet into my flip-flops by the back door. The warm air blew across my skin in silent invitation, and the lights along the wooden path illuminated my way down to the water. The sounds of the morning birds and the lapping waves harmonized my every step.

This tiny spot on Earth had always calmed my mind, clearing the noise and stripping my emotions down to a level that allowed me to actually process them.

By nature, I'd always been wild. I liked getting a reaction or making people laugh, and in my younger years, it was probably how I'd gotten attention from the older kids. Lauren had always been lovely and sweet and perfect, but trying to be that hadn't worked for me. Therefore, I used humor and sarcasm to differentiate myself. Also, having a thick skin had saved me more than once from the constant onslaught of being Calvin's younger redheaded sister. It got me through the teasing and ribbing when Cal and Hudson left me to go off to college.

Brenden had loved my smartass ways, and together, we'd

spent countless nights on the beach, laughing and talking long after the sun had gone down. So that patch of cool sand, ready to warm in the day's sun, was a place that meant more to me than just a spot beside the water. It had been my safe haven when I was younger. A place where I could be quiet and reflect as I matured. And maybe the last place I was truly happy, wrapped in a blanket with a guy I'd met in college who had always accepted me for who I was because, in some ways, he was even wilder.

It was also the place I had come to when I was grieving and then again when I was ready to stop.

I had a very complicated relationship with that sandy spot of oceanfront real estate. But at least while I was there, I could stop pretending.

After I'd spread my blanket out and kicked the flimsy shoes off my feet, I planted my ass on the ground and waited. I never believed in the bullshit of meditation, but as I watched the sun paint the horizon heart-stopping shades of orange and purple, I wondered if that wasn't what I'd done there so many times all along.

I rolled my eyes at myself.

Could you be any more melodramatic, Lex?

Then again, if I had to be caught up in my emotions, that blanket at that hour was the best place for me. There, I could safely unpack the jumbled chaos in my brain. And right then as I dug my toes into the sand, at the forefront of my thoughts was Hudson.

Okay. More specifically, it was me trying to figure out why Hudson was suddenly at the forefront of my thoughts. I couldn't quite figure out if I was just lonely or if maybe I was having actual feelings for him. Which, let's be honest, was just ridiculous. He was my brother's best friend. Hell, he was one of my best *and only* friends. The father of a kid I looked at like a nephew. A man my parents called son. A guy who was a huge part of our family.

Was it terrible that, over the past few weeks—and dates—I'd not only *not* found anyone I was interested in, but I'd had to face the notion that I was slightly interested in Hudson? Because none of them measured up to him.

That was all I needed. Another man who was out of my reach. All right, that was super dramatic. Hudson wasn't dead, just… I didn't even know.

Not for me?

Out of my league?

Too important to lose?

If the feelings I was having ended up being real, there was little chance he'd reciprocate them. Then what?

There was only one thing for me to do. I'd have to wait it out, let it pass on its own. How long that would take, I had no clue.

What I did know was time couldn't pass soon enough. The untimely flashes of attraction, the probably imaginary tension I'd been feeling, the way my body reacted to his touch, and how my heart raced lately when he texted or called or said my name out loud were almost too much.

It was totally fucking annoying and completely fucking unexpected. I didn't *want* to feel like that.

I wanted everything to go back to normal. Deep down, with as much as things were changing and as fast, I knew our small group would never be normal again.

So, as I'd done many, many times before, I focused on the horizon and wished my troubles away.

I wasn't insane, and it didn't always work, but somehow, I usually felt better. There was only so long I could stand hiding from things, and even if I only revealed them to the ocean and the dawn, surely some of the weight would be off my shoulders.

And after an hour, when the sun was finally rising into the

sky, I'd convinced myself I was done with the untimely and weird attraction I had to Hudson. It simply wasn't a thing.

A few minutes later, I was gobsmacked with how fucking delusional that conclusion had been, because hearing only three words from him proved that nothing had gone away or changed.

"There you are," he crooned, stepping off the boardwalk from the house. "I was sure I'd find you down here." Wearing his trunks and a henley, barefoot, he kicked his way through the white sand to me.

"Busted," I said, holding my hands up, not feeling quite as spry as I usually came off. But shit, it was still early and I hadn't had any coffee. There were plenty of hours left in the day for me and my bullshit. As far as I was concerned, it was my time and he'd just happened to stumble upon it.

He stretched, causing the bottom of his shirt's tattered waffle fabric to inch higher up his chiseled stomach. Quickly, I turned my head and stared out to the ocean.

"Beautiful morning," he said and looked both ways down the empty beach. "Your mom is up, making breakfast. Every kind of pancake you can think of."

I smiled, remembering how Jack liked everything pancakes, just like me.

"You can tell her I'll be up there in a bit. I'm gonna sit here for a little while longer." I looked up at him and pulled my blowing hair to my other shoulder, out of the breeze.

Hudson scratched the back of his neck, glanced out into the water, and inhaled so much salty air that his chest swelled to twice its size. When his attention came back to me, he gently kicked my knee and said, "Scoot over."

"What? No. You don't have to stay. I'll be right there." I'd come to my spot on the beach to rid my fucking head of him. Sitting there on the sand *together* was the last thing I needed. "I sort of want to be alone."

When I didn't budge, he plopped down beside my blanket. "Tough shit, Kid."

Without much thought, I snapped back. "Don't call me that anymore, Hudson. I'm almost twenty-nine." I'd always loved when he called me Kid, but now, it felt so wrong and gross.

He rocked into my shoulder with his. "No more Kid, huh? I always knew, when the time was right, you'd make me stop. I had a good run." He chuckled. "Gonna be a hard habit to break."

I tipped my head toward his and looked him dead in his devastating blue eyes. "Well, I don't like it."

"Good. That's a start. What else? I know something has been on your mind. So keep talking."

That was my biggest nightmare—and also what all the searches told me was the right thing to do yesterday when I Googled *what do you do if you have feelings for a friend* and *how to handle wanting to fuck your brother's bff* and a dozen other ways to describe my problem. It didn't matter though. Everything had one answer. Even the Reddit threads all said the same thing.

Talk to him.

Ideally, now would be the perfect time. It was quiet. I wasn't already on his nerves for the day. We were alone. He was sitting beside me, demanding I spill my guts.

Yet I couldn't.

"I'm fine," I said and gazed back at the water. It was much easier than facing him. I also knew he wouldn't give up until he was satisfied. So I added, "I appreciate what you're trying to do, but it's nothing. I just wanted to enjoy the sunrise. That's all." I pulled my feet up and wrapped my arms around my legs.

"Hey. You don't have to ball up and hide from me, Lex. I know you better than that." He brushed my hair away from my face, and it gave me tingles and goose bumps. "Does this place make you miss him more?"

WHEN THE *Time is Right*

I didn't want to do it. I hated it. Every emotion I had in front of someone always came back to this. Even if Brenden wasn't the reason for how I was feeling, talking about him never failed to bring everything about losing him back.

My eyes began to sting, and I swiped a hot tear away with the cuff of my Spelman College hoodie. Then I swallowed, took a slow breath, and met his gaze. "Actually, I feel closer to him here."

Hudson offered me a sympathetic grin. "I remember the first summer Brenden came with all of us. I was kind of jealous."

My heart hammered. *Jealous? Of Brenden? My boyfriend?*

My back shot straight, an odd surge of hope hitting my veins. Had Hudson had the hots for me back in the day?

He huffed, recalling the memory. "It was before Lauren got pregnant the summer my mom died. I was like who is this new asshole moving in on *my* family."

Damn. That made more sense.

"He wasn't moving in on your family, Hud. You weren't replaceable."

"Back then, I didn't know that. All I knew was there was this new kid who Cal thought was the coolest, your parents thought he'd hung the moon, and he had his hands all over you when the three of them weren't looking. It was hard to deal with, okay?"

I remembered that week too.

It was the first time Brenden had vacationed with us, so Mom and Dad strongly urged us to sleep in separate rooms. Hudson had also chimed in how he thought it was a good idea and offered to share his room with Brenden. The memory of sneaking through the halls and waking Brenden without waking Hud was still vivid in my mind. I'd quietly opened the door and tossed M&Ms at my boyfriend until he woke up.

After all that, we still didn't do anything my parents wouldn't have approved of, but the thrill of doing anything in secret was enough. We laughed and talked and kissed all night long at the end of the boardwalk and snuck back inside before anyone woke up.

That was a good memory though and nothing to cry about.

"But you ended up liking him," I said.

His face softened, and his brow relaxed. "I did. Is that why you've been—" Choosing his words, he ran a hand over his cleanly shaven chin. "Well, you've just seemed different this weekend."

My breathing quickened like I was about to jump off the pier. I couldn't just come out and tell him.

What if he laughed at me?

"I'm just working through some stuff."

"Damn it, Lex. How can I help you if I don't know what the problem is?" *Typical Hudson.*

Knowing he wasn't going to give up, I stood and gathered my blanket. My peaceful, quiet morning was over. I was back to being the pain in the ass everyone expected. Otherwise, he was going to nag until I couldn't take it anymore.

"You don't have to help me. I didn't ask for help." I started to walk to the wooden planked path, but he caught hold of my arm.

"Wait."

I shrugged out of his grip. "Stop. Would you *please* quit touching me?"

I froze, sure my words had come out too strongly. But it had been almost torture being around him half naked for the past day. Him with his broad shoulders and perfect tan. Strutting around, taller than everyone else. The way his board shorts hung on his hips. The bulge that need not be mentioned. His chest and stomach hot enough to make a nun break vows.

I'd hit my limit.

"Is that what this is about? Me touching you? You told me

to forget about it. So I *did* cross a line?" He paced in the sand, scratching his hair. "Fuck. I'm sorry, Lex. I feel like an ass. You shouldn't have to deal with that shit from anyone, least of all me."

I felt guilty for hanging him out to dry. What he'd done wasn't that bad, and then there was the other thing.

My chin tucked to my chest, I stared at a tuffet of grass and whispered, "I liked it, Hudson."

His stomping around came to an immediate halt, and he dipped low to catch my eyes. Hudson's were the size of the wheels on the Chevelle.

"What did you just say?" he asked slowly.

I swallowed my pride in the name of him not thinking he'd taken advantage of me, and then I nearly swallowed my tongue as I forced more words out of my mouth. "I said, I liked it."

He leaned back and squinted, his jaw hanging open. "No fucking way," he breathed. His reaction was all I needed to know about where he stood.

So I did what any embarrassed woman would do after confessing she enjoyed when her brother's best friend touched her.

I lied.

"I mean, it's no big deal. But I'm pretty sure I warned you about waving that big dick energy around. I guess I'm just more hard up than usual. Hopefully the date you set me up on this week is a winner, because I am thirsty and it's making me go a little cuckoo." My index finger circled my ear and I made a wild face at him. "Anyway, it's not you. I'm just a live wire right now."

He was like a sand sculpture, but blinking at me.

It was time to get out of there, and I needed everything pancakes like never before. I stepped backward to the walkway—only tripping over my feet once—and then said, "So yeah. If you could just keep your hands to yourself, that would be great. 'Kay? Okay. Yeah."

Then, much like I'd swum away from him after the sunscreen incident, I ran to the house like a little bitch. I was learning avoidance was kinda my forte.

The rest of the day was awkward, but at least on the way home, Jack was in the car with us. Playing road trip games and singing at the top of our lungs, I was able to act like my tiny world hadn't been shaken. Still, Hudson sat in the driver's seat, quiet and stoic as usual, and didn't say much all the way home.

I wished I could say his indifference and reaction to my silly schoolgirl confession had made my feelings for him disappear by the time he pulled into his drive and I got back into the driver's seat, but that would have been another lie.

CHAPTER
Twelve

Hudson

Lex: K

I stared down at my phone, my forehead wrinkled so tight I thought there was a solid chance it would stay that way forever. There were only so many ways I could interpret that one single letter, but over the last week, it had become something of an obsession to try.

Sunday afternoon, when she'd dropped Jack and I off, it had been business as usual.

She'd smiled.

Given my forearm a squeeze.

Forced a kiss on my son.

And then called, "Love you," out of the window as we wandered up the steps to my front door.

I'd mumbled a sad, "You too, Kid," at the Chevelle as she'd backed out of the driveway.

It was all so incredibly *normal* that, to an outsider, her little act would be almost believable.

But, as her taillights disappeared, I knew the truth.

Something huge had happened during the trip to the beach. I could feel it in the air swirling around us. But, most of all, I could feel it inside the aching of my chest. One night staring down a whiskey bottle and I'd somehow managed to alienate the woman I'd viewed as a little sister. Only, if I were being honest, I'd never really thought of her like that. She was Cal's sister...

And one of my best friends.

Then I'd opened my big fucking drunk mouth and told her all about how hot she was.

And because things weren't nearly complicated enough, she'd *liked* it.

Whyyyyy had she liked it?

Better yet, why had I fucking done the fantasy ass-grabbing to begin with?

But regardless of the reason, cause and effect were in full force.

Things had been *tense* over the last week between me and Lex. Monday, she hadn't spoken to me at all, but I was still too damn weirded out to text her, either. Jack and I ordered pizza, and I sat on the back patio, watching him play in the sprinklers and feeling like I'd made a grave mistake.

Why? I had no idea. It wasn't like she was never going to speak to me again. But guilt was a far easier emotion to digest than why I was suddenly having feelings for Lex.

On Tuesday, I'd sent her a montage of funny cat videos. It had taken me hours to pick out just the right one to send and I wasn't proud of my time management that day, but it did temporarily take the edge off when she replied with a simple, *Aw.*

Good news: She didn't hate me.

Bad news: Things were still totally off the rails between us and I had no fucking idea how to fix it.

I wanted to believe she had been right and we were both hard up, sad, and desperate. And in my case, drunk. See, this was why I stuck with beer. Bad shit happened when *I* became the irresponsible one.

WHEN THE *Time* *is* *Right*

But, once again, that didn't explain why she'd liked it.

A simple, "Ew, don't be gross!" would have sufficed. I'd have apologized. She'd have accepted and we would have lived un-awkwardly ever after. As friends. Best friends. Nothing more.

Though that wouldn't have changed the fact that I had found myself utterly unable to stop thinking about her.

Luckily, on Wednesday, Maggie had gone into labor and had her baby. I'd met the woman a few times, but when Lex spent the day spamming me with photos of the baby dressed in at least a dozen monogrammed onesies, I grinned like a maniac each time my phone vibrated. For the first time since our conversation on the beach, things had started to feel normal again.

Thursday passed without much communication outside of a group message between me, Cal, and Lex where she said she couldn't make it to Huey's for darts. Considering neither of us expected Cal to be there much anymore, it was all too telling that she hadn't messaged me directly. After that, Cal asked for a recommendation for a company who could fill in a concrete hole in his backyard. Lex gave him a "shut up and be grateful" lecture somehow without ever mentioning my name or speaking to me directly. Any hope I'd had about things going back to normal because of the cat induced, *Aw*, crashed and burned.

It was now Friday, and I'd just sent Lex the name and meeting place for her date. She replied with that damn *K*, leaving me staring at one letter as though it had been an entire novel written in a different language.

Things she probably meant:
Okay.
Sure.
Cool.
Things I was terrified she meant:
I can't stop thinking about you.

Want to come over for some whiskey?
I had a sex dream about you last night.
Things I hoped she meant:
Okay.
Sure.
Cool.

Things I was secretly—and not at all willing to admit to myself—hoping she meant:
I can't stop thinking about you.
Want to come over for some whiskey?
I had a sex dream about you last night.
Fucking fuck, what the hell was wrong with me?

She put me out of my misery when the next text came through with the details for my date. I spent an exorbitant amount of time formulating the perfect response.

Me: K

Yep. That was it. Shoot me. Just shoot me.

I arrived at Bogart's, a classy little small plate, martini bar that I was positive I was going to hate at seven sharp. No point in delaying the inevitable. I couldn't imagine that *Kate* would be any different than the other Betty Crocker preschool-teacher types Lex had chosen for me. The sooner we got it started, the sooner I could get it over with.

And then what? I'd go home—alone. Maybe I could get there in time to FaceTime my seven-year-old son, who had more of a social life than I did. Then I could spend the rest of the night approving Hud Construction time cards before going to sleep and waking up in the morning to go to work where, every other weekend, I forced an eighty-four-year-old woman to come in on Saturday because growing a business was hard work, when in reality I was avoiding the fact that I had no fucking life when Lauren had my son.

And worst of all, deep down, I knew without a shadow of a doubt all I really wanted was to blow this fucking date, head to Huey's, and sit in a booth, talking and laughing with Lex until the sun came up and quite possibly long after that.

Fuck.

"Hudson?" a woman called.

I tugged at the open throat of my button-down and sucked in a sharp breath before turning to face her. And then I froze.

Familiar blue eyes collided with mine and a warm smile curled my lips. "Oh. My. God."

"Hi," she whispered, her grin matching my own.

Lex was not fucking around with this cat condo anymore; that crazy woman had pulled out the big guns.

Kate Marlow, with all her flowing, blond hair and her low-cut bikini, had been the object of my obsession every summer of my college life. Her family lived in Hilton Head, so when Cal, Lex, Lauren, and I would spend time at the beach house, she was always around.

And always ignoring me.

Brenden and Lex did their best to run wingman for me, but summer after summer, Kate wouldn't so much as give me the time of day. After Jack came along, my priorities shifted and I no longer had the freedom to spend my summers lounging in the sun, chasing the uncatchable woman.

But seven years later, there she stood in a martini bar that suddenly made a lot more sense. Lex hadn't picked that restaurant with my tastes involved. This was for Kate.

I let out a loud laugh and extended a hand, but she batted it away, pulling me in for a hug instead.

"Wow, it's so great to see you again," she said, releasing me without stepping away. She patted my chest teasingly. "I see you haven't given up on the gym."

I chuckled. "Well, you look pretty amazing yourself. How in the world did Lex convince you to drive up for the night?"

"Oh, I didn't drive up. I live here now."

"Since when?"

She shrugged. "Few weeks. I took a job at an architecture firm down in Buckhead. Alexis keeps up with me on LinkedIn, so she messaged me as soon as my feet hit Georgia soil."

I narrowed my eyes. That didn't sound right at all. Lex on Facebook? Possibly. Instagram? Likely. Crazy cat lady chat boards? One hundred percent. But LinkedIn? And the fact that she had never mentioned that Kate had moved to town was all so very...interesting.

"An architect, huh?"

"Oh, don't even feign being impressed with me. I didn't get three miles inside the city limits before I saw a Hud Construction billboard. I hear you're something of a big deal here in town."

I chuckled. "I don't know that I would go that far, but if you want to, I'm not going to stop you."

She let out a musical giggle. "Come on. Let's get a table. I want to hear all about this new-and-improved Hudson Bradley."

After we were seated at a dainty table I barely fit behind, we ordered drinks—a dirty martini for Kate and a beer for me, because no fucking way I was having a repeat of the Whiskey Hurricane from Hell. Then Kate excused herself to use the restroom.

And like any man on a date with a gorgeous, smart, funny, and charming woman, I took my phone out to text a different woman. Yes, I did realize the ludicrousness of the situation.

Me: Kate Marlow, seriously?

Lex: Just keep in mind Boop would like corkboard on her scratching balcony while Beep prefers carpet.

I grinned like an absolute fool. Sixteen words. She'd finally replied with a full sentence.

Me: Okay, slow down there. This show isn't over yet. How are things going with Logan?

Oh, yeah. Lex wasn't the only one who had been busy planning for this date. Logan Winters was a big-name realtor in Atlanta. He was a good guy. Smart, funny, and had the well-dressed badboy thing going, which I knew Lex couldn't resist. Honestly, if I'd known he was single a few weeks ago, he would have been date number one and I'd have been at home waxing my new Chevelle by this point.

Lex: Surprisingly well actually. You didn't do half bad this time.

I smiled at the phone. See? This was totally normal, just two friends chatting about our awesome dates. At least that's what I told myself as a spark of jealousy singed the inside of my chest. Oh, for fuck's sake.

Me: I thought you might approve.

Lex: I do. Now leave me alone. I was just getting a vibe on Logan's big dick energy. Go enjoy your dinner with Kate. Fun fact: She is the only woman in Atlanta Lauren hasn't told how awful you are in bed yet. You've got a clean slate, Buster. Enjoy it.

Choosing to ignore the thought of anything to do with

Logan's cock—especially when it came to Lex—I tucked my phone back into my pocket just as Kate returned.

Dinner was great. Sure, I was still starving when it was over. I was not a small-plate kind of man, but at least the rabbit-sized portions had tasted good enough.

Company was great too. We talked for hours, catching each other up on all the years that had passed and everything in between. I was usually a pretty quiet guy, but that night, the conversation flowed and I found myself carrying the majority of it. Honestly, it was one of the best dates I'd ever been on.

Or so I'd thought.

"Wow," Kate said, leaning back in her seat and placing her empty martini glass on the table. "I didn't realize you and Alexis were so close."

My head snapped to the side. "What?"

"You and Alexis. I mean, I knew you two were tight when we were younger, but I just assumed Calvin was your best friend and she kind of came as part of the package."

"He is my best friend."

She twisted her pink lips. "Then why have you spent the last two hours telling me everything about Alexis?"

I laughed awkwardly, sweat suddenly beading across my forehead. "I didn't do that. I was just telling you stories about my life. She's a part of that."

She nodded skeptically. "She has a muscle car you want. She has two cats named Beep and Boop. She adores your son, and he currently owes her twenty bucks from this hilarious bet they made. She just got a new job at Warren and Warren Consulting. It's only entry level, but you have full confidence that she's going to move up the ladder fast. You've been worried about her in this little fixer-upper she bought, so you've been using your crew to help her out when you really just wish she would let you do a full renovation, but she's way too prideful to ever accept that from you." She shot me a tight closed-mouth smile. "Oh, and at Cal's wedding, she looked gorgeous and it made you uncomfortable, so you told her she looked like a clown."

"I never said that," I defended. And it was the truth, but oh, holy fuck, had I really spent the entire date talking about Lex?

She shrugged. "You didn't have to. You had this big goofy grin when you told me she looked like a clown. It was cute." She leaned forward on her elbows. "So tell me this. Does she know that you're in love with her, or was that just a secret you were planning to share with me?"

It was like a bullet fired from a gun. I lurched from my seat, desperate to avoid it, but I wasn't fast enough and it hit me with the force of a brick wall. "I'm not in love with her. We're friends. Fine. We're even closer than me and Cal these days. But that's *it*."

Do not think about the air ass-grab. Do not think about the air ass-grab. Do not think about—

"I liked it, Hudson."

Oh, God. What the hell had I done wrong in a past life to deserve this shit?

I blew out a ragged breath and raked a hand through the top of my hair. "It's not like that."

She stood up and grabbed her small, black clutch. "Maybe. Maybe not. I'd rather not wait around to find out. But hey, I had a lot of fun tonight. If things don't work out with Alexis, give me a call." She opened her purse and pulled a few bills out.

I quickly waved her off. "No. Please. I've got dinner. I'm embarrassed enough without you offering to pay."

She smiled. "Okay, then. Tell Alexis I said hi."

I scratched the back of my neck, feeling like the ultimate asshole. "Sure thing."

She flashed me one last smile and then she was gone.

My head was swirling as I waited for the waiter to bring me the check. What was wrong with me? I'd spent over fifteen years being immune to Alexis Lawson, and then three words and my name didn't just open that door in my brain, they dropped-kicked it right off the hinges.

"*I liked it, Hudson.*" Her voice rang in my ears, and I could still see her wild, red hair blowing in the breeze and her green eyes dancing with an insecurity I ached to quell.

This couldn't happen. The last time I'd decided I had feelings for one of my friends, I'd regretted it almost immediately. Yeah, Jack was the best thing that had ever happened to me, so it wasn't all bad. But that one night with Lauren changed everything. I couldn't afford to chance that with Lex. I just needed to figure out how to reinstall that damn door in my head and then lock it up tight until she was married with a litter of kids.

Normally when I was in a bad place with something, Lex and I would talk it through. And if she wasn't available, I'd turn to Cal. And if he wasn't available, I'd go to Judy or David. And if they weren't available, I'd go to Lauren.

But I wasn't really eager to talk to any of them about how I was feeling about Lex. Cal would probably have me castrated. Lauren wouldn't even pick up the phone. And with my luck, Judy would set our wedding date.

No. There was only one person I could talk to about this, and as much as I would have rather thrown myself in front of a bus than have that conversation, it had to be said. And then, hopefully, this would be squashed once and for all.

Me: Hey, when you and Logan are done with dinner, can we meet at Huey's for a few? I have something we need to talk about.

Ten minutes later, as I was walking to my car, she still hadn't replied. So I called. It was a dick move, knowing she was on a date, and only about forty percent of why I called instead of letting it go for the night was because she was in fact out on a date.

When she didn't answer, my mind went to places like Logan taking her back to his place for a nightcap. And that was probably only about ninety-nine percent of the reason I decided to text him.

Me: Hey, are you still with Lex? She's not answering her phone.

Logan: Nah. She left about an hour ago. Cool chick. Not sure she was all that impressed by me though.

My jaw got hard as I climbed into my truck.

Me: Did you drop her off at her place?

Logan: She took an Uber. Is everything okay?

My pulse quickened. I had no fucking idea if everything was okay or not, but it had been over an hour since she'd climbed into the back of an Uber, and now, she wasn't answering. After what happened with Brenden, that damn phone was like an appendage for her; she had a plastic baggie she used so she could take it into the shower with her. With my chest tight and unease thick in my veins, I rang up Huey's to see if she'd gone there instead. Carmen said they hadn't seen her all night.

I texted Cal, careful not to tip him off that anything was wrong, but he hadn't seen her.

Then I texted Lauren because where the fuck else could she be? Lauren hadn't heard from her, either.

And with that, the sense of unease in my veins morphed into full-blown panic. I peeled out of the parking lot with my phone held to my ear and the constant drone of unanswered calls throwing fuel on my flame.

CHAPTER
Thirteen

Lex

"Oh, Ben. Oh, Jerry. You devils. I've never had a three-way before. Okay, I have. But only ever with you."

Didn't everyone talk to their ice cream? No? Just me?

It didn't matter, because that night, I was DTF.

Down. To. Fudge.

It was likely the sugar endorphins firing through my body, but I didn't care. I needed the pick-me-up in the worst possible way, because outside my front door, the world was going crazy.

I had the hots for one of my closest friends.

My brother was married off and MIA most of the time.

My parents were on my ass about settling down—a.k.a. finding a spouse.

And lastly, I'd left a perfectly good date early.

Let me clarify. I'd left a date with an insanely handsome man who actually made eye contact when he spoke. Logan had one of those fuck-hot hipster haircuts that I always found sexy. He wasn't too forward, but his smile said a lot. Namely, the way he licked his lips and smiled, but who was paying attention? On top of that, the big dick energy was strong, and he complimented my legs, which I'd always thought of as two prickly stumps.

Just went to show that different men liked different things.

But two things were certain: Logan was into me and I kept calling him Hudson.

Ergo, I'd left early.

As I dug a stubborn chunk of brownie out of the pint, I took a breath and decided that all the shit that was happening—or not happening—was out of my hands. The only things I could control were my spoon, how much chocolate I binged that night, and turning my phone to silent so I didn't have to hear all about Hudson's incredible date.

So be it. My life was left to fate.

The Gods.

Mother Nature.

Maybe even the Illuminati for all I knew.

And whatever they wanted for me, I was willing to accept, because Ben and Jerry would always be there for me.

"So give me whatever you've got, Universe. We're not scared," I said out loud to Beep and Boop who were my captive audience in the kitchen. "Ain't that right, girls?"

Boop licked her ass and Beep meowed, which were both signs of their unwavering solidarity.

Then, as if I'd literally challenged the cosmos, something happened. There was a commotion on my porch and I peeked into the living room to get a look out the window.

Before I could do anything, my door flew open and there he stood.

Hudson.

With the spoon hanging out of my mouth, I asked around it, "What the fuck are you doing here?"

He was all dressed up for his date, whereas I had already taken off my bra and pants and was hanging out in my tank top and undies.

"You didn't answer your damn phone." His chest was

heaving like he'd run from wherever he'd been, and he blew out a long stream of air as he raked his hand through his blond hair.

My gaze bounced around the room as I plucked the spoon from my mouth and then replied, "Well, as you can see, I'm here. I'm fine." *I'm head over heels for you and hiding, so go away.*

"I thought some Uber driver murdered you."

That was our Hudson, sole protector. I swear he was part man and part Australian Shepherd with the way he had to know where everyone was at all times.

"I don't take Ubers. I take Lyfts. Studies show they're safer and more female friendly." I dug around my dessert and took another bite as he stood there panting and staring at me. I did everything I could to not make eye contact.

Actually, my MO for the past week had been no contact period, but that was a little hard to do when the guy you're dodging knows things about you. Specifically, the lock code on your front door.

"You can go home, Hudson. I'm fine." Out of my periphery, I watched him perch his hands on his hips.

"No," he argued. "Not until we figure this shit out."

So he had noticed my ghosting. I hoped he wasn't as good at calling my bluff.

"There is no shit."

"What about what you said at the—"

"Yeah, I must have had a cold or something. Whatever it was, I'm over it."

Lies. Lies. Lies. Hopefully, I'd start believing them.

"Over it?"

"Yep. Hey, how was your date?" My topic-swapping skills were on point. "I expected you'd have a long night with Kate." I had to be careful. I didn't want to come across as jealous, and I was sounding that way. My tone was all wrong and I still couldn't look at him. And for the record, I was jealous as a motherfucker.

But I didn't want to be.

"It was fine. Well, except…" His voice trailed off before he could finish the sentence.

Damn my curiosity. "What was wrong with her? I swear. You're getting awful picky in our old age."

He took a step closer, and I took a step back toward my sink. It was easier to pretend when there was distance between us. But though he was still several feet away, my pulse raced and my breaths became shallow. It was hell.

"The truth?" His booming voice shot back as he crept forward, but I had nowhere else to go. "The truth is the date was a ten. Kate looked great. The food—the finger food more specifically—was delicious, what little there was of it. Our conversation flowed easily enough."

When he stopped, only an arm's length away, I finally seized what scrap of pride I had and looked up into his blue eyes. His big, deep-blue eyes. Then I swallowed.

"So, what happened? Are you seeing her again?"

Hudson huffed. "Well, that's kind of up to you."

"Me?" I dropped the spoon into the sink and put the ice cream down so I could cross my arms over my chest. "What do I have to do with it?"

His lids fell shut, and he tipped his head at the ceiling, stretched his neck from side to side, and then brought his gaze back to mine. "Kate seems to think that, maybe, I have a thing… for you."

My face flushed hot, and I wondered if maybe I'd fallen down trying to get out of my leather skirt earlier and I was dreaming, passed out on my bedroom floor. The issue with that theory was I could smell him, feel the warmth from his body in front of me, and see his heartbeat thumping in the vein in his neck.

This was real, but I still wasn't sure I could handle it.

"Well, that's just, uh, *dumb*," I contended weakly. Shaking my head to rattle myself back to sanity, I asked, "W-why did she say that?" I tried to laugh, but it was as fake as my gusto.

"Because, apparently, I talked about you the whole night."

Okay, I was wrong. I'd thought riding in a car with him and seeing him shirtless and watching him play with Jack and seeing how much he loved my family and having him touch me and avoiding him all week had been torture.

This moment was a whole new level of torment.

"So?" I said childishly.

Because it didn't matter how I felt or what I wanted. I couldn't just leap into his arms and expect everything to turn out the way it was supposed to. That's not how my life worked.

"*So* I need to find out if this, whatever's been building between us, is something."

Wouldn't that be nice? Up until that very second, it had all been so one-sided and I'd racked my brain all week to understand why I'd felt the crazy things I did about him.

"How you gonna do that?"

"We're going to kiss," he stated very matter-of-factly, and then he closed the distance between our bodies.

"We are?" I whispered. My voice had all but left the building.

"Unless you stop me right now."

I wanted to.

I didn't want to.

I was scared.

I was excited.

But mostly, I wasn't stopping him. I was frozen.

He tipped my chin up and I trembled.

"Tell me to stop, Lex."

I said nothing.

He licked his lips and then whispered, "Last chance."

That close, I saw the flecks of sapphire in his eyes as he slowly blinked down at me.

Still, I didn't tell him to stop.

Were we about to ruin everything? Would there ever be a way to go back to the way things had been after this?

Hudson leaned in and then paused. Eye to eye, I could see that he was as nervous as I was. He was doing this for both of us, and for us, I could at least meet him halfway. And a saying from our youth came back to me. *Where we go one, we go all.*

I lifted up onto my toes, letting him know I was all in.

He let out a short exhale and then crushed his mouth to mine. He didn't go easy on me, didn't hold anything back. Instinctively, I tipped my head one way and then the other when he deepened the kiss, mingling his tongue and lips with mine. It was just enough wet. And just enough breath. And just enough Hudson to pull a whimper from my chest.

As if the sound were a shot fired at a starting line, he hoisted me up into his strong arms and placed me on the edge of my sink, never breaking our connection.

My legs wrapped around his waist and the sexiest groan I'd ever heard poured into my mouth.

All thoughts of whether it was right or wrong were drowned out by my hammering heart. We kissed and touched and held on to each other like it was life or death. His calloused hand climbed my thigh and then palmed my ass as he came even closer between my bare legs. My fingers tangled in the longer hair he had on top, and when he moved the kiss from our mouths to my neck, I was lucky to be sitting. Had I needed to rely on my knees, they would have buckled under the weight of it all.

Licking and sucking at my skin, Hudson pressed his erection into my thigh, and fantasies I'd buried in the back of my mind of him doing that very thing when we were teenagers surfaced.

Had I wanted this all along?

"Ahh," I panted as he gently bit my earlobe. Hearing his breathing against me sent fire up my spine.

I wanted more, and that was exactly why, with a hand against his chest, I pushed him away. It didn't take more resistance than that before he broke our contact and took a step back.

We stared at one another, catching our heaving breaths. Hudson's hand smoothed over his jaw and then covered his mouth. The muscles in his forearms flexed and he slowly wiped his lips.

"I have to go," he said, his voice thick, finally breaking the silence.

And just as quickly as he'd barged into my house, he was gone.

I felt like a piece of paper that had been torn into a dozen pieces, and each of those scraps represented one of the emotions I felt. Every time my mind wandered back to what had happened in my kitchen, they all scattered in the wind.

How could one kiss have fucked me up so much?

Part of me had assumed that if anything like that ever happened, it would snap me out of this unfortunate crush. Like it would confirm we were only meant to be friends. That what I had felt was just because I'd had such a long dry spell.

Never in a million years had I expected Hudson's kiss to awaken my entire body. Seriously, I'd been kissed. I'd kissed many. But I'd never been so consumed and swept up in a moment like we'd shared. Then again, what had he ever done poorly—aside from his drunken sexual encounter with Lauren?

That thought only led me back to the *what was I thinking kissing Hudson* corner of my mind. He had a child with one of our friends. He was best friends with my brother. If anyone ever found out, they'd lose their ever-loving minds.

"You're so fucking dumb, Alexis," I repeated for the hundredth time. Scolding myself for letting it happen while deep cleaning my house had taken up most of my morning. The other part of my morning had been spent showering and brushing my teeth. Anything I could do to scrub away what I was sure had been a huge mistake.

But as the conflicting voices in my head had done since the moment it happened, I'd somehow found my way back to Why Do I Want To Do It Again Land?

I needed fresh air.

Needed to do something big to take my mind off it. Off his hands cupping my face. Off his body pressing into mine. Off the tiniest humming sound he made when I'd first kissed him back. Off the fact of how unfair it was that it had—easily—been one of the best kisses of my life. First kisses were supposed to be timid and awkward. How was it even fair that he got to be that incredible right off the bat?

Damn Hudson Bradley.

I needed a task that would give me some control. Some authority. Something monotonous with immediate results. *Power washing.*

Yes, I had my own, and it was a beast too. It had been a housewarming gift from—*shit.*

Anyway, *a friend* had given it to me when I'd moved in, knowing how much I loved the chore. When I was growing up, it was the one outdoor job I always volunteered for at home. My parents had a massive wooden deck in Atlanta, and the beach house usually needed a good washing about once a year too.

I was odd, but that wasn't new.

After I gassed and fired up the machine, I pulled the bill of my cap down to shield the spray back from my eyes and got to it. My old iPod shuffle was in a plastic bag in my pocket and my heavy-duty headphones were on, playing fourteen-year-old Lex's favorite hits.

For a few hours, I got lost in the sweet instant gratification of blowing grime off my siding to the still-iconic sounds of Nick, Joe, and Kevin Jonas. No phone calls. No real-world issues. Just me and forty-four hundred PSI of take-no-shit water pressure.

Then, as I was tugging the power washer through the grass to my backyard, I saw his black truck coming down my street.

Panic set in. Not that he hadn't seen me look way, way worse before, but things were different now whether I was comfortable admitting it or not. Combine that with the fact that I didn't know what to say, how to feel, or what to think about him just showing up.

And I didn't know what he'd say. Or how he'd felt. Or really anything other than he'd bolted less than a minute after I'd broken the kiss.

Normally, I wouldn't care if a guy had ditched me with little to no goodbye. Their loss as far as I was concerned.

That morning, I probably cared too much, and that was what had me hiding in a bush, armed with a spray nozzle. In my defense, it had been half a decade since I'd felt so vulnerable. All these emotions and sensations were brand new to me again.

I didn't know how to handle it, and I needed time to organize my head. However, I should have expected Hudson to come at this whole situation guns a-blazin'. That was who he was.

"Alexis, open up." He knocked on my front door. When

there was no answer, his second knock was louder and more obnoxious.

Not using the keypad today, eh, Buster?

"I'm not home. Go. Away," I mumbled to myself from the refuge of my massive gardenia bush on the other side of the house. When I heard him march back across my porch, I silently thanked the Lord Almighty for having my back, because we both knew I didn't exactly deserve that kind of karma.

I relaxed a little when he got into his truck and drove away, and then I counted to fifty before emerging from the sanctuary of my bush.

I should have been smarter than that.

The second I stepped foot out from my hiding spot, his voice rang through the quiet afternoon air.

"What the hell are you doing?"

I jumped at least six feet in the air—give or take six feet—and spun around, armed and ready.

CHAPTER
Fourteen

Hudson

"Don't shoot!" I shouted, lifting my hands in the air.

She kept the barrel of her pressure washer aimed at my chest as she leaned to the side to peer around me. "Where's your truck?"

"I moved it to the street so you'd come out from wherever the hell you were hiding." A slow grin pulled at my lips, and fuck me, her gaze dropped to my mouth.

Memories from the night before assaulted me from all angles. Her lips on mine. Her hands in my hair. The sweet flavor of her moans still lingered on my taste buds.

I hadn't slept a wink since I'd left her house. When I'd first gotten home after our kiss, I'd spent a full hour sitting in my truck, the engine running, my cock hard as a fucking rock, begging and pleading with my brain to go back.

My brain won out and forced me into a cold shower, where I might or might not have palmed my cock. Twice.

It was Lex.

It was Lex.

It was Lex.

But it sure as fuck hadn't felt like I'd been kissing my best friend with her tight little body pressed to mine and her breasts pillowed against my chest.

No, that hadn't felt like anything even resembling friendship. I'd texted her twice that morning, but in true Lex fashion, she'd ignored me. I swear, that woman was a professional when it came to running from her problems. It had never bothered me before. Though I'd never been one of those problems before. Now, it just pissed me off.

"How do you know I was hiding?" she snapped, a few broken twigs with leaves still stuck in her hair.

I tipped my head to the side and planted my hands on my hips. "You do realize we've met, right?"

Her lips thinned. "Unfortunately, I'm aware." Finally lowering her weapon, she used a hand to shield the sun from her eyes. "What brings you here on this fine Saturday, Hudson?"

I took a step toward her, fully expecting her to retreat, but when she didn't, I plucked the leaves from her hair. "A couple of things, actually."

She peered up at me, her bright-green eyes sparkling in the midday sun. "If any of them begin or end with what the hell happened last night, I'm out."

I sighed. "Come on, Kid. We have to talk about it."

She shook her head and turned on a toe, making herself busy by gathering the hose on the pressure washer. "No, we really don't. And I thought I told you to stop calling me Kid. Seems a little creepy after you shoved your tongue in my mouth last night." She marched to her open garage door, calling over her shoulder, "Which we still aren't talking about, by the way."

I rolled my eyes and followed after her. "If I recall correctly, you did a little shoving your tongue in my mouth too."

After grabbing her broom from a hook on the wall, she hurried back out without so much as making eye contact again. "It was a self-defense move."

I once again fell into step behind her. "See, I considered

that—until I remembered you looping your legs around my hips."

She started sweeping the already spotless sidewalk in front of her door. "It's how octopuses in the wild subdue their attackers."

"Right," I whispered, quickly losing my patience with this discussion and my roaring desire to seal my mouth over hers and see what else she'd learned from animals in the wild. I caught the broom midswing and tugged it from her hands.

"Hey!" she objected.

Dropping it at our feet, I pleaded, "Can you just give me something here? I couldn't sleep last night."

She crossed her arms over her damp T-shirt. "Have you tried melatonin? I hear it works wonders."

"Damn it, Lex," I snapped, raking a hand through the top of my hair. "I'm serious. I feel like I'm losing it right now. I don't know who to talk to. No, strike that. I can't talk to anyone even if I had someone because I don't know what the hell is going on between us."

"I don't know, either!" she exploded, and pissed off as she was, I breathed a huge sigh of relief.

Angry and ranty Lex, I could handle.

"This is new to me too, okay? You're Hudson. The idea of kissing you should be only slightly less stomach-churning than kissing Cal. But it wasn't. And I really fucking enjoyed it and that just confuses me more. Because I can't stop thinking about it. And part of me really wants to so we can just go back to normal." She sucked in a shaky breath that might as well have destroyed me. "The other part of me is terrified that nothing is ever going to be normal between us again. I'm a tad overwhelmed here, okay?"

"Hey," I breathed, closing the distance between us. I rested a hand on her hip and gave her a squeeze. "Easy. It's okay. Don't get upset. We're fine. If you want normal, I can do that. Just relax. We're good."

Looking off to the side, she whispered, "This doesn't feel good."

Damn if she wasn't right. The kiss had felt good. Actually having her in my arms had felt incredible. But the unknown and uncertainty that followed was awful.

You meet a woman, kiss a woman, date a woman, and then shit falls apart. No big deal. You go your separate ways. But what happens when that woman is such an integral part of your life that going your separate ways sounds like not only a nightmare, but also an impossibility?

However, there was some pretty heavy chemistry between the two of us, and I too was worried that after last night there wouldn't be a version of normal when I didn't look at her and fight the urge to take her mouth again. I was just as confused and overwhelmed as she was.

But we were friends first and there was nothing I wouldn't do to make this easier on her.

"Time out," I said, and thankfully, her gaze came back to mine.

"What?"

"Time out. We put a pin in this for now. We get the normal back. You don't ghost me. We don't talk about it. We think about it for a few days, and when you're ready, we'll figure it out."

She offered me a tight smile. "I can do that."

"Me too." I gave her one last squeeze before dropping my hand and taking a giant step back.

We stared at each other for several beats, and then I cleared my throat and gave her back the normal we both needed.

"So, anyway, I hate to interrupt you and your power washing fetish, but I just stopped by to see what you were doing tonight. Lauren called about an hour ago and said Investment Banker Mark is finally free for a meet and greet. What do you say you shave your mountain man leg hair and put on a dress and go with me? I could really use the backup on this one."

She grinned, and it struck me so hard it nearly rocked me back a step. Lex had smiled at me no less than a million times in my life.

Midlaugh after she'd beaten me in a game of darts.

Fake and full of agony as I'd offered her my arm to guide her out of Brenden's funeral.

Teasing from across the room as she'd snuck Jack a bag of water balloons from her purse.

But this one was different, and it struck me like a thousand arrows falling from the sky because I knew to the core of my soul she should have been in my arms when she grinned up at me like that.

"You wearing a suit?" she asked.

"Good God, no."

Her smile grew, and so did the pain in my chest.

"You paying for dinner?"

"Yes, but only because I already checked the menu and they don't serve lobster. And you're limited to one dessert."

"And one to go."

"None to go," I corrected.

"We'll see." She winked. "What time?"

"Seven."

"Okay. I'm in. Honestly, this works out. I've been dying to interrogate this Mark fellow. I don't trust just anybody with my Jackie-boy."

And just like that, things were normal again.

Only not really.

Not at all.

And not even close.

Running on no sleep, I took a two-hour nap as soon as I got home. When I woke up, I was still twisted up over all things Alexis Lawson, but the rest had done wonders for my mindset when it came to meeting Mark. After a quick shower, in which I miraculously didn't touch my cock, I put on navy slacks and a white button-down that I spent entirely too long picking out for it to have had anything to do with Mark, and then I was on my way.

It was the craziest thing. This wasn't a date with Lex. Far from it, actually, but there was a distinct buzz of nerves as I walked down her sidewalk to pick her up. And the second she opened her front door wearing a little black dress, her red hair cascading over her bare shoulders in thick waves, and a pair of black strappy heels, that buzz turned into an all-out earthquake.

"Hey," she chirped, dragging the small diamond at her throat back and forth across the silver chain.

Do not look at her cleavage. Do not look at her cleavage. Do not look at her cleavage.

"Hey," I replied, staring at her eyes so hard that tears formed in the corners of mine from a lack of blinking.

She cocked her head to the side and leveled me with a glare. "Why are you looking at me like that?"

I cut my gaze over her shoulder and took a minute to appraise the expert brickwork my guy had done beside her door, all the while cussing myself for not having jerked off in the shower. "I'm not sure what you're talking about."

She let out a sigh. "Would you stop being weird and just look at my boobs already? It's not like you didn't check them out on the regular before last night. I thought we were supposed to be normal tonight."

My gaze snapped back to hers. "What? I did not check out your boobs on the regular."

She twisted her lips and looped a small, black clutch around her wrist. "Uh, yeah, you did. I always just assumed you weren't breastfed enough as a baby or something. Though, looking back, you did always smile when I caught you. I should have seen your obsession for me coming."

"I did not look at your boobs!" I defended again, but I'd be damned if my gaze didn't drop. And before I could stop it, an involuntary smile tipped my lips.

"There it is." She patted me on the chest as she headed toward my truck, calling over her shoulder, "Good to have you back, Hud."

"Damn it," I mumbled, following after her.

I smiled when I looked at her chest? That shit was not normal. I'd had a baby with Lauren and last time she'd worn a low-cut shirt, I'd thrown a hoodie at her. No smiling involved. Jesus, how long had I been harboring this shit for Lex?

I went straight to the passenger side door, barely able to grab the handle before she did, and tried to open the door for her.

"Nope," she said, jumping back as if I had a leprosy flare-up again. "You opening doors for me is not *normal*. You coming to the door instead of honking when you got here was already testing the limits."

Shit. She was right there too.

"What happened to us not talking about this? I'm pretty sure that was part of the deal we made."

"I wouldn't have to talk about this if you weren't acting like my eleventh-grade prom date out of nowhere." She made a shooing motion with her hands. "Go on. Get in on your side. And try to think of something rude to say when I get in. That's normal, Hudson. Not this crap."

I didn't want to say something rude though. I wanted to kiss her and tell her she looked beautiful and maybe, definitely, probably, sneak a few peeks down her shirt while we laughed over dinner.

I didn't want Lauren to be there or Investment Banker Mark.

I just wanted Lex, and yes, I did realize that was not our usual *normal*.

But damn if it didn't feel *right*.

A few days—that was all I'd promised her. A few days and we could talk. A few days and maybe we could get on the same page, hopefully one where I got to taste her again.

Until then, though, the old normal was going to have to suffice.

I walked around the truck, climbed in, and patiently waited for her to open her own damn door. I pretended not to see the way she closed her eyes and sucked in a sharp breath before plastering on a smile.

"Buster, I'm waiting," she said, sliding into my passenger seat the way she'd done so many times in the past.

"What the hell are you wearing?" I rumbled. "Jesus, Kid, did you need industrial lubricant to slip into that dress?"

Why did I have to say lubricant? That was not helping me in the fucking slightest.

She smiled and put her seat belt on. "Oh, you're one to talk. You look like that cockroach guy from Men in Black who didn't know how to walk around in a human body."

I barked a loud laugh, and I had to give her credit. It did feel normal, even if I did have to fight the urge to lean over and trace the curve of her delicate collarbone with the tip of my tongue.

Yeah, okay, fine. Normal was a stretch.

But I could pretend.

The ride to the restaurant was quiet, more of comfortable silence than stilted though. We arrived right at seven, and I didn't attempt to help her out of the truck or take her arm as we walked inside. And it sucked far more than I ever could have imagined a few days earlier.

"You're here!" Lauren said when we entered the restaurant. Her excitement faded as she shifted her gaze to the woman at my side. "And you brought Lex."

Lex slanted her head. "Good to see you too, Lauren."

"No, I didn't mean it like that." She pulled her in for a quick hug and then did the same with me. "I just meant we only asked for a table for three. I'm sure it won't be an issue though." She laughed awkwardly. "I'll…go tell the hostess. Give me a second. Mark ran to the bar to get me a glass of wine." She offered me a tight smile and then hurried away.

"Well, that was fun," Lex said. "Thanks for not telling her I was coming. It made for a real warm and fuzzy reception. Next time, consider having me jump out of a large cardboard cake. I hear that always goes over well in a crowd."

"I'll keep that in mind," I mumbled, watching Lauren walk away. "Why does she seem so nervous?"

Lex shrugged. "Probably the same reason you brought a dat—*friend* as backup."

"Mmmm," I hummed, something not quite sitting right as Lauren weaved through the crowd on her way back to us.

"Okay. All set," she said. "It will be about ten more minutes until our table's ready. Let's go find Mark at the bar." She paused and craned her head back to peer up at me. "Please be nice."

"Why wouldn't I be nice?"

"Of course." She nodded and then turned on a toe, her heels clipping the tile as she led the way.

Lex and I exchanged suspicious glances and then followed after her.

The bar was packed, not a single seat to be found, so when Lauren stopped behind an older gray-haired gentleman at the bar, I didn't think much of it.

And then he turned.

And then he kissed her.

And then Lex audibly gasped.

And I blinked as my son's soon-to-be elderly stepfather extended a hand in my direction.

"You must be Hudson. Can I get you a drink?"

Stupefied, I clasped his hand and rumbled, "Whiskey. Neat. Double."

"Beer," Lex interjected, extending her hand. "He'll have a beer. I'm Lex, by the way. I'm sure Lauren's told you all about me. And I would *love* a beer too."

Lauren sawed her bottom lip with her teeth. "Mark, you remember Alexis, right? She's David and Judy Lawson's daughter."

"Oh," he said, his eyes wrinkling as he smiled. "You're Calvin's little sister. Yes. Now I remember. Your parents brought you and your brother out on my yacht when you were much younger." He cupped her hand in both of his. "So good to see you again, dear. And all grown up too."

Lex laughed uncomfortably. "Uh, yeah. So…good to see you again, twenty years later, quasi-engaged to my friend. What are the chances?"

"Whatever they are, they were definitely in my favor." He released her hand and kissed Lauren's temple before turning back to the bar.

With Mark's back to us, I bulged my eyes at Lauren in a silent *what the fuck?*

She bulged hers back in a silent *shut the fuck up and be nice?*

But it was Lex's tugging on my arm before pressing up onto her toes to whisper, "Oh my God, I am so glad I came for this," that put the smile back on my face.

I stared down at the mischievous green eyes, the corners of my mouth twitching. "You should have let me order the whiskey."

Her cheeks pinked in the least Lex way possible. "It's going to be a long time before I let you order the whiskey again."

I don't know why I did it.

We weren't talking about *it*. We were pretending to be normal.

For fuck's sake, Lauren was standing right there.

But I regretted nothing as I dipped low, my cheek grazing hers, and put my lips next to her ear. "I was sober last night. Tonight, with you in that sexy-as-fuck dress, you probably would have been safer if I'd had the whiskey."

She went solid and her breathing shuddered as I traced a finger down her arm, careful to block the movement from Lauren's view. The last thing either of us needed was this thing between us getting back to Cal before we'd even had the chance to figure out what the hell it was.

And as the night went on, I became less and less patient with the idea of waiting to do just that.

Dinner was great. I learned Lauren's parents had set her up with Mark's son, Mark Junior. It was an oh-so-hilarious story of mixed-up phone calls, late-night texts, and finally a date before either of them realized he wasn't the Mark she was supposed to be dating. Lex had a field day with that story, gasping and laughing in all the right places. My favorite part was every time Mark would call Lauren a beautiful young lady, Lex would squeeze my thigh under the table.

Luckily, old man Garrett thought Lauren was a seriously

beautiful young lady, and it got to the point where Lex didn't even move her hand off my thigh while he was talking. This meant I spent the majority of that dinner hard or mentally listing construction equipment in reverse alphabetical order.

Honestly though, by the time it was all said and done and Mark and I had argued over the check—an argument I eventually won—I'd forgotten that he was in his mid-fifties. Lauren was right. He was a good guy. He loved his kids and said all the right things about respecting my relationship with Jack but also being eager to be a part of his life. And Lauren, holy shit. I'd never seen her that happy.

So, as the valet arrived with my truck and Lauren pulled me in for a quick side hug, I told her, "You and Mark should take Jack out to dinner one day this week."

Her blue eyes lit. "You have him this week."

"Yeah, I know. But just a quick dinner. Ease him into it. That way, I'll be there when he gets home in case he has any questions or anything. He'll see I'm happy for you. That'll make him happy too."

Her eyes filled with tears. "You are amazing."

I nodded. "I know. But I never get sick of hearing it."

After another round of goodbyes, Lex and I loaded up in my truck and headed home.

I was smiling.

She had a bag with two to-go desserts in her lap, so she was smiling too.

All in all, it was a pretty damn successful night.

"Hey, thanks for going with me tonight," I said as I pulled into her driveway.

"Are you kidding me? That was the highlight of my week. Mark is a dreamboat. You think his son is still single?"

I hit her with a side-eye. Mark Junior wasn't getting within a square mile of the woman in my passenger seat, so there was no point in talking about it. "The highlight of your week, huh?"

She shrugged. "What can I say? I've had a boring week."

"Nothing exciting happened? Like, say, last night? Or this afternoon when you held a man up at pressure-washer point."

"Nothing that I can think of." She swayed her head from side to side. "Though I vaguely remember someone calling a time-out, and after that, it all got a little foggy."

Just as I was about to ask if she was ready to talk about it—because I was—she spoke without even an ounce of bullshit in her voice.

"You were pretty great tonight, Hud. It's got to be weird being connected to someone the way you and Lauren are, but she's really lucky a guy like you knocked her up and not some selfish asshole loser. Jack has a badass for a dad. And none of us tell you often enough, but you're…" She paused, put her hand on the door handle, shook her head, and then finished with, "Well, you're okay."

Not often was I speechless, but a compliment like that, about how I was as a co-parent and a father, it meant a fuck of a lot. Especially coming from her.

"Anyway, don't let it go to your head. You're also a cocky, bulldozing jackass sometimes." She hopped out and said through the window, "So I guess the universe does like balance. I'll talk to you tomorrow. Be careful. I lo—" Her mouth slammed shut, preventing her from saying something we'd told each other for years.

Things were different, not normal or even pretend normal.

She didn't have to say it that night, but as she sprinted to her well-lit front door, I called, "You too, Lex."

That night, the drive home felt wrong. Putting distance between us didn't seem like the right thing to do. Not when even our chaste touches throughout the evening had my blood racing. Not when she looked that sexy and sounded so sweet.

What the fuck was I doing?

No sooner than I pulled into my driveway did I back out.

Home wasn't where I wanted to be that night. Fuck the time-out.

Pulling up on her curb, I watched her swaying in her living room to a song I couldn't hear and drink wine straight from the bottle.

She was beautiful, and I was done wasting time.

CHAPTER
Fifteen

Lex

I didn't hit the word *chandelier* quite the way Sia did, but if history and red wine proved anything, I'd get damn close after the twentieth time on repeat.

It wasn't my first choice in how the night would end, but I couldn't deny that, for whatever reason, I felt good. So, instead of feeding the ladies and going to bed, I decided a night cap, some barefoot dancing, and singing at the top of my lungs were just what I needed.

Sometimes you just have to let shit out. Because of timeouts with sexy construction men and gravely, whispered words in your ear. Because the sheer tension alone from sitting beside him at the table and in the truck had me squirming in my seat all night. And mostly because I wished he hadn't left.

Again, as if my brain had some unexplainable power to make Hudson materialize, there was a knock at my door. I didn't even have to answer to know it was him. I could feel it.

Giddy and nervous, but high on the fact that he couldn't stay away, I opened the door with a grin twitching the sides of my mouth.

"Did you forget something?"

He ran his hand through his hair, stepped inside, and slammed the door. "Yeah, this. Time the fuck in."

Before I could even react, I was in his arms, against the wall, loving the feel of being claimed by him. If there was any doubt that our first kiss had been a fluke because of how incredible it had been, then there was no confusion about it now.

Hudson's mouth knew things. When to deepen the kiss. When to let me lead. When to be gentle and when to roughly rake his teeth over my bottom lip—which was my personal favorite. There was something so raw and sexy about those playful and hungry nips that had me wanting more.

Hudson was by far the most confident, steady-handed man I'd ever known. But with one hand pinning both of mine above my head against the wall as he kissed the hell straight out of me, I could feel the ever-so-slight shake in the touch of his free hand running up my dress and across my hip to palm my ass.

"You wore this dress to drive me nuts," he breathed against my neck.

I couldn't deny how I'd fantasized about him taking it off me when I'd put it on. "What if I did?"

He looked into my eyes, and I couldn't remember a time when he'd ever looked so handsome. His mouth swollen from our kisses and his cheeks flushed. But his eyes. Oh, blue was such a boring word, and his glistening, hooded gaze deserved better. Deep, rushing, cool water. Sunny Georgian skies after a thunderstorm. Sea glass at dawn.

Hudson up close was ruggedly beautiful.

When he released my wrists, my arms fell around his neck, and he cupped my chin and quickly pressed his mouth to mine before he said, "It worked." A grin spread across his face. "But now that you've made me crazy and I'm back here again, what do you want?"

My heart banged through my tight, black dress against his chest.

Words were thick in my throat.

And all the places I usually hid within myself were suddenly too far away.

"I want you," I confessed. "But—"

His index finger covered my mouth, and instinctively, my lips pursed around it.

"Shhh. No buts, Lex. I want you too." Sweetly, he moved to cup my cheek and my eyes fluttered from the sensation of his warm palm against my skin.

"What if you're wrong?" I asked without the mental fortitude to bite my tongue. The question wasn't unfounded. After all, he'd mistaken friendship for desire before.

Surprisingly, he didn't get defensive. He didn't argue. He didn't even make excuses. He only answered with, "What if I'm not?" His Adam's apple bobbed as he swallowed.

We were at the edge of a cliff, not knowing what was at the bottom. Only sure that, after we took the leap, nothing would ever be the same.

I unhooked my legs from around his waist, and he let me slide against the wall to my feet.

If I wanted to take a step away from the ledge, it was my chance.

Instead, I offered him my hand and he took it, kissed it, and threaded his fingers with mine. That gesture alone proved to me that, at the very least, we were jumping together, and that made it worth the fall.

"I guess there's only one way to find out," I said, and then I led him to my bedroom.

The walk to the room at the back side of my house had never felt so long. With each step, I teetered between nerves and excitement. I was eager for more of him but also unsure if it was the right thing to do. And if I were being completely honest with myself, I'd have to acknowledge that it was the first time in over five long years that I was inviting a man into my bed.

Yes, I'd had sex. Yes, I'd been with men in beds. But not here, in my home, and never with someone I already loved and respected.

There was also this nagging voice in my head wondering what we would do if it *wasn't* good. If we weren't compatible like that. If the chemistry Hudson and I were feeling would end when our clothes came off. But like I'd told him in the foyer, there was only one way to find out.

Inside my room, I dropped his hand and moved over to my bedside table to turn the small lamp on. It was barely bright enough to read by when sitting beside it, but it was enough for me to get a look at him in the buff—which I hadn't been able to stop thinking about for days.

I only had two items of clothing on, so I returned to him to even the playing field.

Hudson stood a few feet from the end of my bed, rigid and tall, but his eyes were on me like a predator observing his prey as he unbuttoned his pressed, white dress shirt.

I slipped my hands inside and ran them down his sides to pull the bottom free, and then I pushed it off his broad shoulders. Newly taken with the sight of flesh I'd seen thousands of times, I pressed my lips to his chest atop his oh-too-perfectly-snug undershirt. Hearing his breath catch, I continued by dipping my fingers into the waistband of his slacks and tugging the ribbed tank up his stomach.

With both hands, he reached behind his head and in one swift motion yanked it off and threw it somewhere to the side.

I'd dated a few guys in the past who were shredded, but they'd had gym muscle. Hudson Bradley had work muscle, and believe me, there was a big difference. From the lats flexing at his sides with his arms over his head to the traps flanking his neck, he had a body shaped by years of hard, laborious work, and for some reason, that made it all the more masculine and sexy.

He wasn't just fit—he was strong.

I licked my lips and spread my fingers across his abs like I'd been given the keys to a magical kingdom. Under my hands, he tensed, but he didn't stop me. After running the ridges from his pecs to the mouth-watering V rising like a phoenix from his hips, I grabbed the buckle of his belt and pulled him back with me as I sat on the edge of my bed.

"Alexis." His voice was low and there was a new edge to it that caused a shiver to skate up my spine.

I lifted my gaze up his body and fuck what a sight he was. His chest heaving. His jaw tight. His bottom lip pinched between his teeth.

God. Damn.

"Before this goes any further—because I'm not sure I'll be thinking as clearly in a few minutes *and* I'm damn sure wild horses won't be able to drag me out of this bed once I'm in it—we need to talk about your safety."

My safety? Maybe my head was foggy, but I was certain no man had ever said that to me before sex.

"I have insurance," I said, not entirely sure why. Although I wasn't worried about getting hurt. Wait. *Fuck.* "How big has your dick gotten over the years?"

He chuckled, and the amused sound made my stomach flutter. "No. Not that. Like the condom in my wallet."

I was so dumb. "Oh. Yeah. Don't worry. I have a contraceptive implant. Nexpla-something. I'm good. No need for your ancient rubber here."

Jesus. He had me thinking I was about to deep-throat a fucking aircraft carrier. Then again, if it was attached to the man before me, I'd have given it the good old college try.

No condom was a novel thought, one I'd never had before and one I'd certainly never entertained, but I didn't want Hudson to wear one. I just wanted him. Wanted to feel all of him.

I added, "And I'm clean, I promise, and besides, I trust you. You don't have to wear it. You don't need to protect me. *Especially not from you.*"

He took my face in his palms and leaned down to kiss me, but before our mouths paired, he said, "Don't you get it, Lex? I've had this relentless need to protect you nearly half my life. I have no plans of stopping now."

That was the moment I realized how much he meant to me. How much he'd always meant to me.

He'd been the guy who'd told me my high school boyfriend had been messing around with another girl, and then he'd taken it upon himself to take me to homecoming so I wouldn't have to go alone. He was the guy who picked me up from the first house party I went to when I'd had too much to drink. Only now had it become clear he'd stayed sober that night for me, just in case. He made sure I'd never been taken advantage of by a car salesman, a contractor, or a realtor. Shit, even my vet had been vetted by Hudson.

And when I'd needed him to protect me from the vast pit of agony I'd fallen into after Brenden's accident, he'd been there too. Driving me to and from the hospital at all hours, when he had a one-year-old and a brand-new business. He made sure I didn't starve or fall into a never-ending sleep when Brenden finally passed. He even went as far as rationing out the sleeping pills I'd been prescribed to make sure I didn't take too many "by accident." Without me even telling him, he somehow knew how low I'd gotten and what I'd considered a time or two to ease the pain.

My other friends and family had been there for me too, but

it was the man above me who had driven me to the beach and told me to heal there and say goodbye.

Hudson was right. He'd always protected me, even from myself. It wasn't often when I let my mask slip, when I showed exactly how vulnerable I was, but he was right. With him, I was safe.

As his thumb rubbed a circle on my cheek, I leaned into his palm and kissed his hand, holding it with my own.

"No condom. I want to be the only thing you feel tonight, Hudson."

He growled and claimed my mouth, and I fell under his spell again, not even noticing when he heaved me up the bed to the pillows. The way he moved was so smooth and intentional and effortless. He didn't rush, but he worked with such intensity that my head swam with an all-consuming sensation.

When he couldn't get his hand up the front of my dress the way he wanted, he roared again. I loved the idea of him wanting me so badly. But before I could help him, he slipped an arm under me and masterfully worked the zipper in reverse, and then in one deft motion, my little black dress was a little black pool of satin on the floor.

Holding his weight on one elbow, he studied me with his eyes and hands. His mouth open and his breathing labored, he tenderly traced my peaked nipples and my bare breasts, the line down my stomach, and the outline of my black lace underwear. He cataloged every square inch of me.

For a moment, while I had my wits, I watched him too. It was probably a silly thing to notice, but the way his face had gone slack and soft as he took me in made me feel beautiful, precious. Ever the explorer, Hudson pulled my panties to the side with his thumb and gazed at me bared to him for the first time. His blue eyes flared, and he licked his lips.

Instinctively, I spread my legs, but that wasn't enough for him and he draped my right leg over his hip as he shifted to his side and smoothed his long fingers back and forth over my lacy center.

It felt so damn good and all he was doing was touching me over the fabric, but just as I thought that, he stopped the pads of his fingertips over my clit and rubbed circles until all I saw was the backs of my eyelids.

Then, like he had at the restaurant earlier, his gravelly voice rumbled against my ear, "I don't know whether to be angry with myself for taking so long to do this…or to be thankful. Because I swear to fucking God, Alexis Lawson, if I would have known how fucking perfect you were this whole time, I wouldn't have got fuck all of anything else done."

A moan slipped out of my throat as he moved my panties aside again, but this time, he didn't just look.

He sucked air through his teeth and pressed his forehead against my temple as he slipped through my slick sex, dipping a finger inside.

"Fuck. I was a blind fool."

I couldn't speak, not coherently anyway and not while he worked my body into a firestorm. I tipped my head to face him, but before I could kiss him, he pulled his fingers from beneath my underwear and did something I'll never forget as long as I live. Eye to eye, he slipped the two fingers he'd been using on me into his mouth and moaned.

"Mmmm. All mine."

Was it wrong that I liked it? The idea of being his? The idea of him possessing my body? Even if it was all pillow talk, I was a sucker for it.

Knowing he was in control, I could just be. I could shut the noise in my mind off and trust him because this wasn't sex with a date or someone I kind of knew. It was sex with Hudson, and although he was stubborn and cocky, he'd never hurt me.

Still unable to speak with any semblance of language, I guided his face to mine to pour all my words into a kiss. I needed him to know how much I wanted him. How hungry I was for more. My other hand wandered to the bulge in his pants and stroked him over the fabric, and he twitched against my palm.

As if he could read my mind, in a flash he shucked his shoes and socks and pants and boxer br—*oh my God!*

While pulling my panties off, I froze and swallowed, getting a real, up-close glimpse of Hudson totally naked. I'd joked with him before about his size according to my teenage memories, but this man's anatomy was no longer a laughing matter.

On his knees beside me, he looked down at himself and then lifted his gaze to mine. It had to be written all over my face.

"Hey," he said and lifted my hand to his lips. "You trust me?"

Without hesitation, I nodded, but that didn't do anything to quell the anxiety forming in the pit of my stomach. What if we legit weren't compatible?

Flipping my wrist over, he pressed his mouth on the underside and then spoke against my skin as he worked his way up. "Wipe that worried look off your face, Lex. I know what I'm doing." The sexiest, most playfully wicked grin spread across his face. Confidently, he whispered from only a few inches away, "Relax. I'm going to make you come so hard and get you so wet, there won't be an issue when I push inside you, and I'm going to love every fucking second of it."

My heart all but stopped. How had a man like this been under my nose all this time?

One thing about Hudson: He never lied.

And as he explored me and turned me inside out, he praised my body aloud, telling me over and over, "You're so damn perfect."

With his lips and fingers at my sex for only God knew how long, he pulled not one...not two...but three of the most toe-curling orgasms out of me. With me languid in his arms, he positioned us on our sides, face-to-face, and with his masterful hand, he palmed my ass and then draped my leg over his hip. He shifted ever so slightly and straddled my other leg, making us one tangled mess of sweat and need.

My eyes were heavy with desire, and my whole body was consumed with a euphoria like I'd never experienced before.

Expertly, he slipped his hand between us and guided his tip to my slick and ready entrance.

"Hi." He smiled when I slowly blinked up at him.

"Hi," I mouthed, breathless.

His smile faded, and his blue eyes leveled me. "Let me make you mine."

"Please."

Then, gently, with more control than I'd ever dreamed this powerful man had, he sank into me inch by perfect inch.

We were pleasure and pain.

We were gentle and savage.

We were scratches and tenderness and bites and moans and screams, and before it was all done, I was Hudson Bradley's and he was gasping for air, with his eyes pinched shut, saying my name.

There was no going back.

CHAPTER
Sixteen

Hudson

The bright morning sun warmed my face, stealing me from sleep. With the sweet, well-used ache of my muscles, I could have slept for a million years. My eyes weren't even open, but a lazy smile pulled at my lips as erotic memories flooded my senses.

Though the cool, empty bed beside me left a lot to be desired.

I did a quick one-eyed geographical check, and yep, I was at Lex's house. A few of her red hairs still clung to the pillow beside me, serving as proof for my doubt-filled mind that it hadn't been some fever dream taunting me with what-ifs.

She'd been there.

We'd been there.

Together, moving together, sweat clinging to our bodies, our moans crashing like waves.

We'd fallen asleep, sated and wrapped in each other's arms.

And now, if I knew Lex, she was somewhere nearby, stuck in her head, flipping the fuck out.

I could fix that though. And after last night, there wasn't a job in the world I was looking forward to more.

I knifed out of bed and immediately froze when I found her sitting in one of the two chaise lounges that flanked her bay windows. Her hair was piled on the top of her head, and she was wearing nothing but my white undershirt. I took that as a good sign even as it made my cock twitch.

"Morning," I rumbled, running a hand through the top of my hair.

With her legs tucked tight underneath her, she stared at me, an oversized mug of coffee in her hands, a blank expression on her face. "Morning."

"Scale of one to ten, how bad is the shit happening in your head right now?"

Her lips thinned as she swayed her head from side to side. "Four."

I stood up, the sheet falling away.

And as her gaze raked down my naked body, lingering on my cock, she amended her statement. "Nine."

Chuckling, I padded over to her and took the coffee from her hands. Her emerald-green eyes tracked my every movement as I stole a sip before setting it aside. And then, with no warning or discussion, I shoved one arm under her legs and one behind her back and lifted her off the chair.

"Hudson!" she exclaimed, clinging to my neck.

I carried her back to the bed and placed her on her pillow before climbing over her to my side.

My side. Fuck, I liked the sound of that. One night and I wanted to claim it all—mainly and especially her.

Like a mummy, she lay stiff just the way I'd left her, so without touching her, I propped myself up on an elbow and asked, "What were you doing all the way over there?"

"I needed a little space," she told the ceiling.

I traced a finger over the curve of her jaw and used her chin to aim her gaze at me. "You still need that space?"

She stared in my eyes for a long second. "I don't know."

"Say the word and I'll get dressed and go. But I'd really fucking like it if you didn't. It's still me, Lex." I lifted her hand off her stomach and kissed her palm before resting it on my bare pec. "Same old Hudson I've always been, just wearing slightly less clothes."

She sucked in a sharp breath and then all at once her body sagged into the bed. "Don't go."

I grinned and teased the hem of her shirt. "Good answer. Now, take this off."

Her eyes narrowed. "Don't press your luck."

"What? It's only fair. If I'm naked, you're naked." I walked two fingers up her stomach, stopping at the swell of her breasts to give her a pointed look. "Talking is so much more fun naked."

Rolling her eyes, she moved my hand out from under her shirt. "It's fun because there wouldn't be any talking if we were both naked."

"Oh, so you did have a good time last night."

She rolled into me, tangling her legs with mine. "No, it was awful. All the rumors I'd heard about you in bed were true. This is the part where I let you down easy, tell you we can still be friends, and then urge you to consider joining the church and vowing a life of celibacy."

I laughed, deep and genuine, the way only Lex could induce. "Then this is the part where I remind you that I was subjected to the horror of witnessing your middle school rendition of *Little Orphan Annie* and you are not a good enough actress to have faked one, much less all five of the orgasms I gave you last night." Shamelessly, I slid my hand around to her backside, discovering she'd taken the time to put on panties, and then disregarded them altogether by sliding a hand underneath to palm her ass.

"Damn," she mumbled.

"Seriously, though. You okay today?"

"It was touch and go for a while, but your monster cock didn't break me."

"Good to hear. But not exactly what I was talking about." Sliding my free arm under her head, I used her ass to jostle her closer.

She didn't fight me. Instead, she rested her cheek on my chest, draped an arm across my stomach, and relaxed into my side. "I'm okay," she whispered. "A little weirded out. A little nervous about what happens next. But all in all, I'm surprisingly calm."

Kissing the top of her head, I mumbled into her hair, "Good. Let's try to keep it that way through our date tonight."

Her body tensed. "Our date?"

"Yep."

She tipped her head back, and I put my chin to my chest to catch her green gaze. "Are we dating now?"

"Well, no, not yet. But tonight we will be."

"Yeah, okay, now I'm freaking out."

Dipping low, I took her mouth in a gentle and all-too-brief kiss, unfortunately aware that I needed a toothbrush and shower stat. "Stop it. We've hung out at least twice a week for over fifteen years. I'm sure we can manage once more without the Earth falling out of orbit." I kissed her nose. Then her forehead. Then moved back to her lips one last time before rolling out from under her.

She flipped to her stomach and watched me as I collected my clothes off the floor. "So...like a date as friends?" Her voice was painfully hopeful.

Had I not known her as well as I did, it would have been insulting.

I tugged my pants on and got busy on the button-down, opting to let her keep my undershirt. "Lex, babe, please hear me when I say this. I will always be your friend, but after the last few days, there is nothing even remotely friendly about the things I want to do to you." Fully dressed, I walked over and curled a hand around the back of her neck.

Her breath caught as she peered up at me.

That was the moment I should have said something reassuring to her. I should have been Hud, her best friend, the man who would move Heaven and Earth to fix even her smallest problems.

But she had to know that, as far as I was concerned, this date wasn't a trial to see if we liked each other. I'd loved her for over half my life. It was never quite like this before, but we'd get there. It was going to set her on edge. And she'd spend all day cleaning her house and making up excuses of why she couldn't come, but in this case, that was far better than her sitting around, convincing herself that we were just friends and the past three days had been a total fluke.

And for those reasons, I shot her a wolfish grin and said, "I'll text you the details in a little while. I'm nothing if not a gentleman, Lex, but pack an overnight bag, because fair warning, I fuck on the first date."

Her eyes flashed wide and her sexy mouth fell open, but I simply planted a kiss on the top of her head and then left.

I'd catch hell for it throughout the day, but as I climbed into my truck and caught her peeking through the blinds, I had the most overwhelming feeling that someone had finally set the wheels of my life in motion.

I just had to make sure hers were moving too.

⌒

I made it all the way to lunch before Lex made her first attempt to back out on our date. Truthfully, I'd been really looking forward to her excuses all day. She was nothing if not creative.

Lex: Hello, this is Nurse Mary Jenkins. I regret to inform you that Alexis Lawson has lapsed into a coma and will be unable to attend your date this evening.

Me: Wow, Nurse Jenkins. That is unfortunate. If I may ask, how was she able to relay this message to you if she's in a coma?

Lex: She blinked in Morse Code.

Me: Oh so this coma only affects her ability to talk? Gotcha. In that case, please tell her to be ready for our date at six. She doesn't need to be able to talk for anything that I plan to do to her tonight.

Surprisingly, sex was the one time when she didn't have something to say.

Lex: I hate you.

Me: Lex, is that you? It's a miracle! But now that you're conscious again, go get the Chevelle. We're cruising in style tonight.

Lex: Uh…are you after me or my car?

Me: Technically, you in the back seat of your car.

I laughed my ass off as that text bubble bounced for fifteen minutes without the first response ever coming through. Over an hour later, she was at it again.

Lex: Can't make it tonight. Boop choked on a hair ball, so I'll need to take her to the vet.

Me: Okay, I'll come with. A little public indecency in the waiting room could be fun.

Another hour later...

Lex: False alarm. Beep is fine.

Me: I thought it was Boop who had a hair ball.

Lex: Don't act like you know my children! Anywho, I seem to have come down with a nasty virus. I'd hate to get you sick.

Me: It's okay. With Jack in school, I pound vitamin C like it's my second job. I'll bring over chicken soup and see if I can make you FEEL a little better.

Lex: Hello, Hudson, this is Nurse Jenkins again.

Me: See you at six!

The rest of the day followed the same pattern of shoddy excuses. I was almost to her house when the last one rolled in.

Lex: Fine. Brutal honesty. I didn't want to tell you this, but given what happened last night, I guess I'll need to tell you sooner or later. I have crabs. We should refrain from any further contact until we can get things under control.

I parked beside the Chevelle in her driveway and waited until I got to her front door to type out my reply.

Me: Nah. I'm all good. I have a set of clippers and an all new cartridge of razor blades I'll bring with me. Don't stress. A little time between your thighs and I'll have you fixed right up.

I was barely able to contain my laughter when I heard a loud, "Damn it!" from the other side of her door.

It was funny. I'd spent all day fucking around with Lex so I hadn't really had a chance to consider if I was nervous about all this or not. Sucking in a deep breath, I smoothed down the front of my gray V-neck tee and ran a quick check of my emotional inventory. There was a lot of excitement in there, maybe even a touch of some old-fashioned horniness, but no nerves to be found.

Switching the bouquet of colorful roses to my other hand, I rapped on her door and smiled. She was making this way more difficult than it needed to be. There was no reason why either of us needed to be nervous about—

I choked on a lungful of air when she opened the door.

And yep, there were the nerves.

For as many times as she had tried to get out of this date during the day, she had known good and damn well it would be happening.

Holy shit, she looked incredible. The short hem of her blue tank top dress flowed in the breeze, and the scooping neckline revealed just enough cleavage to make a man question his sanity. Chunky bracelets were stacked up her wrists, and her deep-red hair cascaded over her bare shoulder. And fuck me, she was wearing tan heels that were sexy enough to convert me from an ass man to a leg man.

She was usually a jeans-and-T-shirt kind of girl, and it wasn't a novelty to see Lex dressed up and ready for a night out, but this was so much fucking more.

"You look gorgeous," I said, the words coming out gravelly even to my own ears.

She tucked a rogue wave behind her ear and smiled. "I wasn't sure if I should dress up or not. This was kind of in the middle."

I didn't claim to be an expert on Lex's wardrobe, but when you spent as much time together as we did, you noticed things. And I'd never, not once, seen any of the laid-back, sex-kitten-at-a-sports-bar attire she was wearing now.

"Is that new?" I asked.

Her cheeks pinked. "I might have swung past the mall after I woke up from my coma today. You know, on my way to take Beep—"

"Boop," I corrected.

"Right. Boop to the vet."

Oh no, Alexis Lawson had not been sitting around all day, trying to get out of our date. She'd been out at the mall, setting fire to her debit card in order to find the perfect outfit for our date. And fuck me, she had succeeded in mouthwatering, hard-on-inducing, spectacular fashion.

I thrust the roses in her direction. "Here. Put these in some water and let's get out of here before I decide that I also fuck *before* the first date too."

She squeaked and snatched the roses.

I chuckled as she all but jogged to the kitchen and hastily shoved them into a vase. And yeah, while she was on the move, I did a little ogling of her ass too.

When she returned to the door, she nervously toyed with her long chandelier earring. "They're beautiful. Thank you. Let's go." She stood there staring at me, more than likely waiting for me to move out of the doorway, but I didn't budge.

"C'mere, Alexis," I rumbled.

She swallowed hard. "I am here."

Reaching out, I caught her hand and gave her a gentle tug. She stumbled into my chest and I looped my arms around her hips, bringing our bodies flush. She was stiff for a single breath, and then, with her exhale, she melted into me.

"I don't want you stressing about tonight," I said. "I've been messing with you all day about the things I want to do to you tonight and every single bit of it is the God's honest truth. Especially now that I've seen you in this fucking dress."

She smiled, and as ridiculous as it might have been, my whole world lit up.

"But if you don't feel comfortable, or if you want me to stop making jokes, then just say the word. I wouldn't be heartbroken if tonight ended in my bed, but that's not why I'm here. Okay?"

"Okay," she whispered, her hand sliding up my chest before hooking around my neck. "But, um, my overnight bag is already in the back of the Chevelle."

It was my turn to grin. "That's my girl."

Pressing up onto her toes, she kissed me soft and slow. It was too short and not nearly deep enough for my liking, but I'd take whatever scraps she was willing to throw me.

"I'm not stressing," she murmured against my mouth.

I slid a hand down to her ass. "Now that's what I like to hear."

We eventually made it off her porch. And after a brief argument about who was driving the Chevelle, which by the way I won after pointing out that if she drove there was a solid chance my fingers might make their way up her dress, things settled down. Come to find out, being on a date with your best friend wasn't weird at all. Short of holding her hand and stealing kisses at stoplights, there wasn't much difference in being on a date and just hanging out.

We stopped for dinner at the mom-and-pop barbeque restaurant outside of town. There was no pomp or pretense of her ordering a side salad and water or me pretending I knew

WHEN THE *Time* is *Right*

a damn thing about red wine when the waiter handed me the menu. No, on this date, she ordered the brisket mac and cheese and I got a burger with fries. She even giggled as I wiped sauce off her chin.

We'd been talking about going to the new drive-in since it had opened, but with it being over an hour away, we'd never made the time. Though, when tasked with deciding where to go for this date, a road trip with Lex was never a bad time. We ordered two brownies à la mode from the concession stand and ate them while The Rock tried to save all of humanity on the big screen.

We laughed more than we watched the movie.

Then we kissed more than we talked.

We danced under the stars during intermission with all the other couples to old 50s and 60s music that played through the speakers.

My fingers did eventually make their way under her dress. It was at that point that I realized what a horrible fucking idea taking her on a date over an hour away from home had been.

We quickly made the decision to skip out on the second film to get back as quickly as possible. She made up some weak, stammered excuse about being out too late and having to work the next day. But we both knew good and damn well there wasn't going to be much sleep had that night.

The ride back was painful, mainly because Lex took great pleasure in tracing the outline of my cock over my jeans, which left me hard for the majority of the trip. She dilly-dallied getting out of the car to tease me, so I ended up throwing her over my shoulder and carrying her inside myself. We didn't make it all the way to my bedroom before she was naked and I was inside her.

Eventually, we got to my bed though, and as she snuggled

into my chest, half asleep, all kinds of sweet and sated, she kissed my bare chest, mumbling, "I had fun tonight. Thank you, Hud."

I gave her a tight squeeze and smiled into the darkness. For fear of spooking her, I waited long after her body had sagged and her breathing had evened out before I replied, "Love you, Kid."

CHAPTER
Seventeen

Lex

Monday at work, I could hardly concentrate. So, when Maggie called to check in and see if things were moving smoothly while she and Shane were at home with their new baby boy, I suppose I sort of forgot I was on the phone with her, having a work conversation, until she shouted, "Earth to Alexis!"

"Oh my God. I'm sorry." I shook my head to scatter the memories of the past few days. Well, the past few *nights*, if I was being honest.

"Are you okay?" Maggie asked sincerely. "You sound distracted."

"Um, maybe because I am." I smiled, and since we were friends first and coworkers second, *and* I was dying to tell someone, anyone—well, not Cal or Vanessa, ew—and I couldn't really swoon to Lauren about her baby daddy, not that I ever would… That only left Hudson, and his heads—plural—were big enough already.

Maggie must have sensed that my tone had nothing to do with work. "Alexis Lawson, you ho. Did you sleep with the FedEx guy?"

"What? Hell no." Actually, since the night I'd set Hud up with Sandy and her fetus, I hadn't even given a second thought to the deliveryman. My full and undivided attention had been on my best friend.

"Then who? Did you meet someone? You have that *I've got a dirty secret* sound. So spill. I need some gossip, please."

"I haven't met anyone new, per se."

"Shut the front door! Are you finally sleeping with Hudson?" Her voice rose two octaves, and then she shouted, "Shane, get your old, wrinkled ass in here! I knew something big like this would happen while I was on maternity leave. Damn it."

"Shut up. You have a beautiful baby—"

"Yeah. Yeah. Baby's so cute. Yeah. Yeah. *How was it?*"

I chuckled. "Wait. What do you mean by finally?"

There was a pause, and then she said much calmer. "Oh, I don't know. When we worked at O'Malley's Pub and Grill I thought maybe you two would end up together. It was always so sweet when he'd sit in the parking lot to make sure you got in your car after we closed."

I'd forgotten all about that.

"And when we moved back, I was really happy to see that you two were still close, but I could never get up the nerve to ask why you weren't *together* together, even if he was all you talked about. I didn't want to be *that* friend."

"Oh." I was taken aback. How had she known there was something there before I had?

"So, good, huh?" She giggled. "Do you think he's serious?"

"Hudson? He's always serious. And yes, it was so damn good." I lowered my voice so no one else in the office could hear. "*So good* that I wonder if maybe he's not just using his construction company as a front for being a world-renowned gigolo."

Suddenly, Shane piped up. "Did you think I was as good as a gigolo our first time?"

She answered her husband in a tone I'd heard her use many

times with him: equal parts loving sincerity and bullshit. "Honey, you know how much I love you, but I had to damn near skywrite *Kiss Me* over the Golden Gate Bridge to even get you to touch me on our first date. A gigolo you were not, Shane."

"Oh, whatever, Peach. I'm going to go play with Greyson. At least he still thinks I'm a badass."

Maggie and I both laughed. Shane was definitely nothing like Hudson. They were complete opposites.

"Is it weird since you've been friends for so long?"

My boss had just put words out loud to one of my fears, but as I considered it, I realized maybe it wasn't as weird as I'd originally thought. Surprising maybe, but not weird.

Still, I wasn't naïve enough to think that, after the thrill wore off or after it got around to our friends and family and we were exposed to their questions and commentary, Hudson might eventually think we'd made a mistake. So I wasn't completely believing the fantasy, but he sure made it easy when we were alone.

"It is and it isn't. If that makes any sense at all."

"Trust me. I get it."

"I've never been more comfortable with a man, but who knows what's going to happen. Maybe we'll have a summer fling, and by fall, everything will cool off and go back to normal." Although, in the back of my mind, I knew we'd never be normal again.

"Just take it day by day, Lex. That's all you can do."

I huffed. "Easy for you to say. You didn't just spend the night with a caveman who packs women around on their shoulders."

"Oh, shit. Maybe we should meet up for lunch next week. I love Shane more than anything in this world, but I'm always down for some big, tough-guy stories. Anyway, I have to go. Call or email if you need us, and we'll check in again tomorrow. Maybe you'll have a juicy update for me."

"Ha! I doubt it, unless you want to hear Beep and Boop's review of their new kitty food I'm trying them on later. I'm expecting a nice, calm night."

Famous last words.

No sooner did I get home, out of my work clothes, the ladies fed, and onto my couch to queue up an old episode of *90 Day Fiancé* than I spied two blonds walking up to my front porch with their hands full. I glanced down at my tank top and my jersey shorts and then basically said to hell with it.

I unlocked the sliding chain lock I'd installed the day before and stood in the doorway as they strolled up.

"What are you two knuckleheads doing here?"

Jack ran ahead, leaping up the pair of steps. "We brought your favorites. Pizza and milkshakes, Lex."

I stood my ground against the boy with my hands on my hips. "Did you bring anything else?"

His face lit up. "Yeah, I got your twenty bucks too. When I told Grampa Simon how I lost the bet to you, he gave it to me. He said"—Jack cleared his throat and gave his famous impression of Lauren's nasally dad—"'It'll be a cold day in Hell when Hudson Bradley gets married. Now you know better, son.'"

I laughed.

Jack laughed.

Hudson did not. In fact, his blue eyes wouldn't even meet mine as he scanned the porch's wooden decking at his feet.

"Are we going to stand out here and let the pizza get cold while the shakes melt, or are we gonna go in and eat?"

"Eat!" Jack shouted and ran past me with the shake carrier.

I tilted my head as Hudson neared. "Can't stay away?"

The twinkle in his eyes came back as he explained, "I was going to let you rest tonight. This was all Jack's idea. He asked what I did all weekend, and I told him I spent it with you. He got mad and told me I wasn't allowed to have fun with you without him."

My Grinch-like heart stretched to new sizes on my threshold that humid evening. It was innocent and sweet to hear how Jack liked hanging out with me. So I squashed all the smartass replies I had and just beamed back at him.

He stared at my lips with an expression I was becoming quite familiar with. *Horny Hudson.* I wasn't falling for it though; there would be none of that while Jack was around.

"Cool it, big guy, and eighty-six those fuck-me eyes. Time. Out." I made the T in front of my chest.

He didn't abide by the time-out guidelines, because as we ate at the coffee table, after he'd changed the channel on *my* TV to the ball game, and as if it were no big deal at all, he put his hand on my leg. Right in front of Jack, who was half facing us, stuffing food down his throat, and half watching the game.

I silently mouthed, "Don't." Then pushed his wandering paw away. "Not now."

"Yes, now," he quietly argued.

I swatted again at his approaching limb. "I said no," I told him through my clenched teeth with a smile.

Jack returned his attention to us as the game went to a commercial, and he tore off another piece of pizza. "Where are Beep and Boop?"

"They ate a little while ago, so my guess is either on my bed or sunning in the boring, no-fun guest room." Seeing his disappointment, I took the last loud, slurping suck from the straw in my chocolate milkshake and added, "You watch the game, and I'll go find them." Popping up, happy for the excuse to naturally put space between me and Hudson when I returned, I went on a hunt for my furballs.

I should have known the second I hit my bedroom, Hudson would be right behind me.

"Get out of here," I shouted under my breath and pointed to the door.

"No," he said, mocking my earlier dismissal and stalking toward me. "What is wrong with you?"

"Wrong with me? What's wrong with you?" I crossed my arms over my chest and held my ground. "I might let you get away with perving on me when we're alone, but don't do it in front of Jack."

He rolled his eyes and kept coming at me with a face that would have pissed me off if it hadn't been so charming. "It was just my hand on your leg, Lex."

"So. What about your rules with Lauren and dating?"

He wrapped his arms around me, making me defenseless with mine tucked between us. He parted his legs wide off to his sides to get down on my level. "What about them?"

"Well, don't you need to talk to her?"

His forehead bunched together as if I'd said something totally insane. "Why? She's known you longer than I have. That's just for bringing new people into Jack's life. You knew him in utero for fuck's sake."

My shoulders slumped because I had been serious when I'd told him he was a good father and Lauren was lucky to have him. The very last thing I'd ever do is cause trouble for them or step on anyone's toes.

"Come on. Please. No touching or flirting or anything like that in front of Jack for now. It's important to me. Then when Lauren finally knows—and after he gets used to Mark—we'll tell him. Think about it. That is a lot of change for a kid all at once. Maybe we just wait a while down the line, if there is a down the line."

Ugh. I hated all this crap. I never knew what to say. And even if I thought I was saying the right thing, it still felt like it was coming out wrong.

"You're serious about this, aren't you?" His face softened and he scratched up and down my back. "Okay, you called time-out and Jack's out there, but I'm ready to talk more about this whenever you are. But for right now, we only have about another minute before we have a three-foot-tall one-man search party looking for us. So kiss me and I'll *try* to keep my hands to myself—around Jack."

I'd never say it out loud, but the brute who was holding me had a sweet side I couldn't resist.

"Fine."

The one word was barely off my lips before he planted his to mine, and for the next thirty seconds, we were back in the safety of the bubble we'd found over the weekend. A place where he moaned when my tongue slipped across his. A place where we didn't have to explain what was going on. A place where my heart led my brain.

All too quickly, it was over and he let me go. But first, he pressed his mouth to my ear and said, "I fucking needed that. I missed you all day."

Like it always did, his low voice in my ear made goose bumps sweep across my skin.

⌒

"That's so cool. Dad, have you seen this?" Jack asked, holding Boop beside me as I showed him the plans for the cat condo I was having built one way or another.

"Oh, I've seen it, all right." Hudson could be such a buzzkill, but I didn't let it bother me.

I knew my design was ludicrous, but either I could make dozens of cat houses, each with a separate feature, or I could treat my babies and have an all-in-one prototype.

How was I supposed to sell badass pet houses if I didn't even know if my cats liked them?

I clicked my mouse to the next 3-D rendition of a birdcage that had a cute retractable-blinds feature on it so bird owners wouldn't have to toss towels and sheets over their cages at night. It was pretty ingenious.

"Dad, we need a pet so Aunt Lex can make us one."

Hudson bent to the side and looked around at the graphic I was showing Jack. He didn't laugh or have anything Hud-like to say. Actually, he studied it for a long time before his blue eyes found mine. I wasn't sure what his expression meant. It wasn't like him not to take an easy shot at me and my wild ideas.

Finally, Hudson answered his son. "I'll talk to your mom about it."

"Yesssss!" Jack pumped his fist in the air. "Nolan has a Rottweiler named Satan. Okay, not really, that's just what he calls it. But still."

"Hey. Don't get your hopes up. If it's *your* dog, it'll have to go back and forth, and your mom is allergic to everything with tails. So don't go naming anything yet."

He turned to me as if he hadn't heard a damn thing his dad said. "I want our doghouse to have an automatic tennis ball launcher."

Damn, I loved that kid.

"That's not a bad idea, Jackie Boy."

The rest of the night was relatively normal—until it was time for them to go. Predictably, Jack didn't want a hug or a kiss, but that only opened a window for his father to barrel through.

With my arms at my sides on my front lawn as they were about to load up in the truck, Hudson swept me off my feet in a bear hug. Then he rained kisses, the way I used to do to Jack, all over my face and neck.

WHEN THE Time is Right

I howled as he assaulted me where Jack and the whole neighborhood could see. "Hud… *Ahhh*…Hudson, stop!" I squirmed, but he only held me tighter, swinging me side to side like a rag doll. "Put me down."

"See, Jack? Hugs and kisses with Lex isn't all that bad. You wanna tickle her sides while I've got her tied down?"

"Yeah," the little shit answered almost immediately.

Monsters. They were both monsters.

When I was almost dead from laughing so hard and only seconds from wetting my shorts, Hudson told his son, "Okay, you go get in the truck and I'll hold her back until you're all buckled in."

"Ha! She can't even get me back. This is great!" The heathen ran for the back door of Hudson's pickup. "Bye, Lex. Love you."

"You better," I called after him. Then I scowled at my captor. "Now, put me down."

He squinted and pouted his lips with phony sympathy. "What are you gonna do about it?"

I knew what he wanted. I was no fool. He'd sent Jack away for purely selfish reasons, not to save his child. "I'll kiss you if you put me down."

His hold relaxed and he almost dropped me on my ass, but he caught me a beat later. Before I could even yelp, his warm mouth covered mine and I tasted his smile on my lips.

Okay, so it sucked when they left.

And it sucked as I cleaned up my living room and took the pizza boxes and trash to the bin. It still sucked as I brushed my teeth and washed my face.

So, when I finally climbed into bed, I ended the suck and dialed his number.

"Hello," he answered.

"Hi." I slipped my bare leg over to the cool side of the bed.

"You okay?" Now that I knew what Hudson sounded like in person at my ear, phone calls would never be the same. But they were a close second.

"I'm fine. How are you?"

I bit my lip when he sighed.

"Well, last night about this time, I had my head between your legs. So, honestly, I've been better, but I'm good."

My face flushed hot as I remembered. "That was you?"

"Babe, if you need a reminder, you can drive over and I'll sneak you in my window."

My eyes squeezed shut, loving how playful and flirtatious he was being. It was almost like this side of him was just for me.

"Oh, I remember everything. My jaw is still randomly popping. I might have TMJ."

His boyish snicker sounded through the line and I could almost feel it vibrate against me. "Did you need something?"

"Not really. I just wanted to hear your voice."

Fuck. Why had I said that? It was way, way too honest.

"Really? Since you called… Since you wanted to hear my voice…" he teased in a low, baritone timbre. "I'm glad you called because I have a few things I want to talk to you about anyway."

I sat up and propped my pillow against the headboard. "Such as?"

"For starters, why didn't you tell me the pussy palace was part of a startup business?"

I'd been waiting for that, totally shocked that he hadn't asked me earlier when he'd been here.

"Because it isn't a startup yet. Not really. Right now, I just have some designs and concepts. And a woodworker who is possibly interested in partnering up, but I can't really move forward until I see one in action. I don't want to waste his time until I know what works and what doesn't. What the ladies like and what they piss on." And although I had someone who was willing to do the fabrication on basic models and customs as time allowed, I would be the one footing the bill for materials. So I wanted to make sure the coolest features were the best they could be.

"I'm not saying it isn't the strangest thing I've ever heard of, but, Lex, your designs are damn good. You should go for it. I can help."

And that was the second reason I'd kept my mouth shut. My parents were rich. I had good credit. My brother was always looking to diversify or whatever the fuck he called it with his investments. I had no lack of funding if I wanted to go that route, but I wanted to start small and let the business build itself. Like Hudson had done.

I wanted to make something that was my very own.

"Thank you, but really, I only need the cat condo right now."

He was quiet, and a yawn slipped out of me.

"I'm getting tired," I said. "Anything else you wanted to discuss?"

"Yeah, that new lock on your door. A sliding chain? Really, Lex. You do know I have bolt cutters that will get me inside in less than a minute, right?"

I grinned, already having thought of that after I'd put it up. "Yeah, I know."

"As long as you know. Now, you're yawning and need some sleep. I have firsthand knowledge that you haven't been getting much."

"That's your fault."

"Thank you. I'm proud of it. But you need to rest, because as soon as I find out what night Lauren is taking Jack for a few hours to meet Mark, I'm gonna come find you."

My heart raced. Not only was I getting D on the regular

again, but it was the real good D. And although he was massive in the cock department and I was still getting used to him, I loved every second of it.

"You know where I live. Good night." Then I hung up.

But on Wednesday, my mom told me that Jack was meeting Mark over at Lauren's parents' for dinner, so I might have taken a Lyft over to Hudson's place and let myself in with the key I'd had for years.

Naked on his bed, I heard him pull up, and my phone rang on his nightstand.

"You better be ready in twenty minutes because I'm on my way over."

I swallowed the squeal in my throat. "Twenty minutes? What's taking you so long?"

I heard him shuck his work boots off at the back door, and they thumped when they hit the walls. From down his hall, I could hear his belt jingling as he undressed on his way to where I was waiting.

"I had a dumpster fire today at work and was up to my ass in concrete. I'm taking a shower and then I'm taking you from behind." He waddled into his room with his pants around his ankles, not even dropping the call.

I smiled. "Why not both?"

He suddenly stopped, surprise slapping him in the face. Though it didn't take long for a devilish smirk to curl the corners of his mouth as he tossed his phone aside. Then, for the second time that week, he hauled me over his shoulder.

But I wasn't complaining. I rode a soapy Hudson on his shower bench until the water ran cold.

CHAPTER
Eighteen

Hudson

Thursday night, Lex met Jack and me at the ballfield. She brought a cooler full of Gatorade and orange slices and watched us play a pick-up game of flag football with Nolan and some of the other neighborhood kids until well past eight.

With nowhere to hide from Jack, she wouldn't let me touch her or kiss her good night. And let me just tell you that shit was for the birds. It made no sense.

Jack loved her.

I loved her.

She loved us both, even if she had stopped saying it to me directly since starting our relationship 2.0.

Damn it, things were moving between us. And I wanted them to keep moving—maybe even at a slightly faster pace. This included not pretending we didn't exist every other week when I had my son.

I understood her reasoning. Jack had a lot of changes on his horizon. But when he'd come home on Wednesday after meeting Mark, he hadn't seemed fazed in the least. It was probably easier that he'd never had Lauren and me together under one roof or had to suffer through a nasty divorce. He'd thought Mark was cool. Old—but cool. A sentiment we all shared. I'd spent a lot of time that night letting him stay up way past his bedtime to get a feel for how he was handling it all, but his only concern was to beg me for a pug he'd seen on TV.

Clearly, Lauren's being in a relationship wasn't going to be the emotional upheaval we'd all feared.

I could give it some time—a short time—before dropping the Lex bomb on him. The more I thought about it, the more confident I felt. Lex wasn't new. There was no awkward get-to-know-her stage where we'd all hold our breath, hoping he liked her. There would be no adjustment at all for him, except I'd be making pancakes for three instead of two on the weekends when I had him.

All technicalities and loopholes aside, I did owe it to Lauren, however, to talk to her about things before officially telling Jack. And hell, maybe if Lauren knew, Lex wouldn't have a soapbox to stand on anymore.

So, on Friday afternoon, as I walked Jack up to Lauren's front door, I had a few things we needed to discuss.

"Hey, buddy!" she cooed, squatting down to give him a hug. "Did you have a fun week with Dad?"

"We played football yesterday!"

Lauren's gaze immediately bounced to mine. The football debate was one we'd been having for a while. She thought he was too young and the sport was too dangerous. And I'd vowed to let it go until he was old enough to feel passionate about it.

"*Flag* football. Father/son pick-up game at the ballpark."

Momentarily appeased, she said, "Oh, that sounds fun."

"What's for dinner?" Jack asked.

"Actually, Mark and I were thinking we could go out. Maybe hit the arcade afterward?"

"Yes!" Jack exclaimed. "Sorry, Mom, I hate to embarrass your boyfriend, but Mark is going down on the basketball game."

"I'll be sure to warn him. Now, go warm up your arm. He'll be here in a few."

"Sweet." He turned and threw his arms around my waist. "Bye, Dad. Love you."

"Love you too, bud. I'll see you in a few days."

He nodded and then he was gone.

"See ya, Hud." Lauren gave me an arm squeeze and started to follow after him.

"Hey, can we talk for a second?"

She paused and eyed me curiously. "Sure, what's up?" Fully stepping out onto the front porch, she shut the door behind her.

"First, I'm thinking about getting Jack a dog. It'll live at my place, so I'm not really asking you to do anything. I just wanted to let you know."

"Oh, he'll love that. He's been driving me crazy about some pug he saw on TV."

"Same." I shoved a hand into my pocket and rocked onto my toes. "Another thing. Lex and I are together now. I know we agreed to talk about things before introducing someone to Jack, but that seems pretty useless in this case. Though, if you want the three of us, or I guess the four of us now with Mark involved, to sit down and talk things out, I'm game. Just let me know and we'll set something up."

"Okay," she said flatly.

"Okay?" I drawled. This was Lauren, so I hadn't expected her to freak out or anything. But it was pretty fucking big news for our little crew that Lex and I were a thing now. I'd at least expected her to be surprised. "You do realize I mean *together* to-gether. Like looking at a future *together* together. Having bedroom relations *together* together."

She tilted her head to the side. "I assumed sex was included in being *together* together, yes."

I narrowed my eyes; something wasn't right. "Did Lex already tell you about us?"

She laughed. "Um, no. It's been a long time since Alexis and I sat around swapping stories about boys. But come on, Hudson. We all kinda saw this coming. Actually, I owe Cal a hundred bucks. I thought it would take at least six months after the wedding before you two hooked up."

I planted my hands on my hips. "I'm sorry. What?"

She rolled her eyes. "You two have always been close. Honestly, with the way you reacted after Brenden died, I thought maybe you'd secretly been in love with her for a while."

I scoffed. "What do you mean the way I reacted? We were friends. We all rallied around her after that."

She shook her head. "Not like you though. It's been, like, six years and you still rarely leave her side. It doesn't matter what's happening or where you are—if Lex calls or texts, everything else shuts down for you. You hate Huey's. The beer is warm and the wings are shit. But every Thursday, you prance in there with a smile on your face because you know she'll always be there sitting across from you."

I lifted a finger in the air. "First of all, I don't *prance* anywhere. Secondly…" I trailed off.

Damn, she had a point.

"She's always made you happy, Hudson. And I did see a few sparks between you over dinner this weekend, so I'm even less surprised to hear this now. I wish you could have kept it in your pants until Cal owed me a hundred bucks. But it's a small price to pay to know you won't be going off the deep end in a few years with a midlife crisis, bringing home a nineteen-year-old model who doesn't speak English."

I chuckled and scratched the back of my head. "I'll still probably invest in hair plugs and a sports car."

She shrugged. "Now those I can deal with. But anyway… I don't really think there's much to discuss with Alexis. But maybe the next time the grandparents have Jack for a night, the four of us can go out to dinner. Mark really seemed to like you two."

"Yeah. Sure," I mumbled.

"Anything else?"

That was Lauren: direct and to the point. Not arguing or mincing words. She was happy for me.

"No, that about covers it."

"Okay. Let me know when you two decide to tell him. I'm dying to hear how the whole 'I'm dating your aunt' conversation goes down."

"Probably similar to the 'I'm dating a grampa' conversation you had with him."

"Hey!" She swatted at my arm and I narrowly avoided her wrath.

I laughed. "All right, well, I need to go kick Cal in the dick for being a nasty motherfucker who bet that his best friend would sleep with his sister. But you have a good weekend, Lauren."

She shot me a wink. "You too, Hud."

The real reason I had to go to Cal's house was I'd had a crew there all afternoon cleaning up and putting the finishing touches on the pool, and since they were doing this as a favor to me above and beyond their normal hours, I was paying them all in cash. I usually met them back at the office, but that would take time I did not care to spend driving around town when I could be spending it with Lex.

Giving Cal absolute hell for betting on me and Lex with Lauren was really just a bonus.

I must have looked like a punch-drunk fool grinning ear to ear the whole way to Cal's. It was strange. You'd think the minute I got her clothes off would have been the moment things with me and Lex finally felt real. Now that Lauren knew, it felt like we'd taken it to the next level. And holy shit if that wasn't a high I never wanted to come down from.

It'd been a while since I'd been smitten with a woman. And honestly, even on the brief occasion over the years that I'd met someone, it had been short lived. Probably because the woman I was supposed to be with had been sitting across the booth from me every Thursday night for years.

She was the image in my mind as I hopped out of my truck in front of Cal's, and as I rounded his house and saw the pool already half full, I couldn't wait to see her in a bikini, giving her brother shit for ever being against it.

"Get in there, you sonofabitch," Cal cursed as he kicked an inflatable unicorn into what appeared to be a new all-weather pool shed.

"You kiss your mother with that mouth?"

Over his shoulder, he glared at me. "I'll tell you something you can kiss with yours."

My hands went up in the air and I laughed at the poor guy. "I come in peace. I just wanted to see how the pool looked all finished up."

Finally, he finagled the cartoonish raft into place and shoved the door shut with his shoulder. Turning, he cocked a suspicious eye at me and stood with his hands on his hips.

"What?" I asked, prepared for the never-ending wrath of Dr. Calvin Lawson, MD.

"Why do you look like that?"

I scanned down the front of myself. Boots. Jeans. Black Hud Construction T-shirt. I didn't see anything strange. "Well, this is what a blue-collar man looks like, Cal. Not that you'd recognize it."

"No, jackass. That smirk." He took a seat on one of his new ultra-plush chaise lounges, and I plopped down into a club chair next to him while he examined me. "Let me guess. This will be fun. You plowed over a family of ducks on your way over. No. You conned your way out of jury duty. Nah. Oh, yes. You acquired a building permit to tear down a neighborhood park to build a strip club."

I sat idly by, and mildly entertained, as he defamed my moral fiber and character in a matter of seconds. "Can't a man just be happy to see his best friend enjoying the thoughtful, heartwarming wedding present he so generously gave him?"

"No." He scratched his chin, and then his eyebrow lifted and his lips curled upward. "You got pussy."

That was not what I'd gone there to talk about.

"So the pool should be filled by morning, huh? Vanessa have monogrammed invitations to your first soiree already in the mail?" I pointed at him, begging the universe for him to let it go and fight with me about his new-and-improved, luxurious backyard. "I better get one and a thank-you note."

"That's it, isn't it? You got laid." His tongue did that thing where it pressed against the inside of his cheek, making him look like a half cocky know-it all and half blowfish. "I'm right. Don't fight it, Hud. You can tell me. Did she cry? She threw up? Did she flee the country? Are you going with her? Joining Boners Without Borders?"

"Drop it," I warned.

"Come on. Tell me about your new slam piece."

There was no way he knew who he was talking about, but that didn't matter. Even thinking about someone calling Lex a slam piece had my hackles up.

"I said shut up, Cal. You do not want to talk about this."

"Is it painful having empty, meaningless sex with desperate women who only do it to take pity on you?"

I'd tried to stop him, but he'd never learn. "You know what?

I did get pussy. Woke up with three of 'em just last weekend, in fact."

His jaw fell slack, and his eyes bulged. "Liar."

"It's true. Beep. Boop. And your hot sister. Happy now? Come to think of it, I don't remember her complaining about feeling sick or talking about leaving the country when she was screaming my name."

"Ahhh!" he shouted, covering his ears. "Lalalalalalala. Stop. Make it stop."

Okay, maybe this was fun.

He fell over onto the thick cushion and stomped his sandal-clad feet on the cement. "I'm the one going to be sick now. That joke isn't funny. Leave Lex out of your twisted games."

I didn't reply and waited for him to settle down. After all, she was his little sister and I really wasn't trying to be a dick.

Also, he'd asked for it. Begged for it, really.

After he finished gagging, he sat up and asked seriously, "Okay, for real though, who is it? Anyone we know?"

"Dude, I told you. It's Lex."

It took a minute, and I gave him time to go through the motions of it sinking in. The gamut of expressions that morphed across his face was almost comical. As soon as I saw him take a deep breath and stretch his neck, I knew he was coming back around.

"Are you two like... Like, what are you... Hudson, what's going on? Are you two just..." He couldn't say it and I didn't blame him. Not often were we serious with one another, but when we needed to talk, we didn't mince words.

Putting him out of his misery, I told him what I'd want to hear if I were in his shoes. "It's not like that. I want to be with her."

He sat forward and propped his elbows on his long, hairy legs. "And does Lex want that?"

I nodded. "But you know her as well as I do. She's not one for talking about stuff." In my past, I hadn't been, either, but having a kid changed all that. There was no room for avoiding conversations just because they were sometimes uncomfortable. Still, I was giving her time to come to terms.

He wiped his palms over his face. "Who knows?"

"Just you and Lauren, so don't go telling your parents. Lex is probably going to kick my ass for telling you as it is." Now, I wanted to get down to the meat and potatoes so I could wrap this up and get to her place. I hadn't planned on spending the afternoon with Dr. Nosy. "Are you pissed?"

His brow bunched. "No. Actually—even though I was joking when I agreed to it—I think I won a hundred bucks from Lauren. Besides, why would I be pissed?"

"I don't know. You're my best friend and her brother. It's not going to be messed up for you to get used to?"

"Man, if you're for real about her, it shouldn't matter who gives a fuck, me included. Nobody loves Vanessa, but I don't give a shit. She may not be anyone's favorite except mine, but I love her and she loves me. So to hell with all of you." And that was why he'd been my best friend for almost two decades. Calvin was a damn good guy.

"Good. Thanks."

"No need to thank me. Thank *you*. Now, I don't have to worry about her getting with some prick anymore."

"So we're cool?"

"Baby, we're ice cold."

We both stood and he gestured like he was coming in for a hug and then waited for my approval. When I shrugged, he pulled me in and slapped me hard, really hard, on the back.

Then he said, "And just so we're clear, I never—*ever*—want to talk about you getting laid again. That part of our friendship is over now. We had a good run. Now, get the fuck out of here before I change my mind and drown you in this cursed money pit you built me."

"Deal." I knew when to press my luck and when to fold, and I had somewhere else I'd rather be anyway.

As I drove away from his house, I was feeling pretty damn high. I was two-and-oh on people taking the news well and couldn't wait until Lex and I were out in the open with everyone in our lives.

Maybe then it wouldn't feel like a dream.

Maybe then it would be without-a-doubt real.

CHAPTER
Nineteen

Lex

I missed a call from Lauren when I was in the shower, but she didn't leave a voicemail, so I decided I'd just call her back some other time. A different time when I wasn't scrubbing and buffing every square inch of my body for her son's father's benefit.

To say things were a bit complicated was an understatement. Hell, I was still letting my mind wrap around it.

I smiled at my reflection in the foggy mirror. We'd officially made it to Friday and Lauren would have Jack for the next few days.

And I'd have Hudson.

It wasn't until my phone buzzed again that I got suspicious—and then immediately livid.

Cal: Where should we send the thank-you card for the velvet painting of Beep and Boop you gave us for the wedding? Your house or your boyfriend Hudson's?

I threw my phone down onto the bed without even replying.

It had been a long time since my temper had shown its steaming head, but she was back in full force. And it escalated when I circled back to Lauren's call and could only assume Hudson had told her too.

Why was he trying to ruin this? I was barely coming to terms with the possibility that whatever we were doing wasn't just a fling or a deep-seated morbid curiosity.

As soon as I was dressed in jean shorts and a tank top, assuming we'd go to Huey's and play darts, I sat on the ramshackle Adirondack chair I'd stolen from the beach house on my porch, argued with myself, and waited for Hudson's blabbermouth to get there. I wasn't going to waste even one second before I let him have a piece of my mind.

Let me tell you, he had a lot of nerve pulling his stupid truck into my driveway while wearing a damn smile an acre wide. Before he was even out of his pickup, I was at the edge of my porch and my sanity.

"How dare you tell my family about us!"

"How dare I?" He seemed completely unfazed as he lifted a duffel bag out of his back seat. If he thought he was staying the night, he had another thing coming.

I was pissed.

He couldn't be bothered though and walked right up to me, planted a kiss on my temple—which I tried and failed to dodge—and then strolled his happy ass past me and into my house. *The nerve!*

I stomped in behind him as he made his way into my kitchen and pulled one of my beers from my refrigerator.

Who did he think he was?

"Ahhh, that's good," he said after tipping the cold brew back.

"Hudson. I am mad."

He nodded. "I can see that. It's cute."

"Cute?" I seethed. "*Cute?!* It's anything but cute. Why did you tell everyone?"

He leaned against the counter, cool as a pain-in-the-ass cucumber, and crossed his legs at the ankle. "That's easy. I didn't."

"Then can you explain why Lauren called and why Cal is sending me text messages calling you my boyfriend?"

"Oh, that. Yes. I told them. And, babe, I am your boyfriend."

I was going to lose my mind. Could he not hear how he was talking out of both sides of his mouth?

"Drop the babe shit. Which is it? You did or you didn't tell?"

So help me God if he didn't wipe that smirk off his face.

"I didn't tell everyone. I did tell Lauren and Cal." He squinted and pointed the top of his beer at me. "And a few of the guys at work."

"Why?"

"*Baaaabe*, that's what guys do on jobsites. I was kinda proud to finally have some good stories to contribute. Don't you want me to have fun at work?"

Ugh. Even worse. Now, I couldn't show my face around his shop. At least not for the next few decades.

"That's not what I meant, you meathead. Why did you tell Lauren and Cal? It was a secret."

"Wasn't my secret."

"Don't you think we should have talked about telling people first?"

Unrushed, he took another long drink. "That's a wild thought, isn't it? Us finally talking about this?"

I shot him a dirty glare.

Although he hadn't technically been rushing me into anything, he certainly was eager all of a sudden when it came to defining *us*.

I put my hands behind my head, frustrated. "Okay, talk. What did you tell them *this* is?" I motioned to the empty space between us.

Finally, he put the bottle down and crooked a finger for me to come closer.

It was a trap and I didn't budge.

"No way, Buster. I can't talk to you when you're that close. You're too distracting."

When I didn't go to him, he strutted over but didn't touch me. Looking down into my eyes, he answered calmly. "I told Lauren because she's the mother of my child, and this is going on in Jack's world, so she deserves to know. And I didn't exactly plan on telling your brother, but he could tell I'd *met* someone. When I got to his place, I was riding high because Lauren had taken it so well and I was probably gloating a little about the state of his pool being ahead of schedule. But he sensed something was different with me and wouldn't drop it. Lex, he's been my best friend since I was fourteen. He can tell when I'm getting laid. I had to say something. It's Bro Code."

"Yeah, but he's *my* bro. What about *my* code?"

"Your code is that I almost punched Cal in the face when he asked who my 'slam piece' was. The other part of your code is I restrained myself from burying my fist in your brother's face, but only barely. Come on, babe. He knew. What was I supposed to do?"

My face bunched, I was losing the battle with him and the war with myself. I couldn't truly be angry with him about Lauren, even if it would have been nice to be in the loop. And I had to admit Hudson had been peacocking around like King Dong all week. Even if I hadn't been the one he was sleeping with, after one look at him, I would have known too.

My armor began to chip away under the forceful hammer of my curiosity.

"So Lauren wasn't freaked out?"

Gauging the changing tide, he tilted his head back and stepped closer, perching his forearms on my shoulders. "Nope. I mean, I didn't give her any sordid details, but..." He winked at

WHEN THE *Time is Right*

me and my tummy did a one-eighty Hudson flirty flip. "Actually, she saw it coming and even put money on it."

Was the whole world in on this?

"That's messed up. Maggie saw it coming too."

The instant the words left my mouth, I knew it was over.

His face lit, and his jaw hung open. "You little, sexy, gossiping hypocrite. You didn't keep your mouth shut, either."

All right, I was busted. "Okay, truce. Lauren was a freebie. Cal and Maggie both called us out. We're even."

Outside, lightning popped off somewhere close and thunder rolled right behind it.

"Good. I'm glad that's over. Now, I just checked and you have plenty of beer for both of us already. Why don't you order some Chinese—I want extra egg rolls—and we'll hunker down here tonight. It's supposed to storm until morning." He wagged his eyebrows. "Maybe you'll let me get you drunk and take your panties off."

Damn him and his rough-and-tough art of seduction. I was weak, but apparently, I didn't care, because that stormy night, he made up a new way to eat Lo Mein.

Off my naked stomach.

By candlelight.

After the power went out, we ended up in a heap of sheets on my living room floor, laughing and talking like nothing had changed. It was comfortable and easy being with him like that, which was probably why I was finally ready to dip my toes into the big discussion pool.

I was using his thick, outstretched arm as a pillow while we lay on our backs and went for it.

"Hey, Hud?"

"Yeah, babe," he replied, absentmindedly kicking his foot to bat away a territorial Boop at the end of our sheet.

I turned my face toward his in the dim, flickering light. "Okay. Time in. This really doesn't feel strange to you? Like, us?"

He rolled to his side but didn't pull his arm away, and then he brushed the hair off my sweaty forehead. With no AC and after doing what we had, I wasn't even worried about how totally jacked I probably looked.

"No," he answered without hesitation. "It feels natural to me. Unexpected maybe, but right."

I couldn't disagree, especially in moments like that.

"Now what about you? What's going on in that beautiful head of yours?"

After three beers and three orgasms and three hours of uninterrupted Hudson time, I couldn't hold back anymore. "It all feels right, almost too right sometimes, but I'm scared too." *Damn it.* I hated how my voice cracked every time I let my guard down.

But if we had any shot at this at all, I had to start somewhere and get used to talking to him about stuff. There was a good chance, before everything was said and done, one or both of us would fuck this up on accident. But I knew one hundred percent that we'd never get anywhere if I didn't face the things I'd been hiding from both him and myself.

"I don't mean to scare you, Lex. I'm just being me."

"It's not that. I'm used to you by now, big guy."

"Then what is it?" He cleared his throat and pulled me closer with his free hand. "Are you afraid I can't make you happy? That you're not a priority to me? That I won't take care of you?"

What absolute Hudson things to say.

What sweet, protective, loyal, thick-and-thin Hudson things to say.

I swallowed and smiled up at him. "No. You do make me happy—when you're not driving me crazy. And I'd never dream of being your first priority—that's Jack's spot. And there's no one, not a single soul, on this great big Earth I trust to look out for me more than you. But..."

I was so damn afraid to say it.

His hand cupped my face and his thumb made tiny circles on my cheek. He whispered gently, "Just tell me. I'll fix it."

With a shaky exhale, I pushed on. "I'm so damn scared that I'm falling totally head-over-heels in love with you and then one day you'll just be gone. Without you, who's gonna fix me?"

He rolled on top of me, bracing himself on his elbows, and I cradled him between my bare legs. "I'm not going anywhere."

A different man had told me that once. He wasn't a liar, but he was gone all the same.

I didn't care anymore if I sounded desperate; I was. "What if you don't have a choice?"

Painful understanding flooded his features. "Oh, God. *No, Alexis.* Don't do that to yourself. Come here."

I clung to him, searching for the relief to my long-aching heart. "I won't survive it again. Please. Don't. Don't go."

"I swear. I won't. Never. Shhh. It's me and you now. Okay?" His blue eyes seemed to glow in the darkness, and thunder shook the walls.

I willed our words to be true by saying them back like a vow. "Okay. Me and you."

"That's right. There's my girl." He kissed my forehead, my nose, and my leaky eyes, repeating, "Never. I'm never gonna leave."

I started to believe him, and with every press of his lips against my fevered skin, I believed him more.

"I need you so much, Hudson." Not just for another night or another week. I needed him forever.

With a firm hand, he guided my gaze back to his. The intensity in his face nearly crippled me. "Alexis, don't you get it? I need you *more.*"

Hudson needed me? This strong man who had the world by the tail needed me?

Then I said four words I never in my wildest dreams imagined coming out of my mouth. "Make love to me." And I meant them.

I wanted Hudson in so many different ways, but there on the floor, in the middle of a summer thunderstorm, I wanted his body to convince my heart that it was finally safe.

Drawing my shaking hands above my head, he sank inside me with no resistance. The initial sensation of our connection caused both of us to moan into the other's open mouth. I arched my back and then pressed up against him, taking him deeper than he'd ever been before.

It still wasn't enough.

I wanted all of him. The stubborn man who had little to no regard for my personal space. The gentleman who tried to open car doors for me. The best friend who never let me walk through Hell alone, and the powerful lover who drove into me now as if Heaven were on our horizon.

But more than all that, I wanted to belong to him. Wanted him to own my pleasure and spend it at his leisure. Wanted him to confide in when the world rattled at my feet. Wanted to show him how much love there was left inside me and prove to him there was enough for him and his son. Wanted to be the woman who was blessed with making him happy.

That night, I worshipped him with my mouth and my hands and my body. I gave him everything I had and more. Sometime in the early hours of the morning, I shouted his name and he roared as we found paradise together.

Spent and panting, I collapsed onto his heaving chest.

"Oh my God." I kissed his neck and worked my hungry mouth up to his. "I could do this all night."

His boisterous chuckle shook us both. "I could too, but we have to be at your parents' house at ten."

My head jerked up and I lifted up onto my palms to stare down at him. "What the hell are you talking about?"

Guilty and handsome as ever, he grinned. "Don't kill me, but I sort of called your mom on my way over and told her I was coming over for breakfast because you were going to drop in on them with your new boyfriend."

So he *did* tell everyone. Maybe I was maturing, or maybe I was just tired and surrendered to him being a giant horse's ass, but I didn't argue. What was the point?

Then again, I was no saint, either, because once we'd made our way to my bed on shaky legs, wrapped in wrinkled sheets, I didn't even try to save him from the viscous onslaught of the kitty brigade.

My girls had my back.

CHAPTER
Twenty

Hudson

"Whatcha doing over there?" Lex asked as we drove to her parents' house. With the Chevelle back in its storage locker/tomb, we were in Lex's SUV, and in a very unprecedented deal from me, which might or might not have included her bending me to her will while her mouth was around my cock, she was behind the wheel.

I looked up from my phone. "Emailing the measurements for the cat condo to my custom cabinet guy."

Always cautious, she kept her eyes on the road, but her eyebrows shot up. "What for?"

"Because, after looking at your plans, I think the base would be easier to clean and safer in case of a cat emergency if we put the front on hinges. Easy access to the entire unit. I saw you have a few open areas marked off as storage space. It won't cost but a few dollars more to put a drawer there, and the hinged front would hide it until it's ready to be used."

She pulled into her parents' driveway and put the car into park. Turning in her seat, she gave me her full attention, an Alexis Lawson specialty smile splitting her face. "You're building the cat condo?"

"Well, it's only fair after you sold me the Chevelle."

"I didn't sell you the Chevelle!"

I shrugged smugly. "A bet's a bet, remember?"

She narrowed her eyes. "What the hell are you talking about? I didn't make a bet with you and I sure as hell didn't *lose* a bet with you."

"Yeah, you did. The dates. The rules were if I found you a man, I got the Chevelle. If you found me a woman, you got the cat condo." I flicked a finger between us. "Man. Woman. In a relationship. We both won."

She stared at me for so long that one of her eyes started twitching.

It wasn't long ago that I'd enjoyed nothing more than riling that crazy woman up to the point of insanity. She'd get mad. She'd insult me. I'd tease her. She'd go home and pout and I'd get to spend more time with her the next day when I apologized over lunch.

Fucking hell, Lauren and Cal were right; I'd had it bad for Lex for a while.

Now though, that eye twitching and then going home to pout meant I did not get to drag her back to my place after this lunch, I did not get to sit on the couch and bullshit with her until the early hours of the morning, I did not get to spend the night with her curled in my arms, and I did not get to wake up the next morning with her hair in a rat's nest and her sweet naked body curled around mine.

So, no. The eye twitch was no longer entertaining in the least.

Wrapping a hand around the back of her neck, I guided her across the center console, meeting her halfway for an all-too-brief kiss for fear of who might catch a glimpse of us through the windows. "Babe, relax. I'm giving you the cat condo because I'd be a shit boyfriend if I didn't. Also because I recently found out you have a whole plan for luxury pet home world domination in the works and you need this as a prototype. And mainly because I saw that spark in your eye when you were telling Jack about your ideas. You were so fucking excited, Lex. I remember that feeling. That hunger burning inside you to create something all of your own. I don't necessarily understand the need for a three-bedroom, two-bath pet home inside a three-bedroom, two-bath human home, but whatever. Not too long ago, people didn't understand how a confused kid framing houses to pay for his son's diapers would ever be able to build the largest construction company Atlanta has ever seen. But here I am. People don't need to understand, Lex, because one day, when this company of yours takes off and you're giggling yourself sick on the way to the bank, what they thought or assumed won't matter anymore. So, yeah, I'm building you a cat condo. And this morning, while you were in the shower, I took your phone and deposited a check into your account to buy the Chevelle."

"It was my grandfather's car!"

"I know. Which is why I'll sell it back to you anytime you want. Take the cash, Lex. Use it as seed money and do what you do best and flip the entire pet industry on their ass."

"I don't want your money."

"I know that too, because it's the exact same thing I told your dad when he tried to sink an investment into Hud Construction." I grinned. "I really want the car, Lex. It's purely selfish. No charity involved."

Her eye thankfully stopped twitching, but it still looked like she could squeak out a laser or two. "I'm changing the passcode on my phone."

"Of course. My birthday is easy to remember in case you're taking suggestions." I winked.

"You're the worst. You know that?"

WHEN THE *Time is Right*

"That's not what it sounded like last night." I swayed my head from side to side. "Or in the shower after that. Or when you came on my fingers this morning. Should I keep going?"

Her lips thinned, and she peeled my hand off the back of her neck. "Okay, this conversation is over. I'll *consider* selling you the Chevelle. But first, I have been bamboozled into introducing my annoying boyfriend to my parents. So keep your meaty paws to yourself."

She looked mad.

She sounded mad.

But she leaned over and kissed me one last time, inhaling reverently as she let it linger. "Thank you for believing in me."

I held her sparkling, green gaze as I vowed, "Always."

We got out and made our way up the Lawsons' grand horseshoe staircase. I would have knocked; Lex just walked right in.

"Mom!" she shouted. "Dad!"

"Oh my God, David!" Judy whisper-yelled. "They're here. They're here."

Not even kidding, I heard Judy clap.

That was not the usual fanfare when I arrived, so I assumed it was reserved for Lex's new *boyfriend*.

"In here, darling!" Judy sing-songed.

Lex shot me one last pleading stare, but my only reply was to sweep a hand out to let her lead the way.

We found her parents in the sunroom overlooking the backyard. Two chairs and a love seat surrounded the coffee table I'd made for them as an anniversary present when I was nineteen. I'd thought it was incredible back then, but it was far from being even acceptable now. Above and beyond that, it looked cheap and out of place in what could only be described as the Lawsons' mansion. But Judy had insisted on keeping it, even after I'd offered to make her something new and more elegant. That sitting area with the massive floor-to-ceiling windows was her favorite room in the house, and my chest warmed every time I saw my ugly, rickety table sitting smack-dab in the middle of it.

Judy was perched on the edge of one of the tan armchairs as if she were barely able to stay in her seat. David was beside her, a book in his hand, glasses he'd only recently started wearing poised on the tip of his nose.

He took them off and set the book aside, smiling as he looked up at us. "Well, look who it is, my favorite kids. Don't tell Cal I said that."

Judy's smile fell as she leaned from side to side, desperately trying to see behind us. "Um, aren't you missing someone?"

Lex looked up at me. "Nope, I think everyone's here."

"Oh, honey," Judy whispered, her entire body deflating. "Did you and the new guy already break up?"

"No. Actually, we're doing pretty well. You know, despite the fact that I think there is a solid chance he's a con man trying to steal Grampa's Chevelle, but he's good in bed, so I'll keep him for a while."

"Jesus," I muttered, bulging my eyes at her in a silent *What the fuck?*

She replied with a wicked grin that did not bode well for the rest of this conversation.

She wandered to the loveseat and sank down, and I had no choice but to follow her or face the firing squad alone.

"Plus, he's bossy and controlling. Kinda rude sometimes too. Don't worry though. He's hot, so it will all be worth it one day."

I gritted my teeth and pressed an elbow into her side.

David suddenly inched to the edge of his chair. "Wait a minute. Alexis, he doesn't sound like the man you need around."

"He's a good guy," I interjected.

Judy clutched her literal pearls.

David sliced a glare my way. "You met him and haven't taken care of the chump yet?"

I scowled at the beautiful and astronomically frustrating woman giggling beside me. "Well…"

"Oh, Daddy, relax. He only threatened to throw me into a snake-infested lake once. I'm trying to look on the bright side: He's loaded."

"Oh my God!" I boomed. "They were tadpoles and you were thirteen!"

The room fell silent as the proverbial record skipped to a stop.

A victorious grin grew on Lex's cheeks, and if I hadn't been worried about making things weird for Judy and David, I would have kissed it right off her gorgeous face.

"Mom, Dad, I'd like you to meet my boyfriend, Hudson Bradley." She reached down, took my hand, and intertwined our fingers before lifting them to her mouth to kiss my thumb.

I shook my head and brought our joined hands to my lips, muttering, "Couldn't make it easy on me, could you?"

"You stole my grandfather's car. It seemed only fair." She laughed and then we both turned our attention to her parents, who were staring at us with wide eyes and gaping mouths.

Right, okay. So maybe Lauren, Cal, and Maggie had been wrong and not everyone had assumed we would eventually end up together.

"Oh my God!" Judy cried, pressing a hand to her chest. "Wait, you mean you two are dating, right?"

I grinned over at Lex. "That's what it means."

"Oh my God," she repeated, shooting to her feet. "Oh my God, my kids are getting married!"

"Whoa, whoa, whoa!" Lex objected. "Slow your roll, Judy. We're dating. That's all."

Judy did not let the technicality ruin her moment. After trotting around the ugly coffee table like a prized pony, she leaned down and threw her arms around both of us, dragging us in for a group hug and chanting, "My kids are dating!"

I laughed and hugged her back, pretty excited about the ease in which this was playing out.

"Okay, okay," Lex said, peeling her mother's arms off us. "Stop saying that. It sounds like I'm hooking up with Cal."

Judy put her hands on her cheeks and stared at us adoringly. "This calls for champagne."

Lex rubbed her temples. "Make it two bottles. I have a mental image of me and Cal in my head now that I need to destroy ASAP."

"Help me carry the glasses." Judy grabbed her daughter's arm and all but dragged her from the room.

With the two of them gone, my attention wandered back to David. He was still sitting in his chair, his hands intertwined and his index fingers steepled over his lips, but the dark, ominous stare of a man who had just met her daughter's boyfriend was locked on me.

I swallowed hard. "I just want you to know that I would never—"

He lifted a hand to silence me. "It makes sense. You keep her grounded and she keeps you laughing and out of your head. I honestly don't know how I'd missed it all these years."

I inched to the edge of my seat and put my elbows on my knees. "Oh, no, David. This is *very* new. There was nothing to see over the years."

He nodded, but it was a complete contradiction of the words that came out of his mouth. "You can't do this, Hudson."

Lex was right behind her, already double-fisting it.

David held my stare as his wife passed us both a glass. And then his gaze shifted to his daughter as she sidled up beside me and wedged herself under my arm.

He couldn't hear her as she pressed up onto her toes and whispered, "They've never been this excited for me to get laid before."

But after I shot her a smile and kissed her forehead, our eyes met again, he gave us his blessing by way of a chin jerk.

I loved the entire crazy Lawson family, but I didn't need their approval. There was nothing that could keep me away from Lex. It was the world's longest fall, fifteen years in the making, but then again, fate didn't always happen overnight.

David stood up and we all surrounded that old coffee table, our glasses held out in front of us.

"To Hudson finally stealing my virginity," Lex toasted.

David and I both coughed, strategically avoiding eye contact with each other. Let's be honest, he might have been okay with our relationship, but having sex with his daughter was pushing the limits.

Judy frowned. "Oh, honey, we all know you haven't been a virgin in a long time. I thought I taught you better than to lie over champagne."

"Mom!" Lex feigned injury.

But I just smiled when David clicked his glass with mine and said, "I did mention the no-return policy on her, right?"

"What?"

"You can't do this. She won't be able to handle it if you two don't work out. She depends on you in ways we've never been able to get her to lean on us. Or even Cal for that matter. After Brenden…" He trailed off, shaking his head.

I suddenly rose to my feet, unable to stay seated any longer. "I was there, David. You don't have to remind me about when Brenden passed. But she's not the same woman she was back then. And besides, I'm not going anywhere. If this thing between us doesn't work out, we'll find a way to go back to being friends. But if you want the truth, I don't anticipate us not working out. I'm in this. When have you ever known me to half-ass something? *Especially* when it comes to her?"

"Relax, son. I didn't mean…" His face got soft. "I just worry about her. She's had a tough run. Her mother and I give her hell about finding a man and settling down. But as long as she's happy, we don't care if she gets a herd of cats and starts a one-man band."

I planted my hands on my hips and offered him a tight smile. "Gotta say, I'm not going to ever be okay with her getting a herd of cats, but I swear on my life I can make her happy."

He sighed and rubbed his hands together, a habit he'd had since he was laying down the law to me and Cal in high school. "I believe you, but you can't just date her. You have to be serious about this."

I held his dark stare, making promises with more than just my words. "I never would have touched her if I wasn't serious about this. I know who she is. I know what she's been through. And I know how I feel about her. There is no way I would be standing in front of you right now if I wasn't willing and ready to be the man she deserves."

"Champagne!" Judy announced, still trotting as she came back into the room.

CHAPTER
Twenty-One

Lex

"Lift with your legs, son," Hudson instructed his seven-year-old on the loading dock of his warehouse as we filled his truck bed with the fabricated pieces for my first experimental cat condo.

His cabinet guy had knocked it out of the park that week and I couldn't wait to see how it would all fit together. If it worked, I could potentially move forward with ordering materials since I had a healthy chunk of seed money. Hudson had also found me a perfect warehouse location and had set up a meeting for me to talk to the owner. Things were moving fast with Plush Pet Homes and *Fur...nishings*.

Plus, Lauren had had Jack that week, so Hudson and I had taken full advantage of the alone time. But it was the weekend again, and Jack was with his dad, which worked out great because I had the most fun when he was around. And we had two more hands for my project.

Bonus, Jack was just as excited about it as me.

No one had told him about us yet, but after talking like adults and compromising—painful and awkward as it had been—we'd come to the decision that if it came up or if the time felt right, we'd do it.

"I don't know what you mean, Dad. I'm lifting with my arms just like you."

Hudson stood and wiped the sweat from his face with the bottom inside of his shirt and my mouth watered. That washboard stomach. That V. Those arms and hands. I was a lucky woman.

"Yes, hold it with your arms, but when you bring it up, let your legs lift your load and your upper body at the same time. Let them do most of the work."

Life lessons, y'all.

Hudson was a great lifter. I knew firsthand, because just that morning when I'd been trying to get dressed before he went to pick up Jack, Hudson had lifted me in my closet *with ease*. Who knew closet sex was a thing? Another bonus, I found my floppy garden hat on the top shelf when I had a higher view of things.

Blushing, I heaved a bag of hardware into the back seat, and Hudson glanced at me, his eyes wide, like he knew we were about to have a long day. A laugh slipped out of my mouth and I covered it. I didn't want to offend my free helpers.

"Oh, I get it. That's what I was doing."

"Whatever. You're going to give me gray hair, bud."

Jack struggled, obviously not taking his father's advice, and chucked a board into the bed of the truck.

"Hey, easy. Those cost money," I chided.

Completely disregarding both of us and the job we were doing, he stated, "Lex, Dad has a booklet at home for the animal shelter. I think I'm wearing him down. Maybe the next one of these we build will be for my dog."

Little did he know, I'd gone with Hudson that week to check out a few that were up for adoption, but the workers told us they were getting a litter of pug mixes a few weeks later. So we'd held off.

"Oh, really. You don't say."

"I do say, and I'm going to name him Reuben." He giggled and added, "It's the pig on Minecraft."

"What about if it's a girl?"

WHEN THE *Time is Right*

His face bunched as if he were grossed out by the idea, and he looked at his dad for solidarity.

Hudson's brows shot up, and he placed a rather hefty bundle down.

Did I mention he was sweaty, how his muscles were glistening like a slicked-up Mr. Universe?

Anyway, Hudson waited for Jack to answer me because he'd pretty much decided on a female since he'd found out they were easier to potty train.

"We don't want a girl," Jack continued. "At the Bradley house, we're all men. No girls allowed."

I couldn't help but grimace.

"Is that so?" Hudson asked. "What if I got a girlfriend?"

Jack held his arms out, and I stacked a few small pieces into his hands as he grinned up at me. "She better like Aunt Lex. That's all I've gotta say."

Over his son's head, he shot me a look like *wanna do it now?* and I shook my head. I just wanted to live in that moment a little while. Jack didn't care if a woman came into their lives as long as she liked me. That boy had my heart.

Additionally, the beaming smile on Hudson's face did naughty things to me, and suddenly, I was disappointed that we'd also decided sleepovers when he had Jack were a no-no for the time being, whether Jack knew about us or not.

I wonder what my parents are doing for a few hours later.

"Anyone who doesn't like Lex doesn't know what they're missing," Hudson stated, giving his kid a high-five.

"Yeah," he agreed. "Lex is totally the bomb."

"You two sure do know how to make a girl feel special."

Jack's hand moved from high-five mode to stop right there. "Okay, but don't even think about kissing me. I already tried to give you that money three times."

I made a smoochie face at him but kept my mouth to myself. I was saving all my lip service for the older Bradley anyway.

Hudson did most of the assembly when we got back, but he took the time to teach Jack a few things about levels and making things perfectly square. It was adorable and truthfully miraculous how much patience Hudson had with his boy. He stayed calm when he didn't get it right and never lost his cool when there was a mistake. Then again, Jack was a pretty decent scribe and for the most part followed his dad's every word.

I was a gopher and the entertainment. I kept the tunes going and the lemonade flowing, all the while watching my dream come to life in my guest room.

I'd always felt confident that my plans were good. I'd aced drafting and CAD in school. Seeing everything click into place, I wondered how far I might have made it by now if I hadn't fallen apart and dropped out when Brenden died. Lately, I kicked myself every day for not having gone back.

Oh well. I wasn't going to let all those ugly thoughts put a cloud over cat palace day. Not when I had so much in one room to be thankful for.

"What do you guys want for dinner? My treat."

"Sushi," Jack suggested. "I want fried rice too."

I'd expected him to request pizza, but I welcomed the change.

After swinging by their house so Hudson could change his shirt, we walked into Gochisō.

"Booth or hibachi?" the hostess asked.

"Hibachi," Hudson answered at lightning speed.

Jack followed the young woman through the restaurant, and we trailed behind.

Leaning down into my ear, Hudson's gravelly voice buzzed against me. "Not touching you is killing me."

A smile slid around my face as we kept walking to the grill, where Jack was already drumming with his chopsticks.

"Don't be so dramatic, Hud. You were inside me just this morning," I replied under my breath so only he could hear.

He groaned and pulled out a chair for me between his and Jack's and nodded at his boy. "Good thing he'll be distracted through dinner."

With that, Hudson's hand was on my leg the second we sat down. Had my shorts been any looser fitting, he would have scandalized me by the time the onion volcano erupted.

Also, I fucking loved it, and I suppose I didn't really care about PDA after all, because the minute Jack excused himself to use the bathroom, I planted my lips on his father's. We were the only people at that grill in the back corner and the cook had already cleaned up and taken off.

"Why are you two kissing like that?"

Mid lip-lock—which we might have gotten a smidge carried away with—both sets of our eyes flew open, and slowly, our heads turned to face the music.

"Um," I said cleverly.

"Um," Hudson agreed. "Yeah, me and your...uh, Lex are in a..." His face was almost comical as he scrambled for words.

If my heart hadn't been racing like I'd been caught red-handed by the Feds while pulling cash from a till and not just an almost-eight-year-old who used the restroom at record speeds seeing us kiss—really kiss—for the first time, I would have laughed.

"You're boyfriend and girlfriend?" Jack asked.

Glancing back at each other and then him, we answered in sync. "Yep."

"But we're related. You're my aunt." He walked back to his seat, climbed on top of it onto his knees, and faced us, waiting for an explanation.

Since the subject was sensitive, and not one I'd really planned to have in a restaurant, I let Hudson lead.

"You know how Mom doesn't have any brothers and sisters?"

Confused, Jack answered, "Yeah."

"Well, neither do I. And you know how Grandma Pauline and Grampa Simon are neighbors with Grampa David and Mimi?"

Jack squinted, looking so much like his dad, still trying to sort it out. "Yeah."

"Okay, so when Mom and me and Lex and Cal were younger, we were all best best *best* friends. Then when you came along, you sort of made us all family because we all loved you so much."

My chest felt tight and full, adoring how he was explaining it, and it was all completely true.

"So they're not really related to you, just to me?" Jack clarified.

Hudson thought for a second. "Yeah, I guess if you want to think of it like that. But just so you understand, me and your aunt Lex are *not* related at all."

"Why didn't you just say something, then? I'm smart enough to get it, Dad. Besides, you guys already argue like Grampa and Mimi. So it actually makes more sense now anyway."

He twisted and popped the last piece of his California roll into his mouth, and I couldn't help but love both of them even more.

The table was quiet for a while and we all finished our dinner. It wasn't until they were dropping me off in my driveway when Jack spoke up again about what he'd been told.

"I've got it!" he announced. "Dad, you better catch Mom's leg thing at her wedding so you can marry Aunt Lex. Neither of you have been married yet, so it works."

I coughed, nearly swallowing my tongue.

Beside me, Hudson's laugh filled the cab of his truck. "You know what, that's not a bad idea. Do you think she'd say yes if I asked her?" He'd spoken to the miniature version of himself in the back, but his eyes were boring holes into mine.

"Probably. It's not like she hangs out with anyone else."

Not that it wasn't fun to toy with the idea of it happening somewhere off in the future, but it was a little too weird having the two of them arrange our marriage.

"Okay, that's enough about that. I'm full and wiped out. I'm going in. I'll talk to you guys tomorrow," I said and opened the door, hopping out before Hud could stop me.

I heard him say, "Bud, I'll be right back." Then he followed me to my door.

I punched in the code as fast as I could, but he was faster.

"Hey, don't you run away from me, Alexis Lawson."

I spun and put my back against the wooden frame. "I'm not."

"Good. Are you all right?"

My voice betrayed me, coming out about two octaves too high. "Yeah. Sure. I'm great." And I was, but I also needed to wrap my head around everything that had happened that day. It was a lot. "It's just been a long one. I need a hot bath and my bed."

He hummed. "You, a bath, and your bed sounds too good. Rain check?"

I was about to shove him away, but he caught my hand. I relented. "Deal. Now, go home before we do something on this porch that will emotionally scar your kid."

He smiled, licked his lips, and then tapped his finger on them, silently requesting a kiss. So I went up onto my toes, pressing a palm to his firm chest for more balance. And because I liked touching him, I paired my mouth with his.

Before it went past G-rated, I fell back onto my heels. "Now, get out of here, Buster." I spun to open my door and felt a swat across my ass.

"Don't tell me what to do. I was just leaving anyway."

Over my shoulder, I glared at him as I stepped inside, and he winked and then jogged back to his truck.

He shouted, "Call you later, babe!" as he climbed into the cab.

And call me later he did. By midweek, our nightly calls had turned into a bedtime ritual. Truthfully, if I couldn't have him there with me, talking to him before I fell asleep was the next best thing.

"So the decals worked?" he asked across the line.

"The first few I put on were a disaster, but thanks to YouTube and reading the instructions, the ones after that were a piece of cake." I'd had the idea of using adhesive vinyl to spruce up the aesthetics of Beep and Boop's new pad—which they were loving the shit out of. After ordering some on a whim, I had been pleasantly surprised when they'd arrived early. "I might consider buying my own printer now that I know the decals work and look good. Could be a cost-effective way to upsell and offer a way to get a custom unit that I can do myself in-house."

"God, it turns me on when you talk business."

I giggled. "You get turned on by a stiff breeze, big guy. It's not much of a challenge."

"Watch it," he warned. "I saw your eyes light up when I spanked your ass the other day. I might have to start tanning your hide when you get lippy."

"You like when I get lippy, and don't threaten me with a good time." I turned off the lamp beside my bed and rolled to my side. "I wish you were here."

He chuckled, which wasn't what I had been expecting. I was kind of hoping he'd say that he wished he were with me too.

"What's so funny about that?"

"Nothing. Sorry. I was just thinking about Craig."

I sat straight up. "Gross. Why?"

He laughed even harder, and although I was utterly disgusted, the sound was music to my ears.

"Tell me."

"It's not that big of a deal, really. But do you remember when he left you at Cal's reception?"

"Yeah. The flaky punk didn't even tell me goodbye."

"That might have been my fault. I overheard him with some chick, and they were talking shit about you ignoring him and dancing all night with Jack. So I asked him to leave."

My mouth hung open wide. "No, you didn't."

"Well, *asked* is a stretch. I sort of told him to get his ass out of my sight before I used his tie as a leash and led him out myself."

Yep. That was Hudson. Always looking out for me even when I had no clue.

"At least he was smart enough to go, I guess."

Hudson's voice got lower when he replied. "Nah, he wasn't smart. Craig was a damn fool. He was there with you but left with the other chick. Seems pretty dumb to me."

"Well, you left with me," I said, thinking back on how he and Jack had taken me home. "I guess that makes you smart."

"Maybe, but I wish I would have been smarter sooner. I could have brought you to the wedding too."

Sinking back into my cozy sheets, I sighed. "Don't beat yourself up. You can make it up to me by taking me to Cal and Vanessa's pool party Saturday. And if you're a real good boy, I'll do that thing you like with my mouth afterward. Good night, Hudson."

He groaned. "Uh. Saturday is so far away, babe. But I'll take you up on it. Good night."

We hung up and I slept all night with images of us doing a whole host of naughty things.

⁓

We parked my—correction, his—Chevelle in front of Cal's place and both took deep breaths.

"Are you ready for this?" he asked from the driver's seat.

Everyone had been too busy that week, not like they ever showed up at Huey's anymore anyway, so it was the first time we were going to be around the whole brood…as a couple.

"I'm not worried. Between your brute strength and my unmatched ability to browbeat verbally, I think we can handle them if they give us too much shit." I turned in the leather seat and grabbed his hand. "But really, I don't think they're going to say anything. It might be awkward at first seeing us together, how we are now, but they love us. We wouldn't be here with them instead of naked at one of our places if they didn't."

He kissed my fingers, and I wondered how I could have been so blind to how much I cared for him for so long. I suppose all things happen when they're supposed to, but I was grateful to be in the place we were. Somewhere with intimacy and fun. Together, sharing more than just our company. Literally hand in hand, walking up to a party with all our friends and family.

For the first time in years, I was deep-down-into-my-bones unbelievably happy.

"There they are," Cal said, bobbing in the crystal-clear water. "The looooovebirds."

"Shut up," I warned him, although I wasn't all that upset. However, he was my brother and it was my duty to be a pain in his ass when he was being an idiot. "Don't you need some

WHEN THE *Time* *is* *Right*

floaties, Cally? Maybe a nose plug? Then again, you're so full of shit you probably float better than most."

He flipped me off but didn't fight back.

"Lex, watch me!" Jack shouted from the diving board before launching himself off it. When he popped back up, kicking and paddling to the side, I clapped for him.

"Nice form, Jackie Boy. I give it a nine-point-five."

"Dad, you've gotta try that thing." He didn't even look back at us as he talked, making his way to the ladder again.

"Okay, I'll get in there in a few minutes. Be careful."

I spotted a few empty chairs at one of the umbrella-covered tables. It was the first time I'd been to Cal's since the pool had been installed, and by looking at all the new furniture and things they'd added, you'd never know that Cal had been opposed to the whole thing. That and the massive smile on my brother's face while he watched Jack go off the board again.

Hudson's warm hand landed at the small of my back and he leaned in. "I'd offer to put sunblock on for you, but I'd rather not walk around with my dick hard in front of everyone. I'm already making mental lists of power tools to think about, knowing you'll be at arm's reach and half naked all day."

I smiled up at him and gazed into his eyes, shining as blue as the water only feet away. "If you and your big dick are looking for sympathy, you've come to the wrong place."

His voice grew even lower, and I bit my lip as he replied, "Me and my big dick don't need any sympathy, babe. We just need you."

How did he do that? Make me forget everyone else was even there. Make me feel like the only person for miles.

Well, until my mom broke me out of my Hudson daze.

"Alexis, come show your dad pictures of the cat house. I've been telling him all about it."

Begrudgingly, I left Hudson, took my phone over to where all the old folks were gathered, including Mark, and told them all about it while averting my eyes from the sight of Hudson stripping down to his trunks and diving into the deep end like something straight out of a wet dream.

Other than my brother making a comment about us when we arrived, shockingly no one else seemed to be fazed by us. Of course, Hudson and I were on our best behavior and kept our hands and wandering eyes mostly to ourselves. Then again, he did swat my ass again as I got out of the pool in front of him when Vanessa called everyone out when the food was ready. And as we ate, Hudson squeezed my leg nothing short of ten times under the table.

When the meal was finished, my brother and his wife shared a glance that sent up red flags all over the place. Standing, he lifted his drink into the air.

"Thank you all for coming today to help us open the pool officially, and even though I fought Hudson every step of the way, we're really pumped to share more summer days like this with all of you. Our family. And in a few months, when our family grows, there will just be more of us to enjoy."

My gaze landed on Vanessa and I couldn't deny the pure joy on her face as Cal leaned over and placed a kiss on her head and a hand on her stomach.

"Does that mean..." My dad began to ask and then trailed off.

"We're expecting!" Vanessa exclaimed.

Suddenly, almost everyone rose to hug the couple and congratulate them.

"It's about time!" Jack shouted from his chair, obviously not understanding exactly how babies worked. "I'll finally have a cousin to play with."

WHEN THE *Time* is *Right*

I didn't even let my mind wander to the place it usually did around the subjects of marriage and babies. This was Cal and Vanessa's moment and I was happy for all of us. When the moms and dads had finally made their way back to their seats to look at the ultrasound pictures Vanessa snuck out from under her plate, I leaned over and threw an arm around Cal's neck.

"Congratulations, big brother," I said, giving him my biggest shit-eating grin. "If it's a girl, I expect her to be named Alexis."

"No," he replied.

"I like the name Hudson for a boy," the man at my other side suggested.

"No," he said again, shutting us both down. "I'm not sure I like you two teaming up. You're bad enough on your own."

Hudson pulled me out of my chair and propped me on his lap. "Well, get used to it." He smiled up at me and my heart melted when I saw how truly happy Hudson was.

I couldn't resist planting a kiss on him right there.

"David, all our babies are happy. Look," my mom said, fawning from down the table. "Lauren is getting married. We're getting another grandbaby. And Hudson is taking Lex off our hands."

I shot her a playful glare over Hudson's broad shoulder, loving when she showed her facetious side. "That'll be enough out of you, Judith."

But she was right. We were all getting what we really wanted.

The next month or so felt like a movie. The Plush Pet website was almost finished, and James, my business partner, was churning out overhead like crazy. Maggie and Shane were so supportive and helped me pro-bono with marketing and advertising. I'd even lined up a few trade shows for the fall and made some great headway with independent pet stores.

Hudson and I only grew closer, even if I hadn't believed that was possible. And for the most part, we followed the rules and slept at our own houses when Jack was around. But I'd be lying if I said I hadn't snuck in once or twice on the weekends when he was asleep.

Although none of it was as I'd planned, my life was turning into one I was proud of and at the very center of it all was love.

CHAPTER
Twenty-Two

Hudson

The Chevelle rumbled as we rolled into the parking lot of the storage unit facility.

"Why do we have to stop now?" Lex complained. "I'm starving and you promised me pizza. That was false advertising."

"Well, if *someone* had remembered to get the cover for *my* Chevelle like I've been asking for the last, oh, month, you'd be two slices in by now."

"It lives in your garage, Hudson. Trust me, I'm all about taking care of *my* Chevelle, but this seems like overkill, especially when I'm hangry and a damn car raincoat is standing between me and a supreme pizza."

"Then I suggest we hurry."

She let out a loud groan and swung the door open. I climbed out at the same time and met her at the trunk. Hangry as she was, when I puckered my lips, she lifted onto her toes and pressed a kiss to my mouth.

Being with Lex was nothing short of incredible. She'd been a fixture in my life since I was fifteen but the last few months were different—a different I couldn't get enough of.

Earlier that week, she'd gone with Jack and me to pick up the new puppy. After listening to over an hour of him groaning about getting a girl dog, she'd tickled him into submission.

Together, they'd named the poor pup Jesse. Lex had been sneaking into my place every night that week to endure the torture of three-a.m. puppy potty training with me while Jack slept right through the incessant whining—mine, not the dog. With Jack back at Lauren's, we'd decided to try to introduce Jesse to Beep and Boop for a few nights. Boop thoroughly traumatized Jesse, but much to our surprise, Beep was a nurturer. At least that's what Lex told me a million times as she followed them around the house while I sat on her couch and drank a beer.

Regardless of who was sleeping where and how many pets were swirling around beneath our feet, Lex and I were together every night. Finding her in my house when I got home from a long day's work was a high I was seriously getting used to.

"Cover for the Chevelle then pizza," I mumbled against her mouth. "But just a heads-up, we are getting it to go and you are eating it naked."

She smiled. "I didn't know I was allowed to eat with clothes on when we have the house to ourselves."

God, I loved her. Not that I'd told her yet. Well, I mean, I had, but never when she was conscious since we'd made things official. But fuck, if I didn't think it would freak her out, I'd be saying it every day until my lungs ran out of air.

Intertwining our fingers, I gave her a tug toward her storage unit.

Her phone rang and she dug it out of her pocket. "Oh, crap. This is Mom. She's already in panic mode planning Vanessa's baby shower. I told her we should probably wait until she's more than twelve seconds pregnant, but you know Mom when someone says the word baby." She extended a set of keys in my direction. "Go ahead and grab the cover. I'll talk her off the ledge of pink and blue streamers." She shooed me away and then answered the call, saying, "Talk to me, Judy."

Chuckling, I sifted through the keys on the ring and walked to her unit. I hadn't been there often, but I'd come with her to put the Chevelle away a time or two. She was pacing and informing her mother that a gender reveal was radically different than a sex party when I put the key into the lock. I twisted, but it didn't budge. I tried again to no avail. Leaning back, I checked the number on the unit. I could have sworn that she had 107. Though maybe it had been 106. I moved one to the left and tried the key in that lock. It popped open immediately.

With one arm, I shoved up the rolling door, and then time stopped.

Or maybe it didn't stop as much as it transported me into the past.

A knot formed in my stomach as I swung my gaze around the dust-covered trip down memory lane.

Dirt Bikes. Trophies. A motorcycle. Boxes stacked as high as the ceiling. Fishing poles lined the back, and there was an entire shelf of custom helmets.

I recognized each and every one of them because they'd all belonged to Brenden.

The wave of grief that rolled out of that storage unit was almost enough to knock me on my ass, and it completely stole my breath.

Why the hell did she still have this stuff? Brenden had been gone for over six years. Short of a few photo albums and a box of his stuff in the top of her closet, I'd had no idea she'd kept anything. As far as I had known, when Cal and I had moved her out of the house she and Brenden had shared, everything he'd owned was going to his parents.

So how the hell had she ended up with all of this?

And, worse, why did she still have it?

There had to be an explanation.

"Um, Lex," I called out, putting my chin to my shoulder to catch her gaze.

Her green eyes collided with mine, but as they drifted to the open door, her wide smile melted away. "I've got to go, Mom. I'll call you later." She quickly hung up.

Silently, I watched as she hurried my way, trying to force her mouth into a grin even as the color drained from her face.

"That's the wrong unit, silly." She grabbed the cord and gave it a tug, attempting to close the door, but I caught the top and propped it open. "Hudson, stop. The cover for the Chevelle is next door." Her voice shook and it rattled me to the core.

If there was an explanation and she wasn't hiding this, why did she seem so fucking nervous?

"What is this?" I asked.

"Nothing."

"Doesn't look like nothing, Lex. It looks like you're still holding on to half of Brenden's life locked up tight in a storage unit."

She became fascinated with her brown sandals. "Okay, so maybe it's a little bit of that too. But I'm not holding on to it. I just haven't gotten around to getting rid of it yet. It's not a big deal."

It felt like a big deal.

It felt like a betrayal.

And I had no right to feel that way. We both had a past. We'd each had front-row seats for those pasts.

But this was the present and she was mine. I beat back the flood of jealousy because it wasn't fair. Sure, it seemed like a really long time to still be procrastinating even for Lex, but I had no reason not to believe her.

"Okay, well, then let me help. I know a guy who owns a bike shop out in Roswell. I'm sure he'd take the bikes on consignment. Maybe the rest of it we can—"

"That's okay. Don't worry about it. I'll take care of it. Come on. Let's lock up and go get that pizza." She gave the door a hard yank, but with my hand still at the top, it didn't budge.

I narrowed my eyes at the side of her face. She wouldn't even look at me. "If it's not a big deal, then let me take care of it."

"I don't *need* you to take care of it." Another pull from her. Another block from me. "Obviously you do. It's been six years and it's still sitting here like you're expecting him to come bac—" I didn't get to finish before she exploded.

"I know how long it's been!" Tipping her head back, she finally lifted her gaze to mine, and it was the most confusing mixture of agony and anger I'd ever seen. Squaring her shoulders, she looked me right in the eye. "You do know it's completely possible for me to do something without you stepping in to fix it, right? I'm a big girl, Hudson. I don't need you swooping in to save the day every time I get so much as a fucking splinter."

My back shot straight as fears I'd never even considered I needed to have rained down over me like a storm of rusty razor blades. Brenden wasn't an issue for us. I'd been there every grueling day as she'd put her life back together. She fell into the darkness hard after we'd lost him, but eventually, she moved on. It was a process, but little by little, she started smiling again. They were all fake at first, a mask she used to hide her true devastation, but piece by piece, the real Alexis Lawson had come back to us.

Currently, I was unconditionally and irrevocably in love with that woman. But for some reason, she was still holding on to him.

I should have been gentle. Brenden was always—and understandably—going to be a sensitive subject for her.

I should have given us both a minute to calm down and talk about this without emotions heating our words.

For fuck's sake, I should have at least let her close the Goddamn door.

Instead, I swung an arm out, motioning to the belongings of a ghost. "This is not a fucking splinter! This is me sharing your heart with another man when I've always given you every single fiber of mine."

Her eyes flared wide and she immediately started shaking her head. "Hudson, no. That's *not* what this is."

I ignored the overwhelming need to rub the center of my chest and performed the herculean task of lowering my voice. "Then why do I feel like you've been hiding this? Why do I feel like this is a lie? Lex, you tell me everything. Just last month, you spent two hours talking to me about cat litter. And in six years, you never thought to tell me about this stuff? If you weren't strong enough, you know I would have helped you get rid of it."

Tears filled her eyes as she whispered, "I wasn't ready to get rid of it."

"And what about now?"

Her shoulders swayed as if the anxiety was trying to find a way out, and she frantically chewed on her bottom lip.

"Lex," I pressed.

"Time out," she breathed.

"No. No time-outs on this one. I need to know what I'm up against here. Are you ready to get rid of it now?"

She turned her gaze back to the storage unit and rocked her jaw from side to side.

As the seconds passed without her answer, a vise cranked down on my chest until I wasn't sure if I'd ever breathe again.

"Babe," I whispered, but even to my own ears, it was a plea.

"I don't know," she croaked.

Who knew three words could feel like a shot through the heart? The silence that followed was salt to the wound.

"Right," I mumbled, releasing the top of the door. Without

looking at her again, I extended the keys in her direction. "I'm gonna wait in the car."

She took the keys, her fingers brushing mine, lingering longer than necessary. "Hudson, please."

Gripping the back of my neck, I stared over the top of her head. "Please what, Lex? Go ahead. Ask me anything. You know I'll do it. But before you tell me this isn't a big deal again, I want you to really think about it and be sure. You know the man I am. You know there is nothing I wouldn't do for you. So if you can honestly stand there and say this is not something I should be worried about, then go ahead and ask me to let this go."

"Hudson," she begged.

I gave her back my gaze, staring deep into the emerald greens that in one way or another had owned me for the majority of my life, and repeated, "Ask me."

Her entire face crumbled, and a sob shook her shoulders, but she respected me enough not to lie.

I needed a few minutes to collect my thoughts, so I left her there to lock up. Not even climbing behind the wheel of the Chevelle soothed the bullet ricocheting inside me.

Truth be told, I wasn't mad at Lex. I was pissed all to hell and back at myself for not having seen this coming. I'd sat on that beach with her when we went to pick up Jack. She'd felt closer to him there. I'd been so damn wrapped up in suddenly having feelings for her that I'd let that little tidbit of information sail right over my head.

I should have been able to read her better.

I should have been there.

I should have asked her if she needed to talk.

She put on a good show, but I'd always known she hated when anyone worried about her. Especially me. She didn't want to be a burden, but I never could get through to her that loving someone—being there for them—wasn't a hardship.

It was just that, now, I was worried about *us*. No, strike that. I was worried about *me*. But this wasn't about how my heart felt. I hadn't gone into this relationship blind. She had baggage. For fuck's sake, I'd been holding that baggage for almost a decade. It wasn't fair to assume that it had all disappeared now that I was in love with her.

This was likely why people warned you not to date your friends. Though it wasn't like I'd had a choice in the matter, either. My heart had fallen in love with that crazy woman long before my head ever had.

I blew out a ragged breath when I saw her approaching in the rearview mirror.

She opened the passenger side door and shoved the cover for the Chevelle into the back seat before quietly sliding inside.

"Hey," I rasped as she clicked her seat belt.

Her red-rimmed eyes immediately jumped to mine, the tiniest flicker of hope dancing within them.

I caught her hand and gave it a reassuring squeeze. "Just tell me that's it. Tell me there are no more surprises. No more secrets. Tell me we got that out in the open and now we can figure out how to move forward."

She lifted our joined hands and gently rubbed my knuckles across her lips. "We need to go for a ride, Hudson."

Fuck.

CHAPTER
Twenty-Three

Lex

The old farmhouse looked tragic.

Frankly, the old farmhouse *was* tragic.

I hadn't been out there for years, and it seemed the lawn care company I'd been paying hadn't kept up the property like they'd assured me they had. And like it had since the accident, being there only caused me dread.

Dread for the memories we'd planned to make there.

Dread for memories I'd made alone instead.

Dread to face what had happened, and even more for admitting to myself I hadn't really faced anything at all.

Hudson cut the engine and let me have a moment. Or maybe he was taking one for himself. He'd been there. He knew what the place almost was and could've been. He had to be shocked at what we were sitting in front of.

Silently, his hand crossed the seat and linked with mine.

After Brenden died, all I saw was him out there. From the dirt track he'd cut into the pasture to the shop he'd dreamed of fixing up and making his full-time garage. The swing he'd bought me to sweeten the deal. Even, yes, the fucking pond. That farm had been so alive.

We had been so alive.

Now, it was just there.

Around the lump in my throat, I said, "I was so angry when he bought this place. He'd just started making the big money he'd always dreamed of, and I'd told him to save it. That, when I finished my last year of school, we could talk about buying a house." I laughed, but there was little humor in it and the space in the car started to disappear and feel tight. In true Lex Lawson fashion, I made an awkward joke while trying to get a grip on the flood of emotions claiming me. "But I suppose I have a type, because the men in my life rarely listen." My quip fell flat.

Tipping his head to the side, he didn't argue.

"He'd said, 'Lexie Girl, what good is all this money if I can't take care of you with it?' But I refused to move in for weeks. God, I was mad."

The air in the car got stuffier and close and hot, so I kissed his hand and opened the door, not knowing where exactly I was headed. I needed some breathing room.

Hudson followed behind me up the gravel driveway to the sidewalk that led to the front door. The house had a corner porch, which was odd-looking at first. Brenden had hated it. Then again, he'd bought the property mostly for the land, but I liked the quirky, big double door in the corner and at one time had planned to paint it black to match the shutters.

Under my feet, the deck boards creaked, and I made sure to watch my step as I went. I strolled to the right, tipped the now barren planter to the side, and found the hidden key we'd put there after I'd locked myself out.

Some things never changed. Even my heart felt like it was shredding all over again.

Hudson still didn't speak, but as I slipped the key into the lock, he put his hands on my shoulders and gave them a tender, supportive squeeze.

Inside, it was just as I'd left it.

My things had all been moved out, but a few random items remained, covered in dust cloths. His ugly hand-me-down recliner. The dining room table and chairs his parents had bought. Although I didn't walk down the hall, I was sure our bed was still there, collecting dust like everything else.

Tears streaked my face and my breath caught in my chest as the pain reignited.

Using the wall by the fireplace to hold me up, I saw a photo lying on its back.

"I don't even recognize these people, Hudson. It's like neither of them exist anymore."

"Lex, you're allowed to change."

I drew a lungful of musty air, knowing he was right, but that didn't erase my shame or the embarrassment I had for the mess I'd left behind. "I never wanted to be here after that day but didn't have the strength to let it go, either."

Hudson paced behind me as if in that place he was forbidden from touching me when it was all he wanted to do. "Why didn't this all go back to his parents when he passed? You were only twenty-two."

I never imagined it would come out. Especially not to him, like that, and not while we were standing right in the middle of it all.

"Oh, because we were stupid kids in love and one weekend…" My voice broke, but I had to get it out. Once and for all. "Brenden had a race in Jacksonville, and he convinced me we should go a few days early, so I took a long weekend off from school. When we got to the beach our first night, he told me he didn't want to wait anymore. That he wanted to marry me the next day." I laughed, remembering how excited and goofy he had been about all of it. "I can't totally blame him though. I didn't want a big wedding. I just wanted him. So the next morning, we went to a walk-in chapel and walked out husband and wife."

I put the picture back on the ledge and turned to face Hudson. He tried to cover it for my sake, but the surprise was painted all over his handsome face.

"He raced," I continued. "He won again. He got offered a spot on the circuit. One step closer to big time. So, knowing how busy he'd be, we came home and decided to keep what we'd done a secret until we knew we could plan a reception and set some dates. My parents would have killed me. His family didn't really care either way as long as he was happy. In fact, they'd given him their blessing to elope." I grinned, feeling the burning in my eyes, when I met Hudson's gaze. "But the very next weekend, he went fishing...and you know the rest."

I'd never told a soul, and saying it out loud felt like both a confession and a betrayal.

My shaky fingers covered my mouth, and Hudson's face was totally blank.

"I was married for eight days. With school, I didn't even have time to change my name. I made his mom and dad swear not to say anything. I gave them money from his insurance policy to pay for and make the arrangements, but I insisted they only refer to me as his fiancée in the paper and at the service." What a coward I had been, but I'd also been so damn lost. "It was just too much to deal with."

He stared at me as if I were a stranger, and that hurt too, but I deserved it.

I'd lied to everyone I knew. I'd pushed the truth aside because it was more than I could handle. More than I could bear. More than I could ask anyone to help me sort out.

No one could fix it—not even Hudson. Not even if I'd given him the chance to try.

The weight of it hadn't been that heavy in so long, and just like it had six years ago, it felt as if I were being crushed all over again. Yet somehow, this time, it was different too.

Before, it had been my sorrow dragging me under.

Now, it was my guilt.

Sharing what had happened didn't make it any better, and I wondered if I'd made another massive mistake. The thought of that made me weary and sick to my stomach.

"Hudson, I want to go home." I sobbed into my palms. "Please?"

I could feel my legs getting weak; the urge to crumble was overwhelming. But before I did, he swept his arm behind my knees and lifted me up into his embrace. I cried against his chest as he carried me out the door and down the driveway, and when he put me in the passenger seat, he pressed a kiss that seemed to last a day to my forehead. Then he rounded the car to drive me home.

The ride was a blur.

When the car pulled up into my drive instead of his, my instincts screamed that this was far worse than I ever could have expected. Yet I couldn't move. Couldn't get out, and neither did he.

"I can't compete with a ghost for your heart, Lex. Do you still love him?"

My neck twisted his direction and I saw his white knuckles gripping the wheel. "Hudson, you can't love a ghost. They never love you back."

He finally looked my way, his brow pinched. "That's not an answer, babe."

My lip trembled and I blew out a stream of air to ground myself. "I love *you.*"

"You can't have one foot in the future and one in the past."

"I don't want the past anymore."

"Then you have to let it go, but I can't help you, and it's going to slay me every single day. But I'll never be able to hold on to you if you're still holding on to him. And as your friend…"

Oh, God. He'd said it.

We were back to friends, and fire raged inside me, scorching the new path I'd been on with Hudson. My eyes screwed shut, and a silent sob racked my body.

"Listen to me. *Please*." He grabbed my shoulders and squared them with his. "I will always be here for you. There isn't a world that exists where I'm not gonna be around *for you*. Where we go one, we go all. Remember?" He swallowed, and the anguish in his voice was like a firing range. With each word, he peppered my soul with holes, and I prepared for the kill shot.

I readied myself for the *but*.

Then it came.

Trying to smile and failing, he continued, "But, Kid, I'm in love with you. Right now. You hear me? Right now, I'm so Goddamned in love with you I can hardly fucking breathe. I never knew feeling like this was possible, but I'd bet everything I have that I've loved you for years. Only something wasn't right and now I know what it is. I can't help you let him go. Not now. Not as your man. Because I have to know it's your choice. Even if everything in my body is screaming for me to take care of this—to take care of *you*. It's all I know. But not this time, babe. It has to be you. Otherwise, I'll never be sure you're really mine."

Then, lightning fast, his lips were on me. My mouth, my neck, my collarbone. He marked and devoured me as if it would be ages before he tasted me again—if ever.

And I let him because I was in love with him too.

His kiss told me everything would be okay, but then I learned you can't really read the meaning in a kiss. Sometimes two mouths connecting is just that.

Because when he broke it, breathless and unsatisfied, he said, "Time out."

CHAPTER
Twenty-Four

Hudson

The first week almost killed me.

I didn't want a time-out. I just didn't know what else to do.

I wanted to hover over her every day, keeping my fingers on the pulse of the situation.

I wanted to kiss her and swear to her that everything was going to be okay.

I wanted to fall asleep with her in my arms so she'd never forget I'd always have her back.

I wanted to sit on her couch and force her to talk about Brenden so I could really figure out how deep this truly ran.

I wanted to drag her to Huey's and share a pitcher of beer just because I needed something—anything—to feel normal again.

Most of all, I just wanted her back.

A week of space for two people who hadn't gone more than a few days without speaking in almost a decade felt like a lifetime. My nerves were shot, but I fell into a monotonous routine without her. It felt a lot like watching my favorite movie in black and white. I went to work, came home, ate dinner, played with Jesse, and then I'd lie in my bed, wishing I could rewind to the days when she'd been lying there with me.

By Friday, I had Jack back, so at least my life was in color again, but he asked about her incessantly. I had no idea what to tell him. We hadn't broken up exactly, but I had no fucking idea how long I was going to have to wait for her to come back. I'd told him she was busy with Plush Pets and *Fur...nishings*, and I wasn't too proud to admit that, when I'd taken him out to lunch on Saturday, I'd gone the long way so we could drive past her warehouse. Her car was there, so I guessed it wasn't a lie.

On Sunday afternoon, I was sitting on the back porch, watching Jack play with Jesse, when my phone dinged with an incoming message. I nearly fell out of my chair when I saw her name on the screen.

Lex: So just to be clear, are you giving me the silent treatment or am I giving you the silent treatment?

A tsunami of emotion crashed into me as I read it over and over again laughing like a maniac. It wasn't that funny, but I was so damn relieved that she'd finally reached out.

Me: How ya doing, Kid?

Lex: I've been better. Any chance you want to beat up my boyfriend for me? I miss him and it's been a week and he hasn't called me or anything.

My chest got tight, and I scrubbed a hand over my face. I could have ended it right there, and as my fingers flew over the keyboard, I almost did.

Come over, I typed only to delete it.

You want to meet me and Jack for dinner? I deleted that too.

WHEN THE *Time* is *Right*

Time in. I wanted to send that one the most. But what would it have fixed?

There was no future for us while she was still holding on to the past. If I knew Lex half as well as I thought I did, that week apart had been hell on her too. That text was the olive branch, one I would have given anything to be able to accept.

Nothing had changed though. It would have been all too easy to pretend. If I just loved her hard enough, in time, maybe she wouldn't have any room in her heart left to cling to his memory.

But even with as desperate as I was, that wasn't fair to either of us. I deserved a woman who loved me completely, and she deserved a man who would wait until the end of time for her to be ready. I'd be miserable until she came back, but inviting her over and essentially putting a Band-Aid on a bullet wound wouldn't solve anything.

Me: He's probably just trying to give you some space. But if you don't think it would be too much like him picking your splinters, I bet I could kick his ass until he agreed to text you more often.

Lex: That would be amazing. Try not to punch him in the dick though. I'd like for that to still be intact when I see him again.

I smiled, my whole damn face nearly splitting in half, and it had little to do with the thought of my dick and more about the seeing-her-again part. Yeah, okay, fine. My dick and seeing her again in the same thought didn't hurt, either.

Me: I miss you so fucking much.

Lex: I love you, Hud.

Me: I love you too, beautiful. Come back to me.

Lex: I'm trying. I swear, I'm trying.

I didn't reply that night, and neither did she. But I read that text more times in the following days than I would ever admit. It was my lifeline on the nights when doubts would invade my mind.

True to my word over the next few weeks, I checked in with her every couple of days.

Sometimes she'd reply and we'd talk for a while via text. Nothing about Brenden, the house, or the storage unit, but only regular day-to-day stuff.

Sometimes she would only reply with a single word, and as much as those days stressed me the fuck out, I hoped like hell those were the days she was making the most progress.

Either way, those interactions were nothing but a fix for an addict. I still craved her on every level.

The following week, she sent me a picture of the invoice for her very first cat condo sale.

I had flowers and a bottle of champagne delivered to her house. It stung, not being there to celebrate that with her. I wanted her to know how damn proud of her I was, but I didn't trust myself to take it over in person. If I saw her and held her in my arms, there was a solid chance I'd never be able to leave.

She replied a few hours later with a silly picture of her making a kissy face that I promptly saved, and had it not been for the picture of her tickling Jack on my home screen, I would have set it there too.

I was well aware how pitiful I was, but it was Lex. I had not one single fuck to give what anyone thought about how I was handling things.

WHEN THE *Time is Right*

Not that anyone noticed. As far as our friends and family were concerned, our relationship was still sailing on smooth waters. I would have known if Lex had told her parents or Cal that we were having trouble. Since no one had beaten down my door yet to demand answers, I didn't feel like it was my place to tell them, either. Besides, admitting that there was a problem would have seriously hindered my delusions that everything was going to work out if I just gave her time.

Lex: Houston, we have a problem.

It was a bright Sunday morning and Lauren had taken Jack for the night to meet Mark's kids. I was still sitting in bed, sipping a cup of coffee, and scrolling through the news when her text had come through. I replied immediately.

Me: What's up?

Lex: Judy has demanded our presence at brunch.

I set my coffee down and leaned back against the headboard. It had been three weeks since I'd seen her. And while brunch with her family was not in any way how I wanted our reunion to go, I was a desperate and weak man, willing to accept whatever scraps of Alexis Lawson I could get.

Me: Okay. So how do you feel about that?

Lex: I feel like she's going to commission a tornado to drop a house on me Wizard of Oz style if I don't show up. I can tell her you have to work if you want.

No, I didn't fucking want that. I wanted Lex to show up at

my damn door and tell me that she had her head and her heart aligned and we could finally be an us again. I wanted her waiting for me at home every afternoon and in my bed every night. I wanted a life with her, and while I had promised her I'd wait, I was getting really fucking impatient.

Me: Nah, I'm good for brunch. Jack's with Lauren though.

Lex: You do realize my parents think we're still together.

I gritted my teeth.

Me: You do realize that I think we're still together too, right? We're just working through some shit. That's all.

Lex: That's not what I meant, Hud. I'm just saying, my parents are going to want to see us together, together. Or we're going to have a lot of explaining to do. You know my family isn't known for their subtlety.

Me: Look, if you don't want me to go, say you don't want me to go. Your family. Your call.

The text bubbles bounced for entirely too long and I stared at them as if they held all the secrets of the universe.

Lex: I brought dessert to your house last night.

I sat straight up in bed. Since I'd had a ham sandwich for dinner, no dessert, and gone to bed alone, I knew how this story ended. But my heart still kicked up like maybe it had hopes I'd developed a case of amnesia.

WHEN THE *Time* is *Right*

Me: What?

Lex: Yep. I picked up a chocolate cake and a six-pack and came straight to your house. I parked out front, but I couldn't convince myself to knock on your door. I miss you so damn much, but I still have so much work to do on me. But just know, this is not an issue about whether I want you to come to brunch or not. I would give absolutely anything to see you again.

I swallowed hard, and my stomach sank. I hated knowing that she was struggling, but a part of me hoped like hell it meant she was on her way back to me. I wasn't sure how much more of this I could take.

Me: You should have knocked, babe. You ever find yourself within a ten-mile radius of my house again and you don't stop by, I'm gonna be pissed, okay?

Lex: Come to brunch, Hud. Please.

My fingers had already sent my answer before I had the chance to consider the hell I was getting myself into.

Me: Pick you up at ten.

She must have heard the Chevelle, because as soon as I put the car into park, she came walking out of her front door.

I'd been a mixed bag of emotions as I'd swirled around my house to get ready that day. But it wasn't until that moment that I realized what an astronomical mistake I'd made. Her hair flowed in the breeze as she walked down the steps wearing a little purple dress that pretty much guaranteed I'd be hard for at least half the day.

It only got worse when she smiled. My whole fucking body tried to pull a mutiny on my brain and break free of that car, but I forced myself to wait for her to climb inside.

She glided the tips of her fingers across the hood of the car, and I swear to God I felt them trail down my back.

"Hey," she chirped when she opened the door.

I had to clear my throat and covertly adjust my pants before I was able to reply. "Hey, Kid."

This was the part where, a few weeks ago, she would have leaned over and planted a hard kiss to my lips that would have no doubt become frenzied in a matter of seconds.

Instead, she gave me a stilted grin and toyed with her purse on her lap.

God, this was going to suck.

We made small talk on the way to her parents' house. She'd sold two more pet homes to friends and was preparing for a soft launch on her website.

I told her that was amazing and maybe soon she'd let Jack and me take her out to dinner to celebrate.

She got quiet the rest of the trip and I considered throwing myself from that moving car in order to keep from reaching over, taking her hand, and promising her that everything was going to be okay.

I sighed when I saw Cal's BMW parked in the driveway when we arrived. Convincing Judy and David that things were smooth sailing would be one thing, but convincing Cal was a completely different story. I'd been avoiding him for weeks for that very reason.

Lex and I got out at the same time, and we met at the front of the car.

Her green eyes sparkled in the morning sun. After three weeks of craving her touch, she was more beautiful than ever.

She extended a hand my way. "You ready?"

I sucked in a deep breath and slid my palm into hers. I wasn't even surprised when it felt like two puzzle pieces clicking together. "Ready as I'll ever be."

It was a lie. That brunch was quite possibly the most terrifying thing I had ever experienced. And not because anyone clued into things being strained between Lex and me. Oh, on the contrary. All of them—including Cal—bought it hook, line, and sinker.

Why?

Because Lex was fucking *good*.

She smiled on cue.

Laughed on cue.

Curled into my side like she hadn't spent the last three weeks anywhere else.

She held my hand, rested her hand on my thigh, and more than once mindlessly kissed the underside of my jaw mid conversation. She was so damn convincing; I swear I heard Judy and Vanessa sigh a few times.

At one point, while I was talking to David, she hooked her fingers through mine so sweet and natural that *I* forgot things were strained between the two of us.

Suddenly, the way she'd been able to hide a marriage, house, and storage unit from all of us for the last six years became a lot clearer. Unfortunately, with her hands all over me most of the day, the other thing that became blindingly clear was that I was done waiting for her to figure this shit out and ready to start my life with her again.

After we ate, everyone congregated on the back deck, so when Lex excused herself to use the restroom, I waited a few seconds before following after her.

The stars aligned for me when I heard her feet bypass the bathroom in the hall and head up the stairs to the one in her old bedroom. The door had just closed when I grabbed the handle and slipped inside after her.

"Uh, I'm kinda in here?" she snapped, standing in front of the sink, a face full of surprise—and tears.

My stomach twisted at the sight, but an unlikely smile tipped my lips. Oh, my beautiful girl wasn't immune to this little show she was putting on, either. I hated that she was hurting, but at least she was feeling again.

Her gaze followed the movement as I pointedly twisted the knob. The click of the lock was my only warning before I plowed forward, lifted her off her feet, and carried her until her back hit the wall.

Shock registered on her face, but I lost sight of it when my mouth roughly found her neck.

"Oh, God!" she cried out, threading her fingers into the back of my hair. She slanted her head to the side to allow me better access.

With all the finesse of a hurricane, I kissed and sucked my way up to her ear, rumbling, "Are you done yet?"

"Hudson," she moaned. "I'm trying."

I bit the sensitive flesh below her ear and then set her on her feet, but only so I could palm either side of her gorgeous face. "Try harder. Do you understand me?"

Her mouth hung open, and unable to stop myself, I pressed my lips to hers in an equally punishing and erotic union. Our mouths sealed and our tongues tangled with the brutal strength of passion. We were both panting when I came back up for air.

"Get out of the fucking past, Lex. You don't belong there." I released her face and slid my impatient hands down to her ass, using it for leverage as I ground into her. "Don't you get it? You belong with me. You have *always* belonged with me."

She kissed me again, the salt from her tears mingling on our taste buds. "I'm yours. I swear I am."

"Then show me. Let this shit go and come back to me. I am wasting away over here, babe. Do what you have to do, but please, just hurry the hell up." I rolled my hips, my thick cock pressing against her stomach.

"I am," she whimpered, her hands diving between us to the button on my jeans.

That was all the permission I needed. Shoving her dress up, I hooked a finger in her panties and tugged them to the side. When she finally freed my length, I lifted her off her feet and drove into her with a feral possession I'd never be able to control with her.

"Hudson," she moaned, her arms folding around my neck.

"Say you love me."

"I love you."

I raked my teeth over her bare shoulder. "Say this is it for you. Tell me this will be over soon. Then it will just be me and you forever."

"I promise."

I drove into her again, more determined with every thrust. "Soon, Lex. *Soon.*"

"Stop talking," she begged, her core tightening around my cock.

"Then say the fucking words I want to hear."

"I love you. I'm yours. Me and you forever. Soon. I swear to you. And everything else in between, Hud. Now, stop fucking talking. I'm about to come."

I was about to come too, but I still smiled. God, I'd missed that woman.

We were upstairs and relatively quiet, but I couldn't have cared less if the entire world had heard us. The weight lifted off my shoulders in that bathroom was monumental.

It wasn't an immediate fix. Lex still had a lot of work to do before we could jump back into things. And damn if that space I was going to have to continue to give her wasn't going to hurt even more now, but as we walked back down the stairs, hand in hand, the first real smile I'd felt in three fucking weeks pulling at my lips and her promises of soon still ringing in my ear, I had renewed hope that the end was near.

Little did I know that fate was just getting started.

CHAPTER
Twenty-Five
Lex

Three weeks. It took three weeks—and one big reminder in my childhood bathroom—that, yes, being emotionally ready was one thing, but actually doing something about it was another.

I was ready, and now, I had a plan of attack.

As the phone rang in my ear, I wondered if maybe they'd had it disconnected and the number belonged to someone else now. Just as I was about to hang up, I heard, "Hello."

"Mrs. Parker?"

"Yes," Brenden's mother, Lisa, answered.

"It's me. Alexis."

Over the line, I heard her draw an audible breath. I'd never purposefully quit talking to them or intentionally put distance between us, but after those first few months when I'd nearly slipped away from everyone, there were just some people I never found my way back to. That included the entire Parker family.

Waiting for her to say something—or possibly hang up—I scratched Beep's head at my kitchen table. Over the last three weeks, I'd made a list to tackle and it started with people. Hudson was right. I'd been hiding and that was no better than lying. Now that I was finished lying to myself, I figured it was time to come clean with everyone.

That's probably why admitting you have a problem to yourself and others is the first rung on a twelve-step ladder. It opens the door.

"Sweetie, is everything okay? How have you been?" It was impossible to ignore the quiver in her voice. "It's been so long."

"I know it has, and I'm sorry I fell out of touch."

"Oh, Lexie. We know all too well what you went through. We understood. All we did was remind you of Bren. Everyone heals differently and in their own time."

"Thanks for saying that, but the truth is, to move on, I just hid everything away instead of dealing with it." I huffed to myself, because for the longest time, it sort of had worked. "Only, now, I am ready to deal with things I couldn't before, and that's why I called."

"Okay. What can we do to help?"

I tucked a hair behind my ear and admitted, "I still have all of Brenden's things, but it's time for me to part with them. I have a storage unit where I've kept his belongings for years. So, before I sell anything, I want to know if you guys—or friends and family—need or want any of it."

It was the right thing to do.

"We'd love to come look. I'm not sure if Allen and I need any of it, and the girls both moved out to Colorado, close to where I'm from, for school and then stayed after graduation. Can you believe that? But we still see some of Bren's friends around every so often. I could ask around if they wanted anything special or something sentimental, you know?"

"That would be great. I'll be at Westside Storage off Gilmore on Saturday around noon. You can drop by then. There's also some of his stuff still at the house."

She gasped. "Alexis. Do you live out there?"

"No, but I still have it. I'm disappointed to say I let it go

WHEN THE *Time* *is* *Right*

pretty bad though." I straightened my back and found my resolve. This wasn't about me feeling guilty about it anymore. I was proud of myself for facing it. *For myself.* "But I'm taking care of it now. Hopefully, I can get it cleaned up and on the market sooner rather than later."

"Good for you. I can't believe you've been hanging on to all that."

What I'd told Hud was true, but I wasn't in love with Brenden anymore. But it had taken putting space between a life that wasn't ever going to happen in reality and my new life after him to accept it. Had I stayed where I was, drowning in my pain six years ago, I might not have made it to the other side. So, although the choices I'd made probably weren't right—probably were all-out freaking wrong—they'd led me to where I was.

A weak smile bent my lips.

I was in love with Hudson, and he deserved my whole heart. And every minute I spent taking care of and making plans for what was left of my past, I could feel myself getting closer to my future.

Our future.

"Yeah, it finally feels like the right time to let it all go. Plus, there's so much stuff that shouldn't go to waste. Brenden would lose his mind if he knew everything was collecting dust."

She laughed. "I'm sure he knows, but you're right. He'd be tickled knowing you're giving his things a second life. Honestly, knowing him, he'd have traded or sold most anything you've been holding on to by now anyway. That boy was always on the move. Always looking for the next best thing. Well, except when he found you."

She was so damn right. Why hadn't that ever occurred to me? He'd buy a bike and then the next thing I knew it would be gone, replaced with a bigger and better one.

I bit my lip and the flood of relief and peace about what I was prepared to do washed over me. Brenden wouldn't have given a shit about any of *my* stuff had the tables been reversed. He'd have only wanted me.

Again, she giggled, but this time, it was joyful, and it made me grin just hearing it.

"What's so funny?" I asked.

"I was just thinking about something he said right before you two left for Jacksonville. I'd asked him if he was sure he wanted to elope—really, I was trying to advocate for you. I didn't know if he was springing it all on you or if you'd talked about it. Most young women want a wedding, you know? He said there was no way in hell he could ever have a big wedding because he'd be too embarrassed that your groomsmen would be bigger than his."

I chuckled, remembering him telling me that too on the beach the night before we tied the knot. Brenden was larger than life, but only about an inch taller than I was. Hudson and Cal towered over him.

"He did spring it on me, but I was fine with it."

"Now forgive me for being nosy, but tell me about what's going on with you. Married? Kids?"

"Nope. None of that yet. But I do have a boyfriend, even if he put me on a time-out to take care of my shit."

"*Men,*" she snickered. "Well, I hope he treats you well and he doesn't keep you on restriction too long. But, honey, it's probably making him crazier than it is you. They can be such tough guys on the outside and big old babies on the inside. So listen, I'll talk to Allen and we'll stop in on Saturday to see ya."

And they did.

Surprisingly, it was good to hug Brenden's mom and dad. They even took one of his older bikes. Allen said it was one of his

WHEN THE *Time* *is* *Right*

firsts and he'd always wanted it. Other than that, all his fishing gear, and a few small items, they left me with the rest. His mom said whatever pictures and keepsakes I didn't want she'd take from the house to go through with the girls when they were back for the holidays.

I spent most of that week racking my brain about the place Hudson said would take stuff on consignment, so Sunday night it was the perfect excuse to send him a text.

Me: Hey, knucklehead.

Only about a minute passed before he replied.

Hudson: You rang.

Me: I need the name of that bike shop you mentioned that's close by. I can't remember.

Helpful as ever, he shot a link to my phone with all their contact info and directions to the shop in Roswell.

Me: Thanks.

Hudson: You doing okay, babe?

How could one silly nickname always give me so much hope?
And for the sake of talking the talk, I was done hiding things from him. Besides, he'd asked.

Me: I'm getting there. Still missing you like crazy.

My phone rang immediately.

"Hi," I said and curled into the pillow he used on the other side of the bed.

"I miss you too." There was something about the tone of his voice that was utterly comforting, and even if we weren't together like either of us wanted at the moment, hearing him made me feel so much better. "I had a conversation with a little birdie," he said.

"Oh, yeah? What did they say?"

"Told me you talked to your family about *everything*."

I knew it would get back to him quickly, but hell, I'd only been home from Mom and Dad's for a few hours. Cal had come alone since Vanessa was not feeling great, and even if it'd sucked and most of us had cried and I felt like I'd been through an emotional washing machine, it also felt freeing to have it all out there.

"Is your little birdie a geeky dude who wears dress pants on the weekends?"

"No, it was the geek's dad."

My father? David Lawson? I'd be reminding Daddio that loose lips sink ships the next time I saw him. On the other hand, I'd dropped a bomb on them, and they knew that Hudson had found out too. You could say I was on an honesty-is-the-best-policy journey as of late.

"Yeah, well, if all of you gossiping Gertrudes were planning some kind of intervention, you can shit-can it. I'm sort of kicking ass in the get-right-with-the-Lord department lately."

He chuckled and it made my skin tingle. "I'm proud of you, Lex."

I felt a sting in my eyes, but I wasn't having it. This was a good moment, and damn it, we deserved one.

"Yeah, yeah. I'm proud of me too. Whatever. So does this time-out include phone sex or what?" I had my doubts, but there was no harm in trying.

He sighed. "No. But that won't keep me from dreaming about being inside you all night. At least, it hasn't so far."

"Fine. If you're going to be stingy with your big cock, while you've got your rolodex open, do you have the contact information for a good gigolo on my side of town?"

"No. You still belong to me. So shut up and go to sleep."

I exhaled and pulled the pillow closer. "You're no fun. Good night, party pooper."

"I'm all the fun you'll ever need. Now keep showing the world who's boss. Eating Lo Mein off of Jesse's big fat belly just isn't the same as yours."

I laughed—really laughed—and it was a balm to my weary soul. If I'd needed another reminder of how much I loved him, I'd gotten it with one silly call. He was worth fighting for.

We both were.

"Good night, Lex," he said and hung up.

On Monday, being the model employee I was at Warren and Warren, I spent most of my workday answering emails for Plush Pet, printing out the handful of orders I'd received over the weekend, and taking a peek at the couple of custom order quote requests in my inbox. I'd work on them at home, but I was excited to dig into the new projects.

And I made a call to the guy in Roswell. He'd known Brenden, remembered him well, and wanted me to send photos of the stuff I had. He was thrilled to have the first shot at the whole collection and even said he'd be interested in buying all of them if the price was right.

That evening, after texting him photos of what was in the storage unit, he offered me twenty-five grand for all of it, explaining to me what every item was worth. Since he'd made the offer, as is and sight unseen except for my pictures, I told him it was a deal.

He would come later that week with a trailer and a few guys to haul them all away.

That left only one thing.

The house.

So, after having some landscapers out to clean up the yard and getting it inspected by a guy Shane had recommended, I found myself cleaning it top to bottom every night after work the whole next week. There'd only been a few minor things that needed to be fixed, and since I wasn't trying to make a ton of bank off of it, I was told the property was in fine condition to sell.

After all, we'd done a lot to it in the short time we'd lived there, and then it had gone untouched for years.

It was shocking how little I felt connected to the house after all the furniture had been donated and the Parkers had taken Brenden's personal things. It was empty and didn't feel like the same place I'd once lived.

It wasn't my home anymore, so it was time to say goodbye.

For real this time.

I was sitting on the freshly mopped wooden floor in the living room, leaning back on my arms, when the unfamiliar urge to talk to Brenden hit me.

"Hey, Bren. It's been a while, huh? I'm not really sure what to say, but leaving without saying anything doesn't feel right, either. God, we had big dreams for this place, and it's sad to see them go with it. But when you left, nothing felt right for a long time. This house. Your things. Our life. It just didn't belong to me without you."

I coughed and cleared the lump in my throat.

"You know how much I loved you, but you went on a journey where I couldn't follow, and it almost killed me, being left behind. And it's taken me a lot of years to find the right way to start moving again, but I'm ready now. So, if you're watching down

WHEN THE *Time is Right*

over me, I hope that makes you happy. Because, wherever you are up there, I pray the track is fast and the big fish are biting."

I pulled my lip through my teeth and pushed forward, wanting to get everything remaining in my heart for him out.

"Your mom and dad and sisters are okay, and so am I. And, Bren, I'm in love again and I want you to know that will never change how I loved you, but it's different with Hudson. Good different. He's a great guy. The best, and you knew that too. He's perfect for me—the me now—but I can't give him half of my heart and keep the other half frozen in time, where you're still here, out of guilt. Because you're not here."

I climbed to my feet and walked to the door.

"So this is where I finally say goodbye. And tell my Grampa, if you see him, not to be mad I lost his car. Hudson will take care of both of us."

After closing the wooden door and locking it up, I walked to the edge of the yard near the road and stuck the for-sale sign in the dirt. As I drove away, I looked out over the pasture where he used to spend hours doing laps and waved goodbye to my past one last time.

By the time I got home and showered, I felt a new sense of accomplishment. All the sadness and finality from earlier eased, and the weight of how much that baggage had been was once and for all off my shoulders.

I'd done it. On my own. On my terms.

Then I wondered how long I should wait before I called Hudson or questioned if I should just go to his house instead. I missed him, and the urge to tell him what I'd been able to do in the last few weeks made me antsy.

I put lotion on, slipped into a silky bra and panties set, and then put on a cute romper that tied on my shoulders and would make him crazy when he tried to get into it. I let my hair air dry into waves and left it down, and then I threw on a coat of mascara and some lip gloss. Giving myself one last glance in the mirror, I smiled.

"It's time to get my man back."

I threw my purse over my shoulder, checked the cats' food and water, and then headed to my door. But just as I opened it, I startled, finding him standing on the other side.

I gave him the biggest grin I had, hoping he'd know without me having to say it, that *soon* was over and there was nothing in our way now.

"Fancy meeting you here. I was just headed to your house."

He ran his fingers through his hair and darted his gaze around as he shifted his weight from one foot to the other.

Something was off.

"Hudson, are you okay?"

He huffed and stepped up to me. "We need to talk."

We did need to talk, and I had a lot to say. It was evident that he was at the end of his rope with this time-out, and my news was clearly coming just in time before he lost his patience.

"Okay. Let's go in." I reached out for his hand, but he breezed by me into the living room and paced in the center of the floor.

I hadn't really prepared a speech or anything. I sort of just guessed I'd tell him everything conversationally, over dinner or as he puzzled his way into my outfit, and then that would be it. But the way he was acting made me want to rush to get it out. So I grabbed his hands, making him stop the frantic back-and-forth.

Before I could get a single word out, he said, "She can't do this. I won't let her."

I wasn't the she he was referring to, and that only left one other person. "What did Lauren do?"

"Lex, I didn't know where else to go. I know things are weird with us right now, but I need a friend. You've gotta help me figure this out." He shook my hands away and balled his fists at his sides.

"Hey, calm down. Whatever it is, we'll figure it out. Tell me what's going on."

Hudson was tough and broody, but the times when I'd seen him genuinely furious, seething angry, had been few and far between. But knowing he was so upset, I sat on the couch to give him space.

"She's taking my son." He threw his arms over his head and turned on his heel to face me. "To Portland. Oregon. It might as well be another fucking country."

"What? For, like, a vacation?"

"To live!" he roared.

My stomach sank, but it still didn't make sense. "She can't do that."

"That's what I said. But she sure as hell thinks she can. She and Mark are moving. Mark is already out there house hunting. Something about he got a big job offer and blah blah fucking blah. I couldn't hear the rest. The only thing I give a shit about is the fact that my kid, my only flesh and blood, is leaving."

He was spiraling. Losing his mind. And I couldn't fucking blame him. The thought that I wouldn't get to see Jack on a regular basis broke my heart, but it would all-out kill Hudson. That boy was his world. Furthermore, Jack thought his father had hung the moon. And trust me, if Jack asked him to do just that, Hudson would find a way to make it happen.

How could she do this to them? I'd known her nearly all my life, but this was the most selfish thing I'd ever heard.

My mind raced; there had to be a way out of this. "Don't the two of you have a custody agreement or something? Surely a cross-country move had to have been covered?"

He suddenly stopped and stared at me. "Yeah. For me. I can't leave a sixty-mile radius. But her dad's attorney drew up that paperwork a million years ago. It says dick all about *her* moving. She was all too ready to throw that shit in my face tonight too."

Oh, fuck. Oh. Fuck. That was not good. The Raffertys were good people, but, it wouldn't have surprised me in the least if her dad had made that agreement as favorable to Lauren, his twenty-two-year-old and unmarried daughter, as possible.

"There's got to be a way to fight that, Hud."

"Oh, there is, but we're talking months before anything is done. And at what cost? Do I really want to be the man who keeps his son from his mother? I am beyond fucking livid with Lauren right now, but Jack didn't sign up for this. I didn't spend almost eight years shielding him from the same instability I'd had growing up just to dump it all in his lap now. But I'm not giving up my son. It's too much, Lex." He finally sat down beside me, and when his eyes met mine, the turmoil swirling in his baby blues cinched my chest.

I scooted closer and wrapped my arm around his back the same way he'd done with me hundreds of times over the years.

Then, lost and desperate, he asked, "What am I going to do?"

There was only one option. One I hated to give him.

He loved me and I belonged to him, but this was bigger than either one of us. It was going to destroy me, but without a shadow of a doubt, Hudson would have fixed the entire world for me, even at the cost of ripping out his own heart.

I slipped on my everything-is-okay face, beamed at the only man alive I'd ever put before myself, and then fell on my sword for him.

He searched my face, likely taken aback by my calmness, as I said, "You have to move to Portland, Hud."

CHAPTER
Twenty-Six

Hudson

I blinked at her for several seconds. No fucking way I had heard her correctly.

Portland? Was she seriously telling me to move to fucking Portland?

Though moving did solve my problems. I'd been wanting to expand the company, and while I knew dick about Portland, construction wasn't a regional career. I could do it anywhere. Plus, if it meant I got my son more than once every few months and two weeks during the summer without having to wage legal war with Lauren, I'd do any-fucking-thing.

Well, almost anything.

I stared at her, an eerie ease to her smile, and announced, "Then you're moving to Portland with me."

Her lips twisted to the side. "I can't move to Portland."

"Why not?"

"Uhhhh, because I have a house, and a business, and family, and quite honestly, it rains too much for me to ever live in Oregon with this hair."

I shot her a scowl. "I'm not fucking around, Lex. Come with me. We can put both of our houses on the market, pool the money, and find a nice place together."

"Oh, wow, how very economically romantic of you."

"I'm not trying to be romantic. I'm trying to keep you!" I boomed, once again lurching to my feet.

She opened her mouth and shut it several times. It wasn't often Lex was silent, so I took the moment to pounce.

"Look, I know you're still working through some things, but no matter when or how it happens, you and Jack are my endgame." I thrust a hand through my hair. So many different balls were in the air all at once that my mind was struggling to keep up. "I've had less than an hour to process all of this, and you're right. Moving isn't the worst idea. But if I'm gonna pick up my whole fucking life and move across the country, you better believe I'm taking my *entire* life with me. And, babe, you are at the very top of that list."

Blankly, she peered up at me from the couch, so utterly unfazed while I was in the middle of a nervous breakdown that it was impossible to get a read on her.

"Say something," I rasped.

"I don't have any Brenden stuff to deal with anymore."

I planted my hands on my hips and slanted my head. "Come again?"

She smiled weakly. "The storage unit is empty, and there's a for sale sign up at the old house."

My heart exploded, and my panic about Jack and Lauren momentarily ebbed. Finally, some fucking good news. In three strides, I closed the distance between us and dropped to my knees in front of her.

"Babe," I whispered, framing her face, pride and relief surging in my veins.

"I feel good about it too. Brenden and I had a long talk and I honestly think he'd be happy for us. Mainly for you because I'm a pretty amazing catch. But he did always like you, so he's probably at least a little happy for me too."

I smiled and traced my thumb back and forth across her cheek. "So you're ready to come back to me?"

"I'm ready," she confirmed with a grin, but as much as she tried to hide it, the slightest quiver of her lip told the real story. "I'm ready but you're moving to Portland."

"No," I breathed, feeling as though she'd punched me in the gut. "I didn't agree to moving yet." I leaned in to kiss her, but she dodged me.

She stood up and headed for the kitchen. "You have to go, Hud. It's the only thing that makes sense. Jack needs you."

"Then you're coming with me. End of story."

Crossing her arms over her chest, she leaned against the counter, an entire ocean in the shape of her bar dividing us. "I have a life here. And after today, I feel like I'm finally ready to start living it. My parents are getting older, and Cal and Vanessa are pregnant. I spent the last six years leaning on everyone around me. I'd kinda like to be here to return the favor. Not to mention, Plush Pet is really starting to take off. I have inventory and new orders rolling in every day. I'd take a huge loss financially and especially in momentum, one I'm not sure a new, small company can recover from, if I paused things now. It's just not feasible."

I didn't want to ask the question. I didn't even want to hear the words roll off my tongue. But I didn't have the power to stop them. "And what about us?"

She sucked in a ragged breath. "Well, I, uh, I hear long distance is a thing."

"Fuck long distance. I've been on the verge of losing my Goddamn mind for over a month without you. You're not making me do this. I won't choose between you and Jack."

"There is no choice!" she yelled, her calm, cool, and collected demeanor finally snapping. "Jack is priority number one for you, and I've known that since the first time he was laid in your arms.

That's the way it's supposed to be. If for one second I thought there was any chance you'd pick me, I'd break up with you on the spot. You're a good dad. It's part of why I love you. But I can't go to Portland with you. Not right now."

I stared at her, every word hitting me like a knife to the chest. If I'd stopped to think about it, I could have understood where she was coming from. She'd just gotten her life back together, and there I was, asking her to uproot everything she knew and everything she'd worked her ass off for.

It went against every fiber of my being not to gather her damn cats, throw her into the car, and kidnap her. Or at the very least drop to my knees and beg her to come with me.

But where would that have left us? Bitter, angry, and resentful.

Jack had always been my number-one priority. And I'd known for over fifteen years that Alexis Lawson was the most fiercely independent woman I would ever meet. She loved me. There was not a beat in my chest that made me doubt that, but it felt like we kept hitting dead end after dead end.

After sitting on pause for six years, she deserved the chance to finally press play on her life. I wanted that for her more than anything in the entire fucking world. I just wanted her to fall asleep beside me every night while it happened.

Though maybe that wasn't in the cards for me and Lex. At least not right now, and fuck me if that didn't burn like the hottest fire.

As I stared at her across the bar, everything I knew about my life suddenly faded into nothingness.

I was stuck between a rock and a hard place.

My son and my soul mate.

I wanted to wage war with the universe in order to keep them both—to fix this for all of us. But no matter what path I chose, one of them would suffer.

WHEN THE *Time is Right*

And I would lose half of my heart.

"I promised I'd never leave you," I whispered. "I *swore* that to you."

She lifted a shaking hand to her mouth as though she could feel the promises I'd sealed against her lips. "You aren't leaving me. I'm telling you to go."

My lungs burned as I stood there, all the oxygen in the state of Georgia somehow evading me. "I love you."

"I love you too, but…"

In the pause, I heard every single broken shard of her heart clatter on the floor at her feet.

"It's just not the right time for us yet."

Blood thundered in my ears. The urge to march around the bar and snatch her into my arms screamed so loud it was almost deafening, but that beautiful, crazy woman who had stolen the other half of my heart long before I'd ever realized it stopped me in my tracks.

"Go. Please, Hud. Just go."

CHAPTER
Twenty-Seven

Lex

When the door clicked shut behind him, I buckled, covering my mouth as sobs rocked my entire body and I slid down to the floor.

My hands shook and I couldn't breathe. It felt like the tears were seeping from my soul.

I cried and cried, and when I didn't think I could cry anymore, I saw his anguish on the backs of my eyelids and I cried some more. Time passed in simultaneous slow motion and fast forward, every emotion imaginable slicing me to the core.

"I promised I'd never leave you," echoed in my head, so I plugged my ears, trying to escape. But the sound of my heart, which beat only for him, was too loud to ever silence.

I sat there weeping for what could have been minutes just as easily as it could have been hours, but after a while, I realized that those tears weren't just for me.

They were for Hudson.

For Jack.

For Cal.

And for my parents.

We were all losing an integral part of our lives.

I'd just gotten him back, and soon, he'd be gone for good.

I'd had to make him leave. Stubborn, beautiful, loyal

WHEN THE *Time* *is* *Right*

Hudson would have stayed and fought me until the words faded into forever. When he made a promise, he kept it no matter the cost. He'd said he wouldn't leave, but I couldn't let him pay that price.

Not this time. It was finally my turn to be there for him. Whatever that meant and whatever it took. Hudson needed me, and finally—after all these years—I was strong enough to be by his side through hell. If it meant giving him peace about making an impossible decision and putting on a brave façade for what was right, then I'd be able to sleep at night.

But that night, I didn't want to sleep alone.

There would be plenty of lonely nights when he left for Portland.

Suddenly, the face of the clock became my worst enemy. I had no idea how much time we had before he'd have to move, but now, the forever I'd hoped to have with him carried an expiration date.

I'd be damned if I let even a second that I could be in his arms pass me by again.

I wiped my face, grabbed my purse off the couch, and went to him.

His house was dark, but I let myself in, and as I walked back to his room, I left my clothes and my pride in the hall. When I got to his door, I saw him lying there with his arms folded under his head, staring at the ceiling. Through the faint light filtering in through the window, I noticed his jaw flex and his brow bunch.

It wasn't anger.

It was pain.

It was fear.

It was heartache.

I knew all too well about those things, and even if I couldn't fix a Goddamned thing, I couldn't let him go through it alone.

He startled at seeing me, but he didn't say a word, only opened the sheet beside him so I could climb in.

Like two puzzle pieces in the dark, we tangled our legs and arms around one another so tightly that I wasn't sure where I ended and he began. It wasn't about sex, although we were both naked and bared to each other. It was about a connection we hadn't expected, a bond neither of us could deny. Even if the world tried to tear us apart a million times, they'd never succeed. Because the ties that bound Hudson and me together were stronger than old baggage and hundreds of miles apart.

We were soul mates, and nothing and no one could change that.

His grip on my body was nearly crushing as he clung to me. And I clung to him as though I could make it stop hurting.

When I finally looked up at his tortured face, I whispered, "Do you feel that?" I ran my fingers through his hair and then anchored them to the nape of his neck, bringing his eyes a breath away from mine. If I could have climbed inside him and calmed his worried mind and bruised heart, I would have.

He pressed his forehead against mine and answered, "I feel it."

"Nothing can change that, Hudson. Nothing will ever take this feeling away from us."

"But, babe, I want you."

"Shhh. I know, and I want you."

"So what do I do? Tell me how to keep you?"

"I don't know. But for right now, we just hang on, okay?" I pressed my mouth to his and squeezed my eyes shut, begging God to convince us both that this would somehow work out. "All we can do is hang on to this. Hold on to me, and I'll hold on to you…until we can't anymore. Try. That's all we can do, because if I've learned anything over the past few weeks of becoming the

WHEN THE *Time is Right*

woman you deserve, ignoring it and fighting it aren't going to solve anything or make it go away, Hudson. We face it. One day at a time. And you fucking hold on to me."

"I swear I'll find a way—"

I silenced him with another kiss before he made a promise we both knew he couldn't keep.

"Me telling you to go to Portland isn't me pushing you away. Neither of us can predict the future, but you have to try for Jack. If I have to lose you to anyone in the world, I choose him. You hear me. I choose him."

"What does that mean for us? For our future, babe? I can't be that far. I can't protect you or be there for you or love you the way I want from across the country."

"Well, right now, there's no good choice. Right now, all we have is this." I tightened my embrace. "And I'm not willing to let go of it yet. Don't you let go, either, big guy."

CHAPTER
Twenty-Eight

Hudson

For over a week, holding on was exactly what Lex and I did.

We'd wake up in each other's arms each morning. We'd bullshit over coffee and breakfast before I'd kiss her a dozen times in the driveway. We'd text most of the day, and when I'd get home from work, she'd be sitting on the couch, playing with Jesse, the aroma of whatever she'd cooked for dinner floating in the air.

At night, she'd curl into my arms on the couch and we'd watch TV after she'd emailed quotes to potential customers, and when she'd yawn, I'd carry her to bed. Sometimes I'd make love to her slow and sweet, as if we had all the time in the world. And other times, it was frantic and frenzied, where I memorized her every curve for fear she'd disappear like sand through my fingers.

But through it all, we held on to each other, pretending the world wasn't imploding all around us.

Lauren and I had a long talk that promptly turned into a war.

She screamed. I shouted.

Ultimately, we became the parents we swore we never would.

She was giddy and excited for her new life in Portland and couldn't understand why I wasn't happy too.

Meanwhile, I was miserable and acting like a dick because I wanted to make damn sure she was miserable too.

Unlike her, I was doing what was best for my son, but I sure as shit wanted to make sure this kind of thing never happened again. I was not a puppet in her life that she got to yank around whenever she had a wild hair to move again. With the help of an attorney, I had a new custody agreement drawn up. I should have done it years earlier, but we'd never even followed the agreement we'd had. If she wanted extra time with Jack, she asked. If I wanted time with Jack, I asked.

We were Team Jack through and through.

Until we weren't.

My new version of the custody agreement was a lot more detailed than the first. With me living in Portland, we were still planning to share custody, but everything was written out, right down to the time she was required to drop him off and who was going to pay for the stamps for him to send letters to his grandparents. It sucked that, after almost eight years of co-parenting, it had come down to that. Lauren was none too happy about the changes, but considering there was a for sale sign in my front yard so her selfish soon-to-be husband could take a new job, she didn't have much of a leg to stand on.

She'd reluctantly signed it, but it only made my reality that much more bitter.

"It's going to be fine," Lex said, giving my hand a squeeze. Dread pooled in my stomach as she skillfully guided the Chevelle into an empty spot in front of the departure's terminal.

"It's not going to be fine. It's going to suck!" Jack complained from the back seat.

He'd been raising hell since Lauren had broken the news of our move to him. He'd seemed relieved when I'd told him I'd be moving too. But leaving behind literally everyone else, including Lex, had been a hard sell, one we were still working on.

"Relax, buddy, I'm just going to get the ball rolling on things. You've got another week before you have to leave." I unbuckled and climbed out, leaning the seat forward to let Jack out while Lex rounded the hood.

I grabbed my bag out of the trunk and he stared at me like a disappointed father picking his son up from jail. "A week isn't going to be long enough. These people are a mess, Dad. Mimi is going to cry again, and Grampa David will just stare at me a lot. Don't get me started on Uncle Cal. Every time I see him, he gives me another twenty bucks. I am not complaining about the extra cash, but I know he's only doing it because he's sad and that makes me sad. This sucks!"

It did suck. So fucking much.

Especially when I looked up and saw Lex leaning against the hood of the car, her red hair cascading over her shoulders and a blank expression doing nothing to hide the tear-filled sparkle in her eyes.

My throat got thick, but I shot her a wink and did my best to swallow it down.

"Why do we have to move?" Jack continued. "I'm gonna hate Portland, and you know it. I won't even have the guys to back me up at the new school."

"You mean Nolan?"

"Yeah," he huffed.

Setting my rolling suitcase beside him, I dropped into a squat to meet him eye to eye. "Bud, you gotta bring it down a notch. We're all struggling here, and I know Portland is going to take some getting used to, but I promise, this time next year, I'll have to drag you away from your new friends to come back to Atlanta for summer vacation." I cupped the back of his neck and drew him closer. "You'll learn to love it. I promise."

He shuffled his Converse and turned his gaze to the

sidewalk between us. "And what about you? Aren't you going to miss Lex?"

My stomach wrenched. I would miss that woman every minute of every day. Every other week, while Jack was with his mother, I would sit alone in my new house, regretting my decision not to kidnap her when I'd had the chance. And most of all, there would be a gaping wound in my chest. One that I had absolutely no way to fix without her.

But he didn't need to know all of that.

"Of course I will." I caught her gaze over his shoulder. "But Lex is going to come visit. A lot." *Until it becomes too time consuming and we inevitably fall out of touch.* "And we're still going to be together." *Until the distance becomes too hard and she meets someone else.* "And we'll FaceTime all the time." *Until the agony of seeing her gorgeous face becomes the only pleasure I know.* "We're all going to be fine. You just have to put on a brave face and trust me and your mom to take care of the rest."

"Ugh!" he groaned, throwing his arms around my neck. "Fine, but my brave face is not a smile. I hope you can live with that."

"I'll keep that in mind." I chuckled and gave him a tight hug until he squirmed in my arms. "Listen, Lex is taking you to Cal's to swim with the rest of her family. If he offers you money, poke out your bottom lip and tell him how the cost of living is more expensive in Portland and see if you can squeeze a fifty out of him."

My boy grinned all toothy and wide, and that was all it took for me to remember why I was doing this. He nodded excitedly.

"After that, you're spending the night with Mimi and Grampa David. Please do me a favor and see if you can do something about that brave face of yours for a little while. I bet if you flashed her a few smiles, she'd stop crying and let you eat junk food all night."

He giggled and it caused a warmth to wash over me. "What about Grampa David?"

"Well, he's a tough nut to crack. Just spend time with him, maybe let him read you a book or tell you a story about when he was a kid. He's going to miss having you around all the time. Give him some good memories to last until he can come up for a visit."

My boy sighed. "I'm gonna miss him too."

"And hey, do me a favor? Keep an eye on my girl for me. I'm gone for the next week. Lex is going to need all the Bradley love she can get while I'm gone. You think you can handle that?"

He put his chin to his shoulder to look back at Lex. She made a kissy face and tapped her cheek.

"No way!" he exclaimed. "No kisses."

Ruffling his hair, I rose to my full height. "All right, no kisses. But hurry up and get in the car so I can give her a few before I have to leave."

"Yuck!" he exclaimed, but he did not waste a single second before climbing back into the Chevelle.

Lex softly laughed as she shoved off the car and walked my way. "Do you think it will help my case if I tell him I'm up to date on all of my cooties shots?"

I circled my arms around her hips and pulled her close. "Not likely."

"Damn," she breathed, sliding her arms around my neck.

I dipped low and grazed my lips over hers. "Come with me. I'll only be gone a week. We can scope out the area together. Figure out where we want to live. Jack leaves with Lauren the day after I get back, so we could spend the rest of the month tying up loose ends before following them out to Portland."

"Hudson, don't."

WHEN THE *Time* is *Right*

"Just say the word and I'll buy you a plane ticket right now. First class. We can pick out a house and find you a warehouse for Plush Pet tomorrow, then spend the rest of the week in bed."

"That would kinda defeat the purpose of you spending a week up there to get things organized on the new branch of Hud Construction."

"Come on now. I've seen your orders. Few more months and I could retire and become a kept man." I teasingly swayed her from side to side. "Once a week, I could come to your office under the guise of making repairs then bend you over the desk and—"

She slapped my chest. "Plush Pet is a respectable place of business, Hud. The only way I'm allowing you in my office is if you put together cat houses in a thong like the rest of my guys."

I shot her an evil glare, but judging by her laugh, it packed little heat. "If I so much as hear about a man in a thong in your warehouse, I'm catching the first flight back to kick some naked ass."

"Good. I'll start interviewing male strippers first thing in the morning."

And just like that, the pretending was over.

She wasn't coming to Portland with me.

And in a few more weeks, I wasn't going to be in Atlanta anymore, either.

Fuck, this was a nightmare. I kept telling myself that she'd eventually come around. Maybe not now, but in a few years, when her life had settled down a bit. But it felt like I was walking a plank by leaving her for a week. How the hell was I supposed to survive the next few years?

"You need to go," she mumbled, pressing up onto her toes for an all-too-brief kiss. But then again, it was Lex. She could have stood there until her lips melded to mine and it still wouldn't have been long enough.

"Just to be clear, you were a hard no on hiring a hitman for Mark instead of me moving to Portland?"

"No. I told you I knew a guy, and then you paced the den and made me swear I was kidding."

I narrowed my eyes. "You were kidding, right?"

She winked. "I guess we'll never know."

I shook my head and stared down at her. God, how had I gotten so lucky—and then so unlucky only a few months later?

I brushed my nose with hers and whispered, "I'll see you soon, babe."

"I'll be waiting."

And that was exactly what I was afraid of.

This trip was only a week of house hunting and meetings to lay the groundwork on Hud Construction's northwest division.

But after that, it'd be one trip after another with no end in sight.

CHAPTER
Twenty-Nine

Lex

The dart board at Huey's took a beating. Hudson had been gone over a week, and I'd broken tips off half my darts. One had even completely lost its fun pink-and-green fluffy bits—and I could relate.

Nevertheless, Hudson had been right as usual. Playing alone was pathetic, and that was now my life.

"I'll take a cold pitcher, Carmen. This one's gotten hot." Honestly, beer just tasted like shit. The wings had been dry. Everything was shit. But I'd forced myself out of the house, refusing to sink like the Titanic.

"Are you sure you just don't want a bottle instead?" she asked.

"Nah, make it a pitcher. I'll share it with her." I spun around and, at the door, saw a giant dork I hadn't expected to run into that Thursday evening, but that dork was there for me. I ran over and threw my arms around my brother.

"Why didn't you call me?" he asked.

"Because if I called and you turned me down, I'd be even more miserable, and I have to maintain a modicum of my ego to prove my dominance over Beep and Boop or they'll eat my face off in my sleep."

"Good thinking. Your face is one of your better features."

I shoved my shoulder into his side and stomped back to my lonely booth.

"So, when does Hud get back?" Cal asked, going straight into it without pulling any punches. Then again, what had I expected?

"Tomorrow," I answered, refilling my cup with the fresh cold-ish beer Carmen had brought us.

"What does this move mean for you two?"

But before I could answer, my phone went off beside my scattered, abused darts.

"That's him. Hold on." After a deep breath, I painted my face with a happy, supportive brush and answered his FaceTime call. "Hi."

"Damn, you look good," Hudson said, grinning at me on camera.

Across the table, Cal sat back and poured himself a beer.

"You look good too," I replied. "How'd it go today? Find a Hudson Bradley–approved location?"

He wiped his scruffy chin with his hand and his brows rose, but there was little excitement on his face. "Yeah, I think so." Clearly, neither of us wanted to celebrate because it was just one more thing making it all the more real. "I suppose I can check the warehouse, office, and at least an apartment off my list."

"Well, that's what you were out there to do. Job well done, big guy." I felt none of the enthusiasm I was trying to emote, but he didn't need me bitching and moaning. He needed me to be strong for him, whether he'd admit it or not.

"I guess. I just want to get back to Atlanta. I even tried to get a red eye out tonight, but there wasn't anything that wouldn't have me in the air for twelve hours just to save six. What are you doing? Are you at Huey's?"

I pushed my shoulder forward and gave him a what-if-I-am

glance, pursing my lips. "Yes, and I'll have you know I just won at darts."

Cal kicked me under the table.

"Okay, I was just playing myself, but why split hairs?"

"Are you alone?"

Thank God I didn't have to lie; Hudson had enough guilt already. "Nope. My big, goofy brother is here. No need to worry."

"Cal," Hudson said and I turned the camera to face my company. "Don't let her get you drunk and play her for money. You might be a doctor, but she'll take you to the cleaners. She hustled me out of fifty bucks last time we played."

Cal chuckled and leaned forward. "Do I look worried? Half the reason I don't come here as much is because I make you guys look so, so sad. You'll never be as good as me, either of you, so it's not really fair to play you guys anyway."

"Whatever. Keep dreaming," Hudson fired back.

I returned the camera to me. "So, you gonna do that thing I like tomorrow night?"

Cal deserved everything he got.

"Which one, babe? The spanking thing or the—"

Cal slapped the table with his hands. "Lalalalalala. Okay, you two sickos win. Shut up."

Hudson wrinkled his nose, looking playful and adorable, and then winked at me. And despite everything we were going through, I would never pass up the chance to see him light up and relax—even if a whole country separated us.

"Okay, well, I love you and I'll see you tomorrow. Come by my place after you see Jack. Your three pussies have missed you. I'll be the bald one on the bed."

Cal gagged. It was awesome and so worth it.

"You know you're the only pussy I want."

"Okay, enough. Wrap it up, you two," Cal begged. "I'm going to be sick."

Hudson laughed. "Hey, that reminds me. Can you do me a favor and drop my truck off at the airport? I'm barely going to make it home in time to see Jack before bedtime. It will save me a trip so I can hurry up and get back to you."

"Sure. Anything that gets you home faster," I said, looking at his face on my screen and wondering how many more times we'd be doing that very same thing in the future.

"Thanks, babe." He placed a kiss to his fingers and then to the lens. "See you tomorrow."

"Bye, Hud." I reluctantly hung up.

Cal shook his head as I put my phone back on the table. "Can I just say something? Like, just put it out there?"

I shrugged and took another drink. "You never needed my permission before. Knock yourself out."

"Why in the fuck are you letting Lauren do this? I mean, I get why Hudson is trying to be fair and prevent Jack from feeling the hurt of a dysfunctional home like the one he had growing up. But you? Why haven't you gone over there and fought for him? Fought for you both?" He glared at me as if I were a stranger and not his little sister. "The Alexis Lawson I know doesn't take shit. Especially from Lauren Rafferty of all people, who right now has her head so far up her ass that she can't see how this will tear all of us apart."

It wasn't like I hadn't thought about it. I bit my lip—just like I'd been biting my tongue—then rolled my eyes and took another drink.

"It just doesn't make any sense, Lex. This shit isn't fair to anyone but Mark, and I have milk at home that's older than their relationship."

I stared over his shoulder because I didn't have an answer

to his questions. I agreed with him wholeheartedly, but I had no idea how to fix this.

"Why are you being such a coward?" Cal pressed on. "That's not the Lex we all love. It's damn sure not the one Hudson is in love with." He slapped the table again. "Hey, Joan of Arc, look at me. Why are you being a martyr instead of fighting for what you want?"

I glared at him, hating how helpless I felt about it all. "I'm the girlfriend. She's the mother of his child. If I wade into the middle of this, I'm going to be the bad guy. What happens if I make things worse for Hudson?"

"Worse? What's worse? He's leaving the only home he has ever known. The only family that has ever given a shit about him. He's starting a new branch of Hud Construction, so rushed and unthought out that he could possibly fuck it all up and lose big time out there. And you, Lex. He's losing you."

I swallowed my rage after having it all thrown in my face like that. "Cal, she doesn't have to listen to me."

"Do you love Hudson? Like building-a-life, starting-a-family-of-your-own, being-a-second-mother-to-Jack, and finally-being-happy *love* him? Or are you just gonna do nothing and hide like you always do when shit gets tough?"

"Hey!" I yelled, and my voice cracked as I pounded on the table. "Shut the hell up. I love him, okay? Yes, like forever. Yes, like I want him to be the father of my children, and there's nothing more that I want than to be a bigger part of Jack's life. A life with him is all I'll ever fucking want, so you can shove your nosy ass questions up your…" I paused because I'd already said ass, but damn it, I was pissed. So I finished instead with, "Up your dick hole."

He grinned. The motherfucker grinned.

"Are you mad?"

"Yeah, I'm mad. I'm furious. How dare you question how much I love Hudson."

"Are you mad enough to fight for him yet?"

Without much thought, I answered, "Hell yeah."

"Good. I'll drive you to Lauren's."

"Does this minivan go any faster?" I bitched from the passenger seat. I'd always assumed Cal would have one eventually, but I hadn't been prepared for it so soon. Then again, the thing had all the bells and whistles, and I'm pretty sure it could drive itself.

"Faster? Since when do you like traveling at traffic speed?"

"Since my whole fucking life depends on it. Now get the lead out, Cally. I'm ready to kick her ass." I turned my head and grimaced.

"What?" he screeched.

"Okay, I'm not gonna kick anyone's ass, but I'm ready to give her a piece of my mind."

"Fine. That's better. I'm not becoming an accomplice to anything."

I laughed and the thought that Hudson would love all of this ran across my mind. Cal fighting for his best friend, albeit using me as the weapon. But I had to hand it to him; he wasn't dumb. Pissing me off was a good way to see how far Lauren was willing to take this.

I only prayed it worked.

I didn't feel much like a weapon as I marched up her sidewalk and banged on her door, glancing back at my brother who was giving me a thumbs-up from the cushy front seat of his new grocery-getter. It wasn't that late, and her car was the only one in the drive since Homewrecking Granddaddy Mark was in Portland already.

She looked out the side light glass and pulled a face when she saw that it was me. She opened the door, and to my surprise, Jack was right behind her. I couldn't blow up in front of him.

"Um, hi," Lauren said like a happiness-sucking ho-bag.

I really needed to get a grip because it wouldn't take much for me to escalate this way past what it needed to be.

I smiled down at Hudson's little mini. "Hey, Jackie Boy. Me and your mom need to talk in private out here. Okay?"

Lauren studied me with a baffled gaze and smoothed her hand over her son's blond head. "Go back in and finish the show. Then it's bedtime."

"Ugh. Fine. Bye, Lex. I hope I get to see you again someday."

He was still being dramatic about it, but I couldn't blame the little fella because I was about to throw the biggest fit of us all. As he stomped off, my heart pinched and my passion for letting my man's baby mama have it surged.

Lauren closed the door and then looked around me and exchanged a wave with Cal, my pussy-ass brother.

"Hey. You and I need to have a conversation."

She straightened at my tone. "I gather that. What's up, Lex?"

"Who do you think you are, ruining this whole family?"

Defensively, she crossed her arms over her fancy silk robe. "What?"

"I just said it. Who do you, Lauren Rafferty, think you are, ripping out the heart of this family?" Meanwhile, my actual heart was racing, but Cal was right. Even if I just told her off, there was nothing more she could do to any of us. And I'd rather go down fighting than wondering for the rest of my life what if.

"I think I'm trying to find some happiness of my own."

"At whose expense? Hudson's? Your parents'? My parents'? Cal's? Mine? Jack's? Why should we all have to suffer for you and some guy we barely know?"

"Well, Lex, I guess because it's my life and I can choose to do whatever I want with it. And don't throw my kid in my face."

"Okay. I get that." I threw my hands up. It was a fair point—a selfish-as-fuck point, but fair nonetheless. "It just sucks so much for the rest of us and it's like you don't even care."

"I care, Lex, but other than Hudson changing our custody agreement, and now you, everyone has been supportive."

I wanted to scream.

So I did.

"Are you really that blind? Can't you see? That's all we've ever done: support you. When you guys got pregnant, who threw you a baby shower? Me and our moms. When Jack was born, who took turns watching him while you fast-tracked the last year of your degree and Hudson was busting his ass? We did. Who's been cheering you on to chase your dreams while you've missed countless holidays, birthdays, vacations, *and even weddings*, Lauren?!"

I glanced back at my brother who was—I swear to God—either watching something on his cell or recording this whole thing. "And maybe everyone else can just sit by and keep their mouths shut, but I can't. Not now. I've got too much to lose. Hud is giving up his company for you—no. For *Mark*. I'm giving up the man I'm in love with for you—no. For *Mark*. Jack is giving up the only life he's ever known for you—no. For *Mark*. My parents are losing their only grandson, your parents are losing their only daughter and grandson, and Cal is losing his best friend and nephew for you—no." I paused and cupped a hand to my ear. "Any guesses?"

She glared at me, but like a coward, she didn't say a damn word.

"For Mark! And honestly, it's not even for Mark. It's for a fucking *job*. I am losing the best thing that has ever happened to me over a Goddamn 401K and benefits package. Please tell me you realize how fucked up this is?"

"I don't know what to say, Lex."

"You don't have to say anything, but I hope you figure it out. Because what you're doing is wrong. And don't you dare take any of my family's silence as support. No one thinks this is a good idea."

Her hands flailed, and then she rubbed her forehead. "Hudson agreed to it."

"He didn't have a choice! It wasn't like you and Mark talked to him before Mark applied for jobs on the other side of the planet. And do you really think he'd just let you take Jack away like that? That Hudson wouldn't follow *him*? He's not that kind of father and you know it! You're moving his whole damn life. And when you get out there, you'll have Mark and Jack half the time. And who will Hudson have? He's been nothing but good to you, Lauren. And this is how you repay him?"

She had the good sense to look sheepish. "You don't understand."

"Then make me understand. Explain to me why you're using a shit custody agreement your dad had drawn up when Jack was born to validate your decisions. Explain to me why you feel like Mark is more important than the rest of us who have been by your side since day one. Explain to me how you can be so damn selfish to a man who has been so damn selfless, even before you two had a baby."

My chest heaved, and I took a second to draw in a breath. As I did it, I took a step closer, as though my proximity might finally allow my words to permeate her thick skull. "This isn't about you anymore, Lauren. Or Mark's big promotion. Or even a new adventure in Portland. This is about Hudson. After all these years of taking care of each and every one of us, he deserves to be a priority." I shook my head and backed away. "I can't tell you what to do. I just want you to know that I think it's the most self-centered, cruel thing I've ever seen." I marched backward to Cal's spaceship on wheels, adding, "Think about what you're doing and who you're doing it to."

In one last show of bravado, she barked, "You're only saying this now because you and Hudson are together."

I chuffed. "Yeah, we're together, but even if we weren't, I'd still be standing right here, fighting for him. Because boyfriend or not, you're fucking over one of the best men I've ever met. Good night. Tell Jack I love him."

I hopped inside the van, and Lauren just stood there on her sidewalk, stunned and—I prayed—gut-punched.

My yellow-bellied brother put it into reverse and sweetly called out his window, as if nothing major had happened, "Bye, Lauren."

She just waved us off.

CHAPTER
Thirty

Hudson

Me: My flight just landed. I'm headed to Lauren's to see Jack, but I fully expect you to be in bed naked by the time I get there.

Lex: Any particular bed? I've had my eye on Cal's four poster for a while, but I'm thinking finding me naked in it might scandalize Vanessa.

Me: Okay, first of all, gross! Secondly, my place is closer to Lauren's, so let's meet there.

A picture came through as I made my way to baggage claim.
Lex.
On my couch.
Nothing but a blanket strategically covering a few of my favorite parts of her body.
Holy. Fucking. Hell.
If my son hadn't been leaving for Portland the very next morning, I'd have left my suitcase on the baggage carousel and run home. Even stopping to find my truck in the parking garage seemed like a gross misuse of time.

Me: Do. Not. Move. I'll be there as soon as I can.

Portland had been a success. Well, I mean, if you could consider ripping my heart out and being miserable while trying to piece together a life that was going to make me even more unhappy a success. Then yeah. Total success.

I'd never been so excited to come home from a business trip in my life. I missed Jack and Lex something fierce, but the lingering unknown hanging over our future put a damper on my mood. The reality was my son was moving across the country, and while I had a few weeks left in Atlanta to spend with Lex, it would also be spent packing up a life I loved.

But that was a pity party for another night.

After grabbing my bag and then finding my truck right where Lex had texted me that she'd left it, I drove to Lauren's house, hoping to catch up with Jack for a little while before he fell asleep.

I jogged up the sidewalk when I arrived. However many seconds I had with him, I wanted every last one.

"Hey," I said when she pulled the door open. After everything that had happened, Lauren and I weren't on the best terms, but I'd managed at least a few civil phone conversations with her over the last week.

"Hey," she whispered, crossing her arms over her chest like she'd caught a chill and it wasn't eight hundred degrees and a hundred percent humidity.

I peered over her shoulder into the doorway. "Where's Jack?"

"He went to bed about an hour ago."

"What the fuck, Lauren? I told you I wanted to see him before you left in the morning and you put him to bed *early*? You've done some—" I suddenly stopped talking when I caught sight of a ceiling-high stack of boxes next to her couch. Both of which should have been gone by now. "I thought your movers were coming today?"

WHEN THE *Time is Right*

She smiled tightly. "They were. But then this morning I told Mark we weren't moving with him, so he canceled them."

My heart stopped as a blistering shock rolled through my shoulders. "What did you just say?"

She smiled weakly and took a step outside, quietly closing the door behind her. "Do you remember when I told you I was pregnant?"

I narrowed my eyes. Where the hell was she going with this?

"Can we go back a step?" I asked. "What do you mean you told Mark you aren't moving with him?"

She ignored me. "I'll never forget when those two little lines turned pink. I was still in college, had drunken sex with my friend, and created a life. That was not at all how I wanted to start a family. But year after year, that's exactly what you gave me—a true family." She paused as tears filled her eyes. "We were never in a relationship so to speak, but you have been the best partner I ever could have imagined, and I don't think I've ever properly thanked you for that." Tears spilled from her blue eyes.

I gave her shoulder a squeeze. "You don't have to thank me. He's my son too. It's my job to be here."

"For him, sure," she croaked. "But he wasn't even alive when you beat the shit out of Doug Goodman when he called me a prude in tenth grade. And he wasn't with me when you drove three hours in the pouring rain to pick me up when my car broke down a few years back. And he wasn't there when you lost your mind on my home inspector for not checking my roof before we closed on the house, nor was he there when you had a crew show up the same day to fix it. If I've ever needed something, Hudson, you have always been there for me. But, recently, I haven't been there for you and I'm so sorry for that."

Utterly stunned, I stared at her. Hope flooded my veins as though I'd been hit by a tidal wave, but I refused to get excited before I had all the facts. "What are you saying? I need you to spell it out for me real clear, Lauren."

"I'm saying your girlfriend is crazy."

I nodded because that much I knew.

"Last night, she came over here and read me the Riot Act about how selfish I was being, and as pissed as I was, I laid in bed all night, trying to come up with all the ways she was wrong. You know what I came up with? Nothing."

"Jesus," I whispered. Yeah. That sounded like Lex.

"That woman loves you so much, Hud. And if there has ever been a man who deserves that kind of love, it's you. And Jack too, because she loves him just as much."

My chest swelled. "I love her too, ya know. I think maybe I always have. Even when I was too damn blind to see it."

She rested her hand over my thundering heart. "And after everything she's been through, *she* deserves that kind of love too. That's why I can't ask you to move."

My chest exploded, an avalanche of emotions crashing into me. "You're staying?"

"I'm staying. Portland is a me-and-Mark issue. Not a Jack issue. Not a Lex issue. And sure as hell not a you issue. You and me, we've made good partners for the last few years, but Lex is your other half. Go get your girl, Hud."

"I can do that," I whispered, overwhelming relief making my head spin. "I can so fucking do that."

"Get out of here." She took a step toward the door. "You can see Jack in the morning if you want. Or if you need some time alone with Lex, that's fine too. Just let me know and we'll make it work."

"Hey," I called. "What does this mean for you and Mark?"

She stood in the doorway and smiled. "That's not your problem. But whatever it means, from here on out, you have my word that it will happen in Atlanta."

My feet remained rooted on her sidewalk for several seconds after she'd shut the door. Thirty years of fighting and searching for where I belonged in the world finally became clear. And as much as I loved my son, that place was not standing in the dark outside of his mother's house.

Not many things in my life had gone as planned, and as I ran to my truck, peeled out of Lauren's driveway, and then sped across town to the only place I ever wanted to be, I knew this would be no different.

I parked in my driveway, the lights in my house lit up like a damn runway. She'd always been shit at remembering to turn them off when she left a room, and I was so fucking stoked to spend the next sixty years arguing with her about it.

Adrenaline ravaged my system, but the ear-to-ear smile covering my face could never be matched. I was going to fuck this up, but I was too damn happy to care.

"Holy shit!" she yelled when I swung my front door open, the crack of it hitting the wall so loud that I was positive I would be replacing some drywall in the morning.

I did not give the first fuck.

She was still naked.

On my couch.

Covered by a blanket.

The most gorgeous woman I'd ever had the pleasure of laying my eyes on.

And she was mine.

No more ghosts or distance or even fifteen fucking years of denial standing between us.

Alexis Lawson was finally mine.

Now…to get her on the same page.

"I want the whole three-ring circus," I announced.

"What are you talking about?" she said, sitting up and

putting her feet on the floor, the blanket barely clinging to her chest. "You scared the hell out of me."

I planted my hands on my hips. "Sorry about that, but it's about to get worse."

"What?" She narrowed her eyes. "Oh, God, what did you do?"

"I didn't do anything, Little Miss Hand Lauren Her Ass."

She bit her bottom lip and cut her gaze off to the side. "I had to say something, and I waited until Jack was out of earshot. You can't be pissed about that."

"Oh, I'm fucking furious." I prowled toward her.

She shot me a scowl. "Well, I'm not apologizing. She had it coming, and you know it."

"She did, but I spent a whole fucking week away from you for no damn reason. I'd have let you go feral hellcat on her a week ago if I'd known that was all it would take." In one fluid movement, I dipped, hooked her around the waist, and dragged her up the couch before coming down on top of her. I caught my weight on an elbow and she opened her legs to allow my hips to fall in between.

She gasped when my lips found her neck, but she shoved at my shoulders. "Wait, stop. What do you mean if you'd known that was all it would take?"

I flashed her a lopsided grin. "She's not moving, babe. Which means Jack's not moving. Which means I'm never fucking leaving you again—*ever*. Which means I want a whole three-ring circus that will make Cal and Vanessa's wedding look like a yard sale."

Tears immediately hit her eyes. "You're not moving?"

I pressed a deep, reverent kiss to her lips. "No, babe. And the time I spent in Portland this week trying to convince myself that I could actually breathe without you is the last bit of time

I'm planning to ever waste again when it comes to us. We belong together. I love you, Alexis Lawson, and I'm done waiting. This is our time. All you have to do is say yes."

A gorgeous smile curled her lips even as a single tear fell from her eye. "Are you asking me to marry you?"

"Yeah."

"Do you have a ring?"

Shit!

I tucked her hair behind her ear and peered down at her. "Um, no. Not yet. But I'll buy you whatever diamond you want. I swear."

She wrinkled her nose. "How am I supposed to take you seriously when you aren't even down on one knee?"

Shit!

"Right. Well…" I started to climb to my feet—or, more accurately, my knee—but she circled her legs around my hips and held me tight.

She licked her lips. "You aren't even naked, Hud. And you're expecting me to say yes?"

Now that I could fix.

After grabbing the back of my shirt with one hand, I tore it over my head. She didn't release me to get my pants, but I was able to slip them down over my ass while she lay beneath me, giggling at my struggle.

"That better?"

Her smile was huge, white, and life changing. "One out of three isn't bad, I guess."

"Say yes." I kissed her slow and filled with promises I'd spend an entire lifetime fulfilling, and she wrapped her arms around my neck as though she could absorb each and every one.

"What if I don't want a three-ring circus?"

I nipped at her bottom lip. "As long as you're at the end of that aisle, I'll find a way to deal. Besides, it's not like Judy is going to let us have a say anyway."

She laughed and it filled my soul in unimaginable ways. Never once in my life had I dared to dream that I'd find a woman I loved as deeply or completely as I did that crazy redhead. We'd traveled through hell together more than once, and I wasn't naïve enough to think that the future would be any different. But as long as we held on to each other, everything else would fall into place.

"Marry me, Lex."

"Yes," she breathed before throwing her head back against the couch as I slid inside her.

Epilogue

Lex

A Little More Than Ten Years, Three Daughters, Two New Cats, and a Goldfish Later...
TL;DR: Jack's Eighteenth Birthday

"Caroline, leave that poor old dog alone and go have Riri help you put your swimming suit on. Everyone will be here any minute."

Jesse, God love her canine soul, lay there while our wild, redheaded three-year-old tried for the millionth time that day to make her wear a birthday hat. Don't even get me started on the things she did to her dad when he was napping. But after Jack and our two other calm, blond children, we'd been asking for it when we tried for another boy. We didn't get another boy, but damn did she make me appreciate the patience Judy and David had had with me as a child every single day.

"Mom, listen. It's Jackie's birthday and Jesse wanted to wear it."

I closed my eyes, tipped my head to the ceiling, and wondered if noon was an acceptable time to start drinking at a birthday party for my oldest kid. But I still had a veggie plate to make and about three hundred other things to do before our family and friends arrived.

I felt two big hands land on my hips and then a kiss on the top of my head.

"Caroline Rose Bradley, what did your mother just ask you to do?"

God, his daddy-tone still got to me. A bolt lit up my spine.

Hudson's voice could be tender and gentle when needed, but I was the first Bradley woman to learn it could also mean business. Just as bossy as ever, he gave little option to disobey. Then again, he'd had decades of experience when it came to taming the fiery, stubborn women in his life.

Caroline straightened the party hat once more and then stood as though she'd made the decision all on her own that she was finished tormenting Jesse. "Riri," she called up the stairs to our oldest daughter. "Can you help me with my 'kini?" Then she lifted her chin and marched to the second floor as if she owned the place.

But let's be real, she did. It was Caroline's world and we were just living in it.

Hudson huffed beside my ear and then said in another familiar tone, "Are you sure you don't want to try one more time for a boy?"

Alone in the kitchen, I spun in his arms and fisted the collar of his shirt. "Listen here, big dick. I have an at-home vasectomy kit in my Amazon cart right now. Do not make me one-click." Despite my threats, I couldn't help but enjoy the thought of another tiny blond boy who'd always have my back.

Hudson would have six more if I agreed to it, and sometimes—especially when he grinned at me with that wicked half smile of his—I considered it. But that wasn't anything I had time to think about that day. That day was about our Jackie Boy and making sure his eighteenth birthday was all about him.

Ignoring his request to procreate again, I wiped a smudge

of grease off his cheek with my thumb. "Did you get it all waxed up?"

"The Chevelle has never looked better. Are you sure he deserves it? I mean, he loves it more than both of us combined, but it seems like a lot of power to give a kid who's barely legal."

Maybe he was right, but Jack was also the most responsible, intelligent, and deserving young man. Plus, it would drive Cal crazy, so it was an all-around win-win for me. Besides, it would be parked here while he was away at college and we could still drive it whenever we wanted.

"He's getting the Chevelle. End of discussion."

He pressed a kiss to my lips. "End of discussion, eh, Mrs. Bradley?"

"I said what I said. My foot is officially down."

His eyebrow rose. "Think he'd still want it if he knew that's where Caroline was conceived?"

I laughed, licking my lips with the memory of that date night. "There's no way you can prove that's when I got pregnant."

"Oh, I know exactly every place I knocked your fine ass up." He leaned down to whisper in my ear, hearing a commotion at the top of the stairs. The hair on the back of my neck stood on end as he listed, "Riley Elaine was our first night in this house right after our honeymoon. You were still sunburned, so I got you from behind over a pile of moving boxes just inside the front door. I still have the scar where Boop mangled my ankle when you screamed my name."

Boop had always had my back, and Boop Two was just as vicious.

I leaned in, enjoying the story and sure he'd continue.

"Melody Jade happened one morning at the beach in our spot. Watching the sun come up, you rode me until you had sand burns on your knees."

I still had a scar from that one, but that sweet baby loved the ocean just as much as I did.

"And Caroline Rose was in the back seat of *my* Chevelle after your mom and dad's forty-fifth wedding anniversary party in the parking lot of the country club like a bunch of teenagers."

I pursed my lips to stifle the chuckle, because I specifically remember what he'd said before that party when he saw me in my dress. In the way only Hudson could, he'd said, "Babe, someone's getting pregnant tonight."

Lo and behold, nine months later, our hellion screamed her way into the world.

"I still have that little black dress," I teased.

His hold on me tightened, and he growled as he playfully bit my lobe. "You better watch what you say before this party becomes part of our family legacy."

"Dad," Jack said, popping his head in through the French door, saving me from three trimesters of swollen feet.

Hudson's chin shot up, but he didn't let go.

"Since you got the SS out, can I drive it to go pick up Nolan?"

I looked up into Hudson's eyes and my heart grew for the billionth time.

"Yes, but no stopping to make out. Get right back. If I have to sit through an afternoon with your aunt Vanessa *for your birthday*, you and your boyfriend do too."

When Jack had come out to us, scared and unsure how we'd take it only a year ago, I'd fallen in love with my husband all over again. At the dinner table after the girls had gone to bed one night, he'd confessed that he thought he was in love with his best friend and didn't know what to do.

Hudson had only smiled at his boy and said, "Like father, like son."

WHEN THE *Time* *is* *Right*

To which Jack almost fell out of his seat.

Under the table, Hudson grabbed my hand and said, "I fell in love with my best friend too once, son. I couldn't care less if you're gay. What I care about is you being a brave man and recognizing love when you feel it. It took me years to understand my love for Lex. So if you love Nolan, then tell him when the time is right and you'll never regret it."

I'd lifted our paired hands to my mouth and kissed my husband's knuckles, thankful he was the father of my children, my lover, my bossy other half, my forever beer, wings, and darts partner, my biggest champion, and—that day and forever—my best friend too.

I smiled at the memory as I gave Jack back my attention. "The keys are on the counter."

"'Kay," Jack said, his gaze slipping down to his father's arms around my middle. "The no-making-out rule also goes for you two though. I don't need any more siblings."

Poor Jack. He'd spent so much of his life as the only child in our giant, crazy family until it seemed baby fever had hit us all at the same time. Cal and Vanessa had been busy with two girls and a boy, and even Lauren and Grandpa Mark had defied the laws of reproduction and had a little girl of their own a few years back. Jack loved them all and had secured a pretty substantial bank account as the family babysitter, but his patience was wearing thin.

"Boy, get out of here before I change my mind about you taking the Chevelle," Hudson rumbled.

Jack rolled his eyes, but like the smart man we'd raised him to be, he snagged the keys and hurried out the door.

Hudson slid around in front of me, his hands dropping to my ass. "We've got a solid ten minutes before your parents get here."

I shoved at his chest. "Right. Which means I need to hurry

up and make my secret recipe salsa before Judy realizes it comes from a jar."

He chuckled and dipped low to lean his forehead to mine. "I can't believe he's actually eighteen. Where did the time go?"

Encircling his neck, I placed a reverent kiss to his lips.

Time had gone to smiles and laughs.

It had gone to making memories and making love.

It had gone to the three little girls laughing and fighting upstairs.

And in ten minutes, it would go to an afternoon of cake and presents with the unconventional family we'd made together.

Although I'd known him most of my life, I'd spend every minute of every day proving to him I'd always bet on us.

"Love you, Hud."

"Love you too, babe."

The End

M. MABIE

STANDALONE **CONTEMPORARY ROMANCES**
Fade In
All the Way
One Week Stand

CITY LIMITS SERIES **SMALL-TOWN CONTEMPORARY ROMANCES**
Roots and Wings
Sunshine and Rain
Smoke and Mirrors

THE WAKE SERIES
Bait
Sail
Anchor

THE KNOT DUET
Twisted Desire
Tethered Love

THE BREAKING TRILOGY
Break My Fall
Break Me Down
Break the Faith

About

M. MABIE

M. Mabie is a writer who made thousands of readers hate to love (and love to hate) the angst-filled contemporary romance, *Bait*.

Mabie lives in Illinois with her husband. She writes unconventional love stories and tries to embody "real-life romance." She cares about politics but will not discuss them in public. She uses the same fork at every meal, watches Wayne's World while cleaning, and lets her dog sleep on her head.

She has always been a writer. In fact, she was born with a pen in her hand, which almost never happens. Almost. M. Mabie usually doesn't speak in third-person.

She promises.

You're invited to stay up to date with M. Mabie. For a look behind the scenes, relevant book news, glimpses into upcoming projects, and more please subscribe to her *real-life romance* newsletter.
www.mmabie.com/Subscribe

If you're interested in being the first to know about sales and new release, as well as recommendations by M. Mabie

Follow M. Mabie on BookBub

For all that and more, join the honeybee family in
M. Mabie's Take the Bait on Facebook

www.MMabie.com

M. Mabie on Facebook

Instagram @m_mabie

Twitter @AuthorMMabie

Also by

ALY MARTINEZ

STANDALONE CONTEMPORARY ROMANCES
Across The Horizon
The Fall Up
The Spiral Down
Release

THE RETRIEVAL DUET
Retrieval
Transfer

GUARDIAN PROTECTION SERIES
Singe
Thrive

THE FALL UP SERIES
The Fall Up
The Spiral Down

THE DARKEST SUNRISE SERIES
The Darkest Sunrise
The Brightest Sunset
Across the Horizon

THE TRUTH DUET
The Truth About Lies
The Trust About Us

THE REGRET DUET
Written with Regret
Written with You

THE WRECKED AND RUINED SERIES
Changing Course
Stolen Course
Broken Course
Among the Echoes

ON THE ROPES
Fighting Silence
Fighting Shadows
Fighting Solutude

About
ALY MARTINEZ

Originally from Savannah, Georgia, USA *Today* bestselling author Aly Martinez now lives in South Carolina with her husband and four young children.

Never one to take herself too seriously, she enjoys cheap wine, mystery leggings, and baked feta. It should be known, however, that she hates pizza and ice cream, almost as much as writing her bio in the third person.

She passes what little free time she has reading anything and everything she can get her hands on, preferably with a super-sized tumbler of wine by her side.

Facebook: www.facebook.com/AuthorAlyMartinez

Facebook Group: www.facebook.com/groups/TheWinery

Twitter: twitter.com/AlyMartinezAuth

Goodreads: www.goodreads.com/AlyMartinez

www.alymartinez.com

Made in the USA
Monee, IL
21 November 2020